PRAISE FOR D[...]

"When six students are tr[...]
reader—helpless to escape u[...] the final page [...]rned. *The Finalists*
is a smart and compelling look at the dark underbelly of academia."

—*USA Today* bestselling author Charlie Donlea

"*And Then There Were None* meets *Knives Out* in David Bell's latest
astonishing thriller. With Bell's customary biting wit and razor-sharp
social commentary, *The Finalists* will have you cackling one minute
while racing through its short, propulsive chapters the next, desperate
to find out whodunit. Utterly riveting with intricate plot twists. Bell
has crafted the summer's most entertaining and masterful locked-
room mystery. I couldn't put it down!"

—May Cobb, author of *A Likeable Woman*

"*The Finalists* is proof positive that David Bell is one of the best
thriller writers working today."

—Alma Katsu, author of *Red London*

"[A] smart, highly entertaining mystery with red herrings galore and
such perfect dialogue, you'll feel like a fly on the wall. . . . The characters will play tricks on your mind, the house will feel like it's closing
in, and the story will keep you guessing until the very end. Not to be
missed!"

—Hannah Mary McKinnon, international bestselling
author of *The Revenge List*

"David Bell is a top-notch storyteller. . . . I flew through this twisting,
riveting psychological thriller."

—Cristina Alger, *New York Times* bestselling author of *Girls Like Us*

"Terrifically tense . . . will keep you guessing until the very end."

—Riley Sager, *New York Times* bestselling
author of *The Only One Left*

STORM WARNING

DAVID BELL

BERKLEY
NEW YORK

BERKLEY
An imprint of Penguin Random House LLC
penguinrandomhouse.com

Copyright © 2024 by David J. Bell
Readers Guide copyright © 2024 by David J. Bell
Penguin Random House supports copyright. Copyright fuels creativity, encourages diverse
voices, promotes free speech, and creates a vibrant culture. Thank you for buying an authorized
edition of this book and for complying with copyright laws by not reproducing, scanning, or
distributing any part of it in any form without permission. You are supporting writers and
allowing Penguin Random House to continue to publish books for every reader.

BERKLEY and the BERKLEY & B colophon are registered trademarks of
Penguin Random House LLC.

Library of Congress Cataloging-in-Publication Data

Names: Bell, David, 1969 November 17- author.
Title: Storm warning / David Bell.
Description: New York : Berkley, 2024.
Identifiers: LCCN 2023050011 (print) | LCCN 2023050012 (ebook) |
ISBN 9780593549995 (trade paperback) | ISBN 9780593550007 (ebook)
Subjects: LCGFT: Thrillers (Fiction) | Novels.
Classification: LCC PS3602.E64544 S76 2024 (print) |
LCC PS3602.E64544 (ebook) | DDC 813/.6--dc23/eng/20231030
LC record available at https://lccn.loc.gov/2023050011
LC ebook record available at https://lccn.loc.gov/2023050012

First Edition: June 2024

Printed in the United States of America
1st Printing

Book design by George Towne

For Molly

STORM
WARNING

PART ONE

ONE

5:14 P.M.

Rain smacks my windshield.

The wipers fight a losing battle. The Elantra's on its last legs, and there's so much water it's almost impossible to see the nearly one thousand feet of causeway ahead of me. Waves pound either side of this narrow link between the mainland and Ketchum Island, sending foamy water sloshing across two lanes of pavement. Constructed of dirt and boulders built up and reinforced over the years. Foot-high guardrails offer only a hint of protection to drivers. The water on the road isn't too deep.

Yet.

I left work early to beat the storm, but I'm barely going to make it back to the island. Even from here, I can see the scattered lights burning in my building. We still have power.

For now.

"Hang on a little longer." I'm talking to myself, and the words help calm my nerves.

The wind whips the car, makes it wobble. The newscaster on the radio provides a grim update: *Hurricane Kylie could soon be upgraded to a Category Three storm. It's bearing down on the east coast of the state and is expected to make landfall in the next few hours.*

"Slow down, Kylie," I say out loud. "Slow down."

She was supposed to go up the Gulf side of the state, leave us alone. But Kylie has a mind of her own. She's already a bit of an outlier—a strong early-November storm, arriving when the season is supposed to be winding down. Now she's made a sudden right turn, cut across the bottom of Florida, and turned north. She's lashing the Atlantic coast, gathering strength, leaving me almost no time to pack and get out before she makes landfall.

The car slams into a pothole, bounces across the pavement like it's a trampoline.

"Shit."

My teeth clap together so hard I wonder if I chipped one. But I keep driving, hands gripping the wheel so tight they hurt.

The sky is almost pure black, the color of charcoal. It's only just past sunset, but there's no light at all. The sun's gone dark. It's a scene straight out of a postapocalyptic movie.

A gust of wind shoves the car suddenly to the left. I lose control. The Elantra careens toward the guardrail. I fight as hard as I can, steering into the wind and righting course just before I'd go over the side of the causeway and plummet into the water below.

"Shit."

My heart pounds in my ears. The air-conditioning blasts, but I'm sweating like a pig.

I reach the far side of the causeway. The island is a narrow spit of land. Fifty years earlier, a developer planted his flag, cleared the land, forcibly removed the alligators and deer, drained the swamp, and erected three large apartment buildings.

Fifty years ago, this place was a dream. A paradise.

Now . . . well . . .

The apartment buildings on Ketchum Island have run their course, spent too many days withering in the relentless Florida sun and fighting the unforgiving winds of hurricane season. It's gotten so bad that all three buildings are scheduled to be demolished within six months.

The palm trees bend one way and then another, nearly kissing the roadway. Garbage blows across the slick, sodden grass. I guide the car right, to the place where I've been living the past six months, the ridiculously named Sunset Manor. I pull into the parking garage underneath the building. The rain stops pounding me, and I ease into my designated spot.

Not that it matters. Only ten units remain occupied in this, the last operational building on the island, and there was plenty of parking even before Kylie set her sights on us.

I step out of the car. My shoe sinks into two inches of water, soaking my foot to the skin. Water backs up out of the storm drains, flooding the parking garage like an oil gusher.

"Lovely."

I splash through the water, rushing for the stairs, while running through my to-do list in my head.

Grab my shit.
Say good-bye to Dallas.
Check on Hazel.
Get the hell out.
Hope like hell the causeway holds.
*Pray the cops haven't blocked the roads on the other side (even though
    I don't pray).*
*If I make it that far—and that's a big if—find something to eat. Fast
    food. A Coke. It's a long drive back to Ohio. I'll need to stay awake.*
Keep moving . . .

I just need enough time to get out.

Get out. Get home. Start over.

Again.

My building—building C—rises ten stories in the air above the parking garage. There are ten units on each level. Each floor is circled by an external walkway. Three sets of stairs, exposed to the elements, rise to the top, on both ends and in the middle. The slow-moving elevator reeks of burning oil and breaks down every other day.

I don't like elevators in the best of circumstances. No way I'm trying my luck in that thing with a hurricane bearing down on us.

My shoes squish on the exposed stairs. At the landing on the second floor, I come to an abrupt stop.

Dallas' door is slightly ajar. Rain blows against me, soaking my
clothes. I hear the waves on the other side of the building crashing
against the island like god-sized cymbals.

I knock below the sign that says MANAGER. But there's no way
anyone could hear me over the wind, the waves, the rain.

"Yo, Dallas. You still here?"

His apartment is spare. Secondhand furniture, nothing on the
walls. It's also neat as a pin. Dallas Bryant knows how to take care of
things. He's the only one keeping Sunset Manor standing. I don't
know how he does it.

"Dallas?"

He comes out of the bedroom. When he sees me, he stops. Surprise appears on his face. "Well, holy fuck. Why are you still here,
Jake?"

He wears cargo pants and a Bears T-shirt. Chicago—his home-
town. Still hasn't lost the accent.

"I need to grab my shit."

"I figured you'd be long gone. Barreling up the turnpike for
Ohio."

"I know, I know."

"Have you been listening to the news? Storm's getting worse.
What on earth could be so important that you'd risk your hide
for it?"

"Just things."

"Shit." Dallas studies me. He's fifty-five, my best friend in Florida. Maybe my best friend in the whole world. Okay, he's more like a
big brother than a friend. Or maybe both. We've spent many an eve-
ning together in the six months I've been in the Sunshine State trying
to reassess my life and figure out what comes next.

He reaches up, adjusts his paint-splattered cap. "What things?"

"You know, clothes and shit."

"I told you I'd look after Hazel. I've been doing it since long before you got here."

"I need my toothbrush too."

"Really?"

"Are you going to make me say it?"

"I am." He laughs a little. "Go on."

"Okay, dumbass. I came back, you know, to say good-bye."

He laughs louder. "How bad is it out there? Really."

"It's bad. Getting worse."

"The causeway?"

"Hanging in. But getting hammered."

"One beer," he says, turning to go to the refrigerator. This is what we do. Drink Jai Alai and watch the Marlins play. "Your last beer as an estranged husband before you return to the land of domestic bliss."

I look outside. The wind slows. A break. Kylie's taking a deep breath before she delivers the knockout blow. Well, maybe she won't be that bad.

Dallas turns around, two bottles in his hands. "Ready?"

"Okay, one last beer before I go."

TWO

The beer's cold in my hand.

We clink bottles and drink. The liquid feels great going down. A pleasant burn. I'm hungry—but there's no time to eat.

I wish Dallas and I could sit on the landing one more time. Watch the sunset. Talk about the past, the present, the future, the what-ifs. But my life is calling me.

Home.

Family.

A chance to fix the past.

I can see our house in Ohio shimmering like an oasis. The red brick and black shutters. Jordan's garden. Mackenzie doing her homework, headphones tuning out the world. My endless list of household projects . . .

Dallas will have his hands full through the night, keeping an eye on the building and its few remaining tenants.

"We're in the crosshairs," Dallas says. "Sitting ducks. I thought with it being November we could breathe easy. But not these days, with the weather the way it is . . ." Dallas looks past me. The rain continues to hit the walkway, splashing right up to his open door. "Well, hell." He takes a long drink.

"I know you won't listen, but I still think you should get out of here. Tonight."

"No, no—"

"Seriously, listen to me. What have you been telling me since the day I showed up here?"

"I told you to figure things out with Jordan and get back to Ohio. To let the past be the past and make a new future together."

"Okay, yes, you told me that. But—"

"And you're doing it, right? You listened to your uncle Dallas. You always said you're never sure when to stay and when to go. That you don't trust your own instincts."

"I don't."

"Does anybody?"

"I don't know."

"Trust me. They don't. But I know—you need to go home. Now is the time." Something flickers across his face—a thought? A memory? "You know, a person's lucky to have a place to go, especially with the holidays coming up. That's where you need to be. With your family."

He holds his bottle out. I have no choice but to clink it again.

Dallas has mentioned—obliquely—having been married once. A daughter he's lost touch with. Grandchildren he's never met.

I can't imagine. My deepest fear would be to never see my family again. It's the stuff of nightmares.

"Okay, Uncle Dallas, I'll go. But what about you? This place?" I gesture to the walls behind us. "You keep saying the building's in shit shape. They've already boarded up and condemned the other two. You said, if a hurricane ever really came through here—"

"If a hurricane ever really came through here and hit us directly, this place might not be standing when it's over. I did say that. Many times. And this one that's about to land . . . Well, shit."

"So get the hell out of here. Tonight. Ride off the island with me. I'll drop you wherever you want to go. Hell, come to Ohio for a while."

Dallas smiles. He takes a long drink and sits in an overstuffed recliner. "We've got—what?—ten units still occupied here, including yours?"

"That's right."

"And who are our fellow tenants? What's their status in life?"

"You know as well as I do." I scan the list in my head. It's an eclectic collection, typical of Florida. Some retirees, some transplants. A married couple down on their luck, a woman in her early twenties with no savings to speak of, a man hobbled by a workplace injury. An elderly curmudgeon, a shut-in, and a quiet middle-aged guy I can't figure out. We're an island of misplaced people. They don't have anywhere else to go. That's why they're hanging on here, in a building that's crumbling around us and slated to be razed. "Everyone still living in this place is only here because they've got no other choice."

He half shrugs, as if the implication of what I'm saying is obvious. It is. I know exactly what he's thinking, but he says it anyway. "Who's going to look out for them if I leave? That's my job."

"But that's not—"

"Even before this hurricane was coming for us, they needed to vacate. The building's being blown up in a few months. To make way for—what's it called? Banyan Tree Villas? Or is it Stingray Suites?"

"Atlantic Estates."

"Atlantic Estates. How could I forget? Luxury condos starting in the fifteens." He points at me. "That's at least one and a half million. And that's where the price *starts*. If you want cabinets or light switches, you're going to spend more. You know as well as I do, the people who live here can't afford that. They've all been handed bad breaks they can't get out from under."

"And then there's Hazel."

"Hazel." Dallas scratches his head. "What is she? Ninety?"

"Ninety-one."

"Wow."

"Exactly." And then I say what he's already thinking. "With nowhere to go."

"And now this hurricane has turned our way."

The wind picks up, blows rain in the front door. As if to support what Dallas has been saying, the building makes a low groaning sound.

"Shit," I say. "Still . . . outside of the wind, this storm seems kind of quiet."

"Hurricanes don't produce much thunder or lightning." Dallas gestures toward the door. "Close that, why don't you? I want to tell you something."

I do what he asks, shutting the storm out. For now.

I remain standing. I'm going to be sitting a long time once I get into the car. I'm not stopping until I see Jordan and Mackenzie again.

"I *am* leaving," Dallas says.

"Great. Glad to hear it."

"After the storm. As soon as it's over. I told you about the job my sister mentioned in Chicago? The one downtown?"

"It came through?"

He nods. "It did."

"Holy shit, that's great."

"No more lizards. No more humidity," Dallas says. "I'm heading up there after Thanksgiving. The building in Chicago is in great shape. And I'll be closer to my sister and her kids. I don't have any other family, you know? I mean—family I talk to. It'll be nice. I kind of miss the snow. And the changing leaves. And a Chicago summer." He lets out a laugh. "All two weeks of it." He takes another drink, emptying his bottle.

"Well, holy shit. I never thought you'd go. I never thought you'd actually make the move."

"I have some surprises left in this middle-aged body." He puts the empty down and holds up his index finger. "And I have one more surprise for you." He stands and leaves the room.

As soon as he's gone, the building groans again.

I put my bottle to my mouth and throw back the rest of my beer.

THREE

Dallas holds a light blue half sheet of paper when he returns. A key fob dangles from his other hand.

"Here." He holds the paper out to me. "This is for you."

The paper has a decorative border and there's the faint image of a seal in the middle.

"What's this?"

"Take it."

I run my eyes over the document. "I *can't* take this."

"Take it." He sounds like a frat boy trying to convince me to do a shot. "For real."

"Dallas, I can't—"

"Yes," he says with a nod. "You can. Look, I know the Elantra is a piece of crap. It's been leaking oil all over my parking garage for months."

"Yeah, sorry about that."

"Well, you're not the only one. Anyway, you need something to get you back to Ohio. Consider it an early Christmas gift."

"Dallas—"

"Now, wait. Listen." He holds his index finger in the air like a teacher. The door rattles in the frame, the wind picking up. "All you've talked about since you came down here is how you need to figure your life out, get back on track, get on top of the debt. I know you need to start saving for Mackenzie to go to college someday. Well, look, I don't need this car. I'm moving to *Chicago*. Shit, I'm sick of driving. I don't even like it anymore. I'm going to ride the El all the time." He grabs my arm. Shoves the key fob into my hand. "Take the car. It's a gift."

I blink a few times. Swallow hard. "No one's ever given me a car. I don't know what to say. My parents could never . . ."

He steps closer, claps me on the upper arm. "Don't say anything. Just take it. Besides, it isn't like it's a Maserati. It's a 2014 Highlander, for God's sake."

"Better than an Elantra."

"Way better. And I've kept it in good shape. It'll get you where you need to go."

I'm speechless, but Dallas has more to say.

"You know . . . I haven't really, you know . . . It's been a while since I had a good friend. Down here, working so much on the building and everything . . . and then you came here, so, you know, I appreciate it." He points at the title. "I filled my part out, signed it over to you, Mr. Jacob Powell. Just take it to the DMV up in Ohio when you get there."

"What about my car? It's down in the garage."

Dallas smiles. "That thing? If you're lucky, it'll get swept out to sea. Become part of the reef. That's about all it's good for."

"That's harsh. But I know you're right."

A second later, we're just standing there, two dudes who have no idea what to say to each other.

"What about your daughter? Maybe she'll want—"

He shakes his head, waves his hand in the air. "*Your* daughter will be driving soon. Pass that Highlander on to her when the time comes. But right now, you need to go upstairs and check on Hazel. Say good-bye. She's worried about you driving all the way to Ohio."

"How is she today?"

Dallas shrugs. "Let's just say, it's one of those days when she's attached to reality by a thin thread. I was up there an hour ago, and she was talking about her stalker again, says he's been hanging around the building. She also claims he can control the weather, says he's responsible for Kylie coming this way. Honestly, man, it's hard to take anything she says seriously anymore."

"That's not good. But, then again, she's ninety-one, so . . . I'll grade her on a curve."

He adjusts his cap, scratches his head. "There *have* been a lot of strangers around here. Squatters. People coming to check on the place because of the pending sale." He shrugs. "But no stalkers of the elderly that I've seen."

A thought pops into my mind. I hand the title and the key back to Dallas. "Here. Hold on to this for a minute."

"Jake—"

"No, really. I'll check on Hazel, get my stuff. Then I'll be back. I have something for you too."

"Not your car. Please."

"No, not the stupid car. A real gift. It'll just be a few minutes. I have to beat this storm."

"Okay, sure. I'll be here getting ready for a long night of not sleeping."

When I open the door, the wind grabs it and blows it out of my hand. It swings open, slamming against the outside wall. The gust pushes me back, and I almost fall over.

Dallas comes up behind me, steadies me. "Careful." He looks around me. "It's definitely getting worse. Landfall's just a couple hours away, and then who knows where we'll be?"

"I'm okay."

"Hurry up, man. Do what you have to do and get out of here."

"I will. I promise."

"And maybe take the stairs. I have no way to get you out if the elevator goes."

"You don't have to tell me."

I grab either side of the doorframe, push off, and lean into the wind as I head for the stairs.

FOUR

I take the stairs two at a time.

The stucco building was once painted yellow, but it's sun faded and sickly now. The pallor of a dying patient. The rain reaches me as I climb, sprinkles my back and head.

Hazel lives on the tenth floor, at the top of the building. She's the only one up there. When I came to Florida, she was down on the second floor, right next to Dallas, but he found mold all over her bathroom, so she had to relocate. The only decent unit was on the top floor. He planned to move her back down, but her old apartment still isn't livable.

By the time I reach Hazel's floor, my hair is soaked. I'm a little winded, but not nearly as much as I would have been when I moved to Florida six months ago. I've spent my spare time working out at the Hammond Point Y on the mainland, getting in the best shape of my life. I lift weights, swim laps, beat the punching bag, run on the treadmill. I've even joined the local Masters swim club. Every Sunday night, we swim across the Intracoastal as the sun sets. I've dropped nine pounds, added a little muscle. Acquired a decent tan.

Hell, Jordan and Mackenzie might not even recognize me.

Hazel's unit is halfway down the walkway, and sometimes she forgets to lock her door. I rap on it, then push it in.

"Hazel?"

"Oh, good," she says in a chipper voice. Like I'm just popping in for tea. "I'm glad you're here, Jacob."

She's sitting on the end of the couch, half-moon glasses resting on the tip of her nose. She wears a housecoat—blue with embroidered flowers—and her white hair is a mess. Hazel taught history at Indian River Community College for over fifty years. Her apartment contains more papers and books than I've ever seen. Every surface is obscured by them.

When she moved upstairs, she allowed a few of us to carry her things only under her strict supervision, losing her temper every time one of us touched a book or placed a folder out of order. She acted like each item was incredibly fragile, like perfectly organized precious eggs. It's hard to believe she's made such a mess in less than six months.

"I just came by—"

"Did Dallas tell you he was back?"

"Who? Oh, you mean . . . the guy?"

"Yes, *him*. I believe he caused this hurricane. You know, when I tell Dallas these things, he looks at me like I've lost my mind." She removes her glasses, considers me. Her eyes are bright blue. Alert. "You don't treat me that way, Jacob. That's why I like you."

"You don't like Dallas?"

"That young man works my last nerve. He thinks he's my care-taker. Always checking on me, bringing me groceries, asking me if I took my medicine."

"Sounds terrible."

"Well, I don't want him to know how much I appreciate him." She winks. "That's our little secret."

"I think he knows."

She gestures at the room. "Now, don't you dare touch any of my papers."

"I'm not here to touch your papers, Hazel. I came to say good-bye."

"Good-bye?" She acts like she's never heard the word before.

"That's right. I'm going back to Ohio. Remember? We talked about this."

She studies me again. There's a mustard stain on her housecoat. Hazel eats hot dogs twice a day, sometimes three times. Dallas says she's been doing it for years, and her cholesterol is better than his.

"This is for the wife and daughter?"

I nod, relieved that she remembers something. "That's right."

"She's taking you back."

"It's not so much a matter of anyone being taken back. We agreed to separate, to take some time apart. We were having some . . . well, some challenges. But now we're going to try again."

"*Try?* You don't *try* in a marriage, Jacob. You commit. You know, I was married fifty-one years." She jerks her thumb toward the framed photo on the end table. Her husband, Robert. Dead for almost twenty years. "I know what I'm talking about."

I've never won an argument with Hazel. Despite her memory lapses, she always manages to turn it on when she has to, instructing me like the professor she was. She likes to cast me in the role of bumbling student.

"You're right. I'm not just going to *try*. I'm committed. We're going to make our marriage work. We're going to raise our daughter together."

"Mackenzie."

"That's right."

"Age fifteen."

"She turns sixteen next month. Are you sure you have memory problems?"

"Are you?"

"Me?"

She taps her glasses against her thigh. "I seem to recall—I know I'm old, but I do remember *some* things, and I do recall more than one conversation with you about how much you dislike your job in Ohio. IT consultant or something? Whatever that is." She dismisses my once and future career with a wave of her hand. "And now you're going back to it? After you've been so happy and fulfilled here?"

"I'm not making enough money."

"And . . . ?"

"I have a daughter who plans to go to college. Her future is more important than mine."

"That's quite noble of you, Jacob." She stops tapping her glasses. "You've gotten over everything that happened in the past? With your marriage?"

"We both made mistakes. We've both learned about ourselves. I've learned what's important."

Hazel gives me the side-eye. "I've been on this earth a long time, Jacob. Until you showed up here, I'd never once in my life heard of anyone having an emotional affair. I mean, people had affairs or they didn't. And an affair usually didn't involve *emotion*, if you know what I mean."

"I do."

"So you've gotten over your problems with Jordan having this"— she clears her throat—"*emotional* affair?"

It's embarrassing to hear Hazel talk about my marriage in such a dismissive way. Thinking about it again—what happened with Jordan—stabs me sharply in the chest.

Am I sure I'm ready to go home? Are we going to be able to make this work?

I desperately hope so.

"I'm going back to Ohio. To a new job. And, yes, it's in IT. But it's a good job. At a better company. A new start. Just in time for the holidays and the New Year. That's why I have to say good-bye."

"Well, okay." Her eyes roam over the room again. "But I was going to show you something I found."

"Is it a piece of paper?"

"Don't be smart." She places her hands on the couch cushions and scoots her body to the edge. She's working hard to stand. "I have something for you."

I go over, offer her my hands. "Here."

"Back off, young man. I'm not an invalid. What do you think I do when you're not here?"

It takes a couple of tries as she rocks her body back and forth, but then she's up. She wobbles a little, places a hand on my arm. She's up.

"If an old lady stands up in her apartment, does she make a noise?" she asks with a chuckle.

She crosses the room to the dining table, where she shuffles papers from side to side. How long will I be waiting while she tries to find what she wants to give me?

"Aha." She lifts a rectangular shirt box that looks like it was gift wrapped by an elf on hallucinogens. "*This* is your going-away present." She brings it over to me and taps it with an arthritis-gnarled index finger. "Don't open it until you're home." She winks. "It's a pajama top. I'll send you the bottoms after you've been home a few weeks."

"Hazel, your mind's in the gutter."

"Okay, it's not that." She holds the box out to me. "But you take that with you. I want you to have it."

The wind rattles her door, shakes the metal hurricane shutters against the building.

I put the poorly wrapped box under my arm. "Thank you, Hazel."

"It's going to be bad out there. That storm's coming in fast." She looks me in the eye. "You drive safe, you hear?"

"Will you please go with me? I can drive you to a shelter or something."

Hazel's mouth opens wide, hangs there for a few long seconds before any words come out. She looks like I've slapped her. "Do you know how many of these I've been through, young man? On this very island? This is my home. I won't leave or . . . or . . . go to a shelter. Not for a measly November hurricane."

"Do you have enough food?" I glance toward the kitchen, which looks bare. "Did you get groceries?"

"I've got enough. They bring me Meals on Wheels, remember?"

"Not after a hurricane, they don't."

"I'll be fine. There are hot dogs in the freezer."

"What if you went to a lower floor? You could stay with Dallas until this blows over."

"You want to put me in that elevator? That thing is an iron coffin. No, I believe I'll stay here. Come what may."

"If you're sure . . ."

"If I die, I'll die right here. With my things."

"Enough paper to build an ark."

"Don't be smart, Jacob. If you were my son, well . . ." She reaches out and pats my cheek, her eyes gazing into mine until they begin to mist. Hazel's son, Paul, died of cancer shortly after her husband. She almost never talks about him.

She stares at me so long it's uncomfortable.

"I wish you could meet Jordan and Mackenzie. Maybe we can visit sometime. Mackenzie's never been to the ocean. We promised her a trip."

"Sure, but I know you're not interested in looking back. I understand that."

"An odd statement from a historian."

"It's not advice. It's merely an observation. Go back, forget the past, focus on the future. Your family. Your new job. Even if it's not quite what you want."

"I want to be with them. This is the way it works."

"Just do me one favor, Jacob: Be careful. . . ."

"I will. The causeway is still clear."

"And watch out for him. That man . . . you know, I saw him again. He's not letting up. He's controlling this hurricane. He wants it to get me."

Hazel must have told me about this man at least thirty times in the last six months. She's also told me her sister—who died in 1958— comes by and cooks spaghetti for Hazel. I never know what to say. Do I try to correct her? Do I just play along?

"Do you remember there were some squatters living in the other buildings? The ones that have been boarded up?"

"Yes, of course. What does that have to do with anything?"

"Maybe that's who you've been seeing: a squatter, not a stalker."

"You know as well as I do, young man, the police chased them off."

"A few times, yes. But they come back."

She jabs her chest with her index finger. "I know what I'm talking about."

This is a losing argument. And I'm short on time. "I'm sure you do, Hazel. So you know what I'll do for you? I'll watch out for everyone and everything that might mean to do me harm. How does that sound?"

"Yes, that's right. Good boy." She pats my cheek again. "Now give an old lady a kiss good-bye."

I move the box out of the way, and she pulls me tight, kissing me on the cheek when she does. Her embrace is surprisingly strong. She smells like hand cream and hot dogs.

When she lets me go, she points to the door. "I mean it, Jacob. Don't look back."

FIVE

The wind buffets me as I take the five flights down to my apartment. It's even stronger now, making it almost impossible to move.

I slip once on the wet stairs, almost tumble.

What if I came this far—so close to returning to Jordan and Mackenzie—and fell on the stairs and hit my head?

I glance to the elevator, but Dallas and Hazel spooked me about it. So I take my time, step with care through the now-driving rain.

Inside my apartment, my already-packed bags stand just inside the door. I don't have much. Some clothes. My computer. A few mystery novels. Toiletries. A couple of photos.

It's all ready to go.

I unzip one of the duffels and move my hand around until I grip the object I'm searching for. It's round and smooth in my palm. An autographed baseball signed by Chicago Cub Ron Santo. I inherited it from my dad, a native Chicagoan and Cubs fan, when he died fourteen months ago. I've never cared much about the Cubs. Or baseball. I keep it only because it makes me think of my dad.

But Dallas does care. He's a *huge* Cubs fan, and he eyes the baseball with barely disguised envy every time he visits. If he's giving me a car—and more importantly, if I'm going to take it—then I want to give him something as well. It's not an equal trade—no offense, Ron Santo—but it will mean a great deal to Dallas.

My dad's death knocked something loose in me. Logically, I could accept his death. Parents die before kids. But emotionally . . . I fell off the beam and never could get myself back on. Jordan recommended therapy. She was right, of course, but I refused to go.

In many ways, Dallas has been more than a friend or a big brother. He's like a father crossed with a therapist.

I stuff the ball in my pocket, zip the bag.

I pause and take one long look around the apartment. There's nothing to it. Used furniture. Dingy walls. A musty smell that permeates every unit. I'm thrilled to leave—really thrilled—but I'll never forget the place.

Even if I never want to set foot in this building ever again.

I grab my bags—one in each hand—and as soon as I step onto the landing, the wind and rain punch me in the face.

I tuck my chin and turn my head to the building as I walk. I don't even bother to lock the door.

The wind catches me, makes me stumble. I adjust my grip on the bags and start down the stairs, moving as carefully as I can. I don't have time to slip.

My heart thumps in my chest, jumps into my throat. Anticipation. I'm eager to get back home. Hope fills me to the brim. This is the most hopeful I've felt in a *long* time.

I reach the second-floor walkway, turn right for Dallas' apartment. The rain blows even harder down here. Dallas' door is still ajar. His apartment must be a lake by now.

"Dallas?"

I put the bags down, dig in my pocket for the ball as I enter.

"Dallas? You here?"

No answer. A giant fist squeezes my chest. Something is wrong. Very wrong. Despite the wind, the air feels still in the apartment. Heavy.

"Dallas?" I say again, yelling over the wind and crashing waves.

A chill runs up my back. I step farther into the room, moving behind the couch.

That's when I see him.

Face down.

Hat flipped over on the floor.

Blood oozing from the back of his head.

SIX

"Fuck, fuck, fuck."

I drop the ball and fly across the room. The ball thuds and rolls away as I fall to one knee on the floor next to him. What am I supposed to do?

"Dallas? Dallas?"

He's not moving. At all. The wind continues to blow, sweeping through the apartment and across both of us. A loose palm frond comes through the door on a gust of rain.

I place my hand against the side of his neck, searching for a pulse. His stubbly skin is warm against my fingertips. My CPR training comes back to me. I find the right spot but feel no pulse.

"Shit."

I try his left wrist, lifting it gently.

I wait, willing a beat below his skin. But nothing comes.

Reality settles over me. My hands start to shake, and then the shake spreads up my arms and into every other part of my body. I'm trembling like one of the trees outside, battered by the storm.

I fall back onto the floor, Dallas' body next to me.

"No, no. This isn't possible. No . . ."

My mind fails to grasp what's happening. I keep talking, trying to summon a different reality into existence before my eyes.

But as the seconds turn into minutes, I know it can't be.

He's dead. Dallas is gone. It's my fault. If I'd stayed with him . . . if I'd talked him into leaving the island . . .

He'd still be alive.

I should have pushed harder. I should've done something.

I shiver again. The shiver seems to jostle my mind so that it turns over, shifting from the initial shock to a more logical state. How did this happen? How?

Some kind of debris must have blown in from the outside, gashed his head, knocked him out. Or maybe something fell from the ceiling.

This shitty building is barely standing. The storm must've knocked something loose. Hell, maybe Dallas fell trying to reach something.

Or maybe he got shocked trying to fix an electrical problem.

He spent the whole day getting the building ready. Putting the hurricane shutters up. Dragging the outdoor furniture into the parking garage. Maybe he overdid it.

I check the floor around his body, looking for the culprit. A branch that blew in. A chunk of plaster that gave way. A picture frame that came off a shelf.

But there's nothing. The carpet is threadbare but clean. Dallas fits the stereotype of the fastidious bachelor. I've never seen a speck of dust in his apartment. Every dirty dish gets washed and put away immediately.

There's nothing on the floor near him. Near his *body*.

Did he fall?

There's no ladder or stool in sight.

The gash is on the back of his head. If he fell somehow and landed hard enough to tear his skull open, he'd still be on his back. Right? But he's face down, his bloody wound facing me.

Like he was hit from behind.

Like he was nailed in the back of the head.

With a heavy object.

But the object is gone. And so is the person who did this.

SEVEN

Dallas was alive and well twenty minutes ago.

Which means the person who did this is very, very close by.

Maybe in the apartment with me.

Hiding.

Waiting—to do what, I don't know.

I could go out into the storm, into the wind and rain, where the person—or persons—would better be able to hide. Their movements obscured by the poor visibility and the noise of the storm.

Or I could stay inside and call for help.

But I have to make sure I'm alone.

I go straight to the front door of Dallas' apartment and shut it. The wind is so strong now that I have to push hard to get it shut. I engage the dead bolt and the chain as soon as it's closed.

Right away it's much quieter. The only sound is from the wind rattling the front door and the hurricane shutters. A second later, I hear a clock ticking in the kitchen.

My eyes roam over the space before me.

My kingdom for a golf club or a baseball bat.

But the only thing I see is a thick glass triangle, an award the local Kiwanis Club gave Dallas back in 2020. It's rock-solid and about the size of a hardcover book.

It will have to do.

I heft it in my right hand and move through the small living room. When I get back to Dallas, I pause, trying to convince myself this is all a mistake. Trying to will my friend back to life.

He's okay.

I was too nervous to detect a pulse.

He fell. Hit his head.

An X-ray, a few stitches, and he'll be good as new.

But no matter how long I watch him, Dallas doesn't move. He doesn't wake up. This isn't a dream. Or a nightmare. It's all very, very real.

My mouth and lips are dry enough to crack. There's water everywhere outside, but I'm dry as a bone.

I leave Dallas and head for the short hallway that goes back to the lone bathroom and bedroom. The bathroom door is halfway open, the light off. I feel like my nine-year-old self, the one who imagined monsters lurking around every corner. Behind every closed door and under every bed.

But the monster who did this is real.

The overactive imagination of my youth has come to life.

No point in hesitating. I spring forward and kick the bathroom door the rest of the way open. I manage to hit the light switch with my free hand as I do it.

The fluorescent lights gleam off spotless white tile. Before I have time to consider, I cross the room and throw the shower curtain open. But there's nothing there besides Dallas' immaculate lineup of shampoo, bodywash, and shaving cream.

The room is empty.

I should feel relieved, but I feel nothing of the sort. Instead I feel angry and anxious. I feel rage boiling inside me. Dallas' bedroom still waits for me down the hall.

I swallow hard before I step out of the bathroom.

The bedroom door is partially open as well. There are no lights on here either. If someone waits inside, they already know I'm heading their way. I've made enough noise to alert the whole island.

I listen but hear nothing. My heartbeat thumps in my ears.

I repeat the same ninja routine: jump into the room, flip the light switch. Again, there is no one here, but . . .

The room has been ransacked.

Every dresser drawer is open, its contents spilled on the floor like litter. The closet door hangs wide, clothes and boxes and shoes vomiting onto the carpet. The bedclothes are thrown back. No way a guy as fastidious as Dallas doesn't make the bed every day.

A robbery? In the middle of a hurricane?

Looting usually happens *after* the storm, not during. The vultures wait until the power's out, the residents gone, their homes trashed and vulnerable.

Did someone get greedy and jump the gun?

But why this place? Where no one has anything of value?

Could it have been one of the squatters who did this?

I need to call for help. The police need to find whoever did this. Before they get off the island.

Before they hurt one of the other tenants.

My hand is shaking when I slide my phone out of my pocket. I put the award down gently on the dresser. Maybe Dallas' sister will want it.

Someone will have to *tell* Dallas' sister. *Shit!* All their plans . . .

I dial 9-1-1 but nothing happens. Nothing.

I try again.

And again.

Nothing.

Service on the island is spotty at the best of times. My phone almost never works when I'm in my bedroom. I walk quickly back to Dallas' living room, hold the phone in the air like an offering to the sky, and try again.

Still nothing.

I decide to risk the walkway. I open the door a crack and look both ways before stepping outside. The blowing rain stings my face like thousands of tiny needles. The roof over the walkway offers some protection, but right now the rain is coming down sideways, nearly parallel to the floor.

I look over my shoulder, making sure I'm not being watched. But no one is there. The call fails again.

And again.

And again.

"Shit," I say, louder than I intend. "Shit, shit, shit."

I have no choice.

Someone has to go to the mainland.

And I'm the only one here to do it.

EIGHT

"Jake?" a voice calls out to me.

I nearly jump off the landing.

"What are you doing, Jake?" The voice gets closer, from the right. Rain splats into my eyes, obscuring my vision.

"Alaina?"

She's one of only two other tenants—besides Dallas—on the second floor. I know more about her than I should. Dallas tells me way too much of our neighbors' business.

For example, Alaina hasn't paid her rent in six months—the whole time I've lived here. Dallas granted her extension after extension. He has—*had*—a soft touch, and Alaina took advantage of that.

"What are you doing out here in this awful storm?" she asks.

Alaina's only twenty-one, nearly twenty years younger than I am. In fact, she's closer in age to Mackenzie than to me, and maybe that's why I've always felt . . . "sorry" isn't the right word. Worried? Concerned? I've always felt concerned for her.

Alaina's thin to the point of being wiry, with light red hair and prominent cheekbones. Her eyes are a deep blue. I'm not sure if she has a job. She speaks vaguely of working but never seems to. Everything Alaina says is a little vague, as if she's intentionally creating an air of mystery about her. Or as if she has things to hide. Dallas thought she had a well-off family. But her mother died last year. Maybe Alaina's spigot got cut off.

Alaina seems simultaneously young and vulnerable but also worldly and indifferent. One of the big reasons I want to head home is that I don't want Mackenzie to go any longer without her father around. Alaina seems unmoored, without anything or anyone keeping her tethered to the ground. I don't want the same thing happening to my daughter.

"Well? What are you doing?"

I reach behind me, pull Dallas' apartment door shut. "Nothing. Trying to make a call."

"Is Dallas home?"

"Didn't you say you were evacuating?" I ask her. "You said you were going to a friend's house inland. The storm's getting worse by the minute."

Alaina moves closer to the building, trying to avoid the rain. She wears a hoodie and jeans and rubs the sweatshirt material on her upper arms. "Fell through." She lifts her chin in my direction. "I thought you were going back to Ohio."

"I was. I mean, I am."

"It sounds nice to me. Ohio. I've never been there." Huddled against the wall, sleeves pulled down over her hands, Alaina looks more childlike and defenseless than usual. "I'm picturing cornfields and red barns. Lots of trees. That seems like what Ohio's all about. Kind of like a dream."

I try to place the call again, but there's still no signal. "Yeah . . ."

She cocks her head. "What's the matter, Jake? You're acting all weird."

I glance at Dallas' closed door, the rain spitting against the side of my face. I turn back to Alaina. "I have some news. But I'm not sure if we should tell anyone else."

"Is something wrong with Dallas?"

"Why do you ask that? Did you hear something?"

"Hear something?" She hesitates a moment. The wind blows her hair out from under her hood and across her face. She brushes it back. "No, I didn't hear anything, but I saw you standing out here, trying to use your phone in the pouring rain. Then you shut the door when I walked up. Like you didn't want me to go inside. Dallas likes to keep his door open, even when it's raining. He likes to be *available* to people. To everyone. I mean, that's his thing, right?"

I move closer to her, catch a whiff of cigarettes. Maybe that's what she's spending her rent money on. "Look, I'm sorry I have to be the one to tell you this, but something happened to Dallas." I glance at the parking lot, hoping for a distraction, but it's hard to make out anything in the storm. I turn back to her. "Dallas is gone, Alaina. He's dead."

Alaina whips her head toward the door of Dallas' apartment. "What the fuck? Did he have a heart attack or something?"

It takes me a moment to say it out loud. I don't *want* to say it out loud. "I think someone killed him. There's blood . . . on the back of his head."

Alaina's mouth forms a small O. A second later she raises her hand and covers the O. "Are you fucking with me, Jake?"

"I wish I were." I shake my head and point to the door. "His bedroom was ransacked, like it was a robbery. Maybe someone was looting. Maybe they thought we were all gone, and then they came across Dallas. His apartment is the first one you see. It's right here by the stairs."

"Maybe it wasn't random like that. Maybe they were looking for something. You know, something Dallas had. Or thought he had."

"What on earth could Dallas have that someone would kill for?"

Alaina averts her eyes. "I don't know." She shrugs. "Maybe it was those squatters. Those people were assholes."

"I thought of that too."

She uses her sleeve to wipe her nose. "Or maybe it was someone he knows. You talk to Dallas all the time, and he's super secretive about his past, isn't he? I mean, look at him. He looks like the kind of guy who had a rough time in life. What about his ex-wife, his daughter? He never talks about them. If they come up, he acts all weird and evasive."

"You think his family came down here and murdered him in the middle of a hurricane?"

"I don't know." She sniffs, wipes her nose again.

I can't tell if she's crying or if it's rainwater hitting her face. Or both. But she's not looking me in the eye.

"I need to get out of here. This building's going to be torn down, and even if it wasn't, I can't afford to stay here." Since she's not looking at me, it feels like she's talking to herself, giving herself a lecture. "I want to do so many things, but I'm just—I don't know . . . stuck. No one I know is really going anywhere. I'm always depressed and"—she looks me in the eye for a split second—"lonely."

Alaina's looking away again, and as we stand here on the landing, the rain hitting the sides of our bodies, she seems to shrink, to become even smaller than she already is. "You're young, Alaina. *Very* young. That's to your advantage. When the storm's over and all of this gets cleared up, you can do whatever you want. You have your *whole life* ahead of you."

"I guess." Big sniff.

"I think you should go back inside. The weather's getting worse and . . . whoever did this to Dallas is probably still around. Did you see or hear anything unusual? Anything at all?"

"Over this storm? Are you kidding? Not a chance. I was in my apartment with the door shut all day."

"What about yesterday? Or any other time? Have you seen anything unusual lately?"

She steals another look at me. "It seems like every few days there are dudes out there in hard hats and construction vests, and they go all over the island looking at stuff and measuring it. I'm sure they're trying to figure out how they're going to build the fancy condos they're putting in. They could at least wait until we're gone."

"Progress waits for no one."

"It's bullshit."

"You're right about that."

"What are you going to do now, Jake? About Dallas?"

"I'm going to go get help. There's no phone service—"

"There never is."

"I'm going to tell the cops. They can come over here and figure out what happened to Dallas. And then I'm heading for Ohio."

She finally looks at me for more than a second, forcing a smile. "Give my regards to the cornfields and the cows."

"There's more to Ohio than that. There are cities and factories and highways."

"Don't tell me that. Let me have my fantasy, okay?"

"Okay, fine. You can picture me in overalls and a straw hat."

She doesn't laugh. "What should I do? Do you want me to get help?" Her offer sounds uncertain, like it's the last thing she wants to do. "I don't have a car. Should I just hide in my apartment?"

"Yes, stay here. Ride out the storm."

I want to do something for Alaina. It seems wrong to just turn around and leave when she's clearly hurting. I get it. I really do. Being lost and confused and stuck doesn't always end when you're young. I understand what she's going through.

I dig in my pocket, bring out the Elantra's keys. "Here." I hold them out to her. "I'm not using my car anymore. It's not in great shape, but it can get you around town. You know, if you decide to . . ."

"If I decide to what?" she asks, although she knows what I was going to say. She's too smart not to.

"Just take the car, Alaina."

"If I decide to what, Jake?"

"I just mean it's nice to have a way to get around, even a lousy one."

"You meant, if I want to get a job. Or go to school. Or any of that stuff. That's what you meant."

"Whatever, Alaina. It's up to you."

She eyes me suspiciously. "How are you getting to Ohio if you're giving me your car?"

"Dallas gave me his car, the Highlander. He's moving to Chicago and doesn't need it. Or he *was* moving there. Before . . ."

"He *gave* you his car? Just gave it to you?"

"He did. You know as well as I do, that's what Dallas is like."

Is? Was. *Was like.*

"So you're driving off in his car, which is way better than your car. And he's dead. So, like, no one can be sure whether he gave it to you or not."

"When did *you* last talk to Dallas?"

Alaina's brow wrinkles. Her blue eyes turn to ice. "Fuck you, Jake. I knew you'd end up saying something like that. You and Dallas sitting around having your bromance while he complains about me not paying my rent. You're just like him. You both seem to think you know better than everyone else. Dallas acted like he was my dad or something."

"Alaina, I just want to—"

"And yet you two are down here all alone. The lonely hearts club. Where's your family, Jake? Where's Dallas' daughter?"

"Alaina, I'm trying to help you. So was Dallas. That's why he didn't evict you."

"Big favor. Letting me stay in this shithole. Fuck you both."

She whips around, her hair flying out in a ring around her head. She storms off down the walkway toward her apartment.

"Alaina, wait—"

She hesitates, freezing in place. Then she turns around.

I toss the keys toward her in a perfect arc, and to my surprise she catches them.

"Good luck," I say. "And be safe."

NINE

The key.

The key to the Highlander is inside Dallas' apartment.

"Shit."

I don't want to go back in there. I don't want to face—

But I have no choice.

Inside the apartment, the air feels even heavier than before. But that must be my mind playing tricks on me, knowing what happened here. My clothes are soaked. Death permeates the air like a virus.

Maybe I made a mistake. Maybe he's still alive. Maybe I was wrong. I'm not a doctor or paramedic. What do I know?

But when I walk up to the couch, it's obvious he hasn't moved. Not a millimeter.

He's dead.

There's no sign of the key fob. Most likely, he stuffed it into his pocket when I handed it back. His *front* pocket. And Dallas' body is face down on the floor. It feels like some kind of violation. To move him. To dig around in his pocket for the keys.

What would Dallas want me to do? He'd want me to get help. He'd want me to do whatever I could to protect everyone else.

"Okay, buddy," I say out loud, trying to act normal. "I'm going to just, you know, roll you over a little. Nice and easy."

I get my hands under his body and lift as slowly as I can. Hot beads of sweat pop out on my forehead as I roll him gently onto his side, his right arm pressed underneath him. It looks painful, but . . .

All of a sudden he's facing me, looking me right in the eye. The corners of his mouth turned down in anguish.

A trickle of blood runs out of his left nostril. Whatever happened to him must have hurt. Bad. Anger surges inside me, threatening to rise through my throat and out of my mouth. *Someone hurt my friend.*

"I'll find out who did this, Dallas."

I hold his body up with my right hand and use the left to search. My fingers dig in one pocket—no keys. It's harder to reach into the other pocket, the one closest to the floor. The sweat runs into my eyes, burning my corneas. I lift my hand to wipe it away. When I put my hand back in his pocket, my fingertips brush metal. I get a firm grip on the key and pull it out before easing Dallas back to the floor.

The gash on the back of his head mocks me like an angry red smile. It's vicious. Nausea washes through me, replacing the anger. The rusty odor of blood reaches my nose.

"Okay, buddy, I've got to go." I pat him on the back a couple of times as if that makes leaving him there any less gruesome. I stand, my knees creaking, and grab my two bags.

All I have to do now is get to the car without the killer finding me. Then try to make it across the waterlogged causeway and get help before it's too late. Before the hurricane makes landfall.

No problem.

No problem at all.

TEN

The rain blows in giant liquid curtains off the roof of the building. It gushes through the downspouts. A foot-long lizard scurries past my shoes, seeking shelter.

Rain and wind are the only sounds I can hear. If someone walked right behind me, I wouldn't hear them.

The stairs to the parking garage go down a half flight and then double back on themselves. If the killer—or anybody else—is waiting around the corner, I won't see them.

But there's no other way down. I'm not getting into the elevator. And the longer I wait, the worse the storm gets.

The farther away Ohio grows.

I grip my bags tighter, potential weapons I can swing at an assailant.

I start down the stairs, taking great care not to slip. Eight steps later, I'm on the landing halfway down. My left shoulder brushes the soaking stucco wall. Rain pounds down on me.

I get wetter and wetter.

Anyone could be right ahead of me.

Lurking.

I propel my body around the corner, so I'm directly facing anyone who might be there.

But there's no one.

My body huffs, my breath coming in great bursts. My lungs hurt. Water runs into my eyes and down the back of my shirt. The parking garage—covered with two inches of standing water—waits ahead of me, illuminated by the overhead lights.

I splash onto the garage floor, my shoes sinking into the water, my feet and socks now completely soaked. Dallas parked the Highlander five spots down from where I usually park. I run across the garage as fast as I can, my pants getting wet nearly to my knees. But at least the rain isn't hitting me anymore.

I hold the bags with one hand while hitting the key fob with the other. I jump in, toss the bags onto the passenger seat, and slam the door shut behind me, immediately locking the doors.

I'm inside. I'm safe.

The storm and the killer are outside.

I've been in Dallas' car plenty of times. It smells like citrus-scented air freshener like it always does. The windows fog. I start the car, blasting the defrost. I adjust the seat a little, wipe water off my face. Then drop the car into reverse. When I back up, the tires plow through standing water.

Just beyond the exit, the water still falls in sheets. When I get there, the headlights catch a figure rushing through the darkness, away from the building. It's a quick blur, a man in a dark jacket moving through the rain-soaked night in the direction of the other two buildings.

I hit the brakes.

The figure disappears into the darkness. I could follow, but I'd either have to get out of the car and go through the rain and slick grass on foot or to go off road in the car.

If he is the killer, he's fleeing the scene of the crime.

Getting away.

There's nowhere to go on Ketchum Island. The other two buildings are closed, boarded up tight without any power or water. A few outbuildings are scattered around the island. But there's no obvious place to hide. *Where are they going?*

My heart thumps in time with the wipers. I need to get out of here while I can.

The police can come and search for this person. Not me. I don't have time.

I hit the gas, and the Highlander lurches forward. The headlights cut through the slashing rain and the deepening gloom.

I'm on my way.

Finally.

ELEVEN

The wind blows across the causeway harder than when I was driving home.

The sky has turned completely black.

The car shimmies, and I fight the wheel. The radio gives me the bad news: *It's official. The National Hurricane Center has upgraded Kylie to a dangerous Category Three storm. That means sustained winds of close to one hundred and thirty miles an hour, causing devastating damage. . . .*

Rain drowns the windshield. The wipers are worthless. My foot eases off the gas as I remind myself not to go too fast. Even though a pressure building inside me urges me on.

Before the causeway washes away.

Before the roads out of Florida are closed.

Before the person I saw running through the dark gets away.

Before someone else gets hurt.

Waves hammer both sides of the road at the same time. The water slams against the barriers and spumes into the air like geysers.

A giant chunk is gone from the road ahead of me, like an enormous sea creature took a bite out of the causeway. The headlights catch it. I can't stop in time—

I'm going in—I'm going in—

A yelping noise of pure terror erupts from my mouth.

Somehow, I swerve in time, taking the Highlander into the oncoming lane to go around the gash, the vehicle lurching from one side to the other.

I slow again, moving back to my own lane. My hands are so wet with sweat I can barely grip the wheel.

I'm halfway across the causeway.

"Five hundred more feet. You can do this."

A light ahead of me comes into focus. It's too close to me to be on the mainland.

The light is moving toward me. I can barely make it out through the wipers and the sheets of falling water, but eventually it resolves into two lights.

Two headlights.

Another car.

Someone is driving across the causeway. Toward the island. Toward me.

"The fuck?"

Maybe it's the cops. Maybe someone in my building called for help. Alaina?

Help is on the way. The pounding in my chest eases.

If it's the cops, I can just keep going, drive right on past the police station and on out to the turnpike. Beat the storm. Start for Ohio.

Everyone will be fine. The cops will straighten the mess out, maybe even get Hazel and some of the others off the island. I slow more. I want to get a good look at the vehicle when it passes. I want to make sure it's a cop's.

The car moves toward me at a low speed—maybe twenty miles an hour. Not the way a cop would drive.

No sirens. No lights. Nothing indicating it's an emergency vehicle.

When it's right in front of me, I squint into the headlights. The high beams.

It's a small car, nothing at all like the vehicles cops drive. I can't see the driver, but the dashboard lights reveal the faint outlines of two people.

Just two regular people heading out to the island.

In the middle of a hurricane.

On a crumbling causeway.

I have a bad feeling. A *very* bad feeling. Are they working with the killer?

Are they going to help him get off the island?

Should I turn around and go after them?

No. I shouldn't. I should keep going. Cross the causeway. Get to the police station. Tell the cops how bad the situation is—how there may be a whole group of people on the island, looting.

And they've already killed one person.

Who or what will be next?

Even with a Category 3 hurricane coming for us, and even with everything else going on, that should be enough to get the cops to check things out.

I wipe a hand across my sweaty forehead, squeeze the wheel tighter, and keep going.

TWELVE

The first traffic light on the mainland blinks red, dancing on the wire like a bizarre marionette buffeted by the wind.

No other cars are out. The soaked streets are littered only with blowing garbage and palm fronds.

It takes a few minutes to reach the parking lot of the Hammond Point Police Station. It's a new building—painted white, topped with a gray metal roof, and fronted by a long Key West–style porch. It looks more like a designer home than like a law enforcement office. There's money to burn in Hammond Point.

I fly into the spot next to the lone cruiser, brace myself for the on-slaught of rain. I dash to the building, head ducked, feet wetter than I could ever imagine. Water sluicing down my neck.

On the porch, I shake myself off like a wet dog. The building's hurricane shutters are all in place, making it look like a fortress. A well-appointed fortress with clean lines.

In the reception area, a single cop stands behind a chest-high counter, talking into a radio. She wears the Hammond Point Police uniform—crisp navy blue shirt, gleaming badge. Her hair is pulled back in a tight ponytail.

"South side. No, the south side. On Highway One. Right—someone was trapped by high water near the back of the Dollar Tree. . . . No,

I don't know how deep the water is. Can you just check on it? And be safe." She rolls her eyes as she puts the radio down. She checks me out, her brow wrinkling. "Are you okay, sir? Do you need help with something?"

The radio crackles, a muffled voice. The officer presses a button, muting it. A computer chimes in some distant corner of the building.

"I—" I hesitate. *How do I say it?* "Someone was murdered. Out on Ketchum Island."

The officer's eyes widen the tiniest bit. She reaches down, grabs a spiral notebook and a pen, both of which she tosses on top of the counter. "I'm Sergeant Fernandez. Can you tell me what happened?"

I step all the way up to the counter, leaving a trail of water on the faux hardwood floors. I give Sgt. Fernandez my name and a summary of events—from the time I drove onto the island until I left again. I include the shadowy figure I saw running away from the building as I drove off.

Fernandez listens patiently, taking notes as I go. When I'm finished, she says, "And you seem pretty certain this man—this Dallas Bryant—really is dead?"

"He's dead."

"I ask because sometimes people see someone with an injury or someone unconscious—"

"Trust me. He's dead."

Fernandez nods. "And you think it was a looter who did this. Because the apartment was ransacked. Maybe a looter came out to the island, thinking the place was deserted, but stumbled upon Mr. Bryant and killed him. Then ran off into the night."

"That's right. But I'm just guessing. You may remember we've had some squatters in the two abandoned buildings on the island. You all came out and chased them off."

"More than once, I believe."

"Yes, that's right."

"But, as I recall, none of them were violent." She nods at her notebook. "Did Mr. Bryant have any enemies? Anyone who might have wanted to harm him?"

"Well, he's the building manager. . . ."

"Does he collect rent?"

"He does."

"Is there anyone not paying?"

"A number of people in the building struggle financially. Folks out there are just scraping by. Social Security. Fixed pensions. Disability. If they were rich, they'd be somewhere else."

"I get it, Mr. Powell. I do. But if there's someone specific who you think might want to hurt Mr. Bryant, it would help with the investigation. . . . Anyone spring to mind?"

Alaina's name sticks in my throat. "I can't think of anyone."

"You sure? Because it seems like someone popped into your head."

I'm shocked to hear her say this. I try to make my face blank before I go on. "Dallas has run that building for years. There are always people he has to come down on. Threaten with eviction. But, look, here's the thing, Sergeant. He's . . . he's just a really decent person. That's the thing you have to understand. He's a decent guy. He looks out for everyone. And they all love him for it. Even the ones who struggle with their rent."

"Right. Sure."

"He *has* butted heads with the owners of the building. The current owners. See, the building's in really bad shape. Not up to code. Electrical problems. Mold in a lot of apartments. Dallas has been trying to get them to do right by the people still living there, but the owners just want to drive everyone out because they're selling. Dallas fights for the tenants. He cares about them."

Fernandez studies me a second before responding. "I know that building is in rough shape."

"It is."

Fernandez drops her attention back to her notebook, continues jotting down notes. "Wealthy owners don't play. They shut down the other two buildings on the island." Fernandez stops writing but doesn't look up. "It sounds like Mr. Bryant made some enemies."

"He was only trying to do the right thing."

"I'm sure." Fernandez closes her notebook. "Well, the thing is, we're in the middle of a major crisis here." Fernandez lifts her hands, gestures at the empty station. The radio crackles again. "In case you didn't know, Kylie is a Category Three now. Folks let their guards down, thinking hurricane season was over. And then—pow."

Did you say the north side of the building, Sergeant? a staticky voice asks over the radio. *The person trapped by water? It's not bad here, and I don't see anyone.*

Fernandez lifts an index finger, then grabs the radio. She clicks the talk button. "South side, Leon. South side."

Oh. Okay. I'll go around back.

"Roger that." She puts the radio down. "Sorry. As you can see, I'm all alone here. And I'm not allowed to leave. And we're trying to deal with the most immediate emergencies as they come in."

"But my—"

"I'm sorry about your friend. I really am. And we'll get someone out there as soon as possible. But those who are still living and the endangered have to take precedence."

"Are you kidding, Sergeant? Look, I know you're all getting slammed and you have a lot of fires to put out, but my friend is dead. *Dead.*" Her blank face doesn't change. "If you're really more worried about the living, I should tell you there are still people in that building. Vulnerable people. And I saw a person fleeing the scene. He could be dangerous."

Something pops into my mind. Something I'd briefly forgotten.

"*And* when I was driving over the causeway, I passed a car. Heading *to* the island. Who would be dumb enough to go *to* an island during a hurricane? Right away I thought they were probably in on it. Maybe they're all working together."

Fernandez's face finally shows some emotion. "Wait—you passed someone? Driving *out* to the island? On the causeway? What kind of car was it?"

"It was a small car, but I couldn't tell the make. It was too dark, too rainy."

"Of all the damn—"

"What is it? Do you know them? Are they criminals?"

Fernandez shakes her head. "Not that I know of. What shape is the causeway in?"

"Crumbling. There's a giant gash in the middle of one lane. The whole bridge is getting pounded. We'll be lucky if it makes it through the night."

"That's why I *told* them to go home, to stay the fuck—excuse me—to stay the *heck* away from that island. But, no, they *had* to go. They were worried about . . ." Fernandez stops midsentence. Her eyes get much wider. It's like she's a real person now, not an automaton. "Wait . . . did you say you're from Ohio?"

"Yes, but how do you—" My heart drops like it's in an elevator shaft. "Why did you ask me that?"

"Is your wife's name Jordan? Jordan Arthur?"

"Yes, that's my wife. We have different last names. What are you saying, Sergeant?"

"I don't know how to tell you this, Mr. Powell, but your wife and daughter? They were just here. Like, fifteen minutes ago. They wanted to go out to the island—to look for you—but I told them to stay the hell away from that causeway. I told them it wasn't safe. And it's clear to me now they didn't fucking listen."

THIRTEEN

Fernandez tells me not to go. She tells me the police can offer me no protection.

She follows me out the door and off the porch and into the parking lot, yelling at my back as I head straight for the Highlander.

"The eye won't be past us until very late tonight," she shouts over the rain. "It's going to be brutal. And you already know the causeway is failing."

I look at Fernandez one last time before opening the car door. We're both getting pummeled by the rain. "My wife and daughter, Sergeant. My family. They're out there with a killer."

"You can't help them if your vehicle ends up on the bottom of the Intracoastal. With you in it. If a car goes into that water, it'll be swept away in an instant. Then you're gone." She snaps her fingers. "Just like that."

I start to open the door of the Highlander, but it slams shut, taken by the wind. "Send help, Sergeant. Please."

"It's going to be a while. That's just a fact."

"Go back inside, Sergeant."

It takes effort, but I finally manage to get into the car. I wipe the water out of my eyes and reverse out of the parking lot too fast, losing control when I hit the deep water collecting in the road. I struggle with the wheel and finally regain control. I put the car in drive and start for the causeway, being more careful as I cruise under the swinging streetlights. The rain falls horizontally, like flying needles. There isn't another vehicle on the road. It feels like the apocalypse.

Jordan and Mackenzie.

Out on the island.

With Dallas' dead body.

And a killer.

What were they thinking?

But I know. *I know.* They're determined to reach me, to make sure I'm safe.

On the causeway, I drive like a grandmother. Like a typical Florida resident. The car crawls along at a glacial pace, the wind shaking it from side to side. Fernandez is right—we don't know how long the causeway will last. I don't even know if I'll make it across.

Or if Jordan and Mackenzie did.

My foot presses down harder on the accelerator, my mind consumed by images. . . .

The car falling into the gash in the road—

Their voices screaming—

The car hitting the Intracoastal with a thud—

Jordan and Mackenzie surrounded by water on all sides—

I slam on the brakes when I see the hole. The Highlander skids across the wet causeway like a carnival ride, slides all the way across the pavement to the very edge of the gash I imagined my family falling into.

The headlights light up the water running off the causeway and into the giant hole. The raw edges where the earth fell away.

The gash is bigger than when I came the other way. It reaches more than halfway across the width of the causeway. It's not clear if there's room left for the Highlander to fit past.

Walking the rest of the way, exposed to the elements, doesn't sound pleasant. On foot, I could easily get blown off the causeway or swept away by a gust of water.

I reverse twenty feet, turn the wheels to the right. Gently, I tap the gas and ease forward, trying my best, in the dark and rain, to line up the tires so they remain on solid ground.

The front of the car clears the hole. My breathing eases a little.

I'm halfway past . . . three-quarters . . .

A strong blast of wind rocks the Highlander from side to side.

In my hands, the steering wheel moves on its own. I tighten my grip so hard the bones in my fingers hurt. A split second later, I feel the rear tire on the driver's side fall backward the tiniest bit. I've caught the edge of the drop-off. The Highlander lurches backward, starts to slide down into the hole.

"Fuck."

A light flashes on the dashboard. The AWD system. It's activating to keep the traction equalized across all four tires. The rear tire catches on something, gains purchase against the edge of the hole.

I apply a little gas, and the car lunges forward. All four tires are back on the surface of the causeway. I exhale the breath I've been holding, choking like I've just been resuscitated.

I'm more than a little shaken, but I have to continue. I drive even more slowly than before. When I reach the island, something inside me calms.

And then it hits me.

There's no way we're going to be able to go back.

We're all stuck on the island now.

FOURTEEN

Jordan's black Prius—the small car I passed on the causeway—sits in the parking garage.

I park next to it and jump out. The wind immediately knocks me off-balance. I push off the wall to get to the Prius.

The car is empty.

A used coffee cup sits next to Mackenzie's earbuds in the cup holder.

"Jake? Hey, Jake?"

I'm not sure I'm really hearing a voice. Maybe just a trick of the wind or the sound of the rain against the building and the trees.

"Hey, Jake."

I tense as a thin figure emerges from a dark area at the edge of the garage. He wears a loose Nirvana T-shirt and long shorts. His legs look like stovepipes that end in black sneakers. He cups a cigarette in his right hand and takes a puff. Ethan. He lives a couple of floors up from me.

Ethan lived with his mother until she died. Now he lives alone with a striped cat named Isaac. He's about thirty and works remotely, maintaining the website for a chain of fried-chicken restaurants based in Georgia. Ethan doesn't socialize much. The few times I've spoken to him, he's been friendly even though he's seemed to be struggling to do so. The first time I met him, he told me he'd recently been diagnosed as neurodivergent and was still working to understand it. He rarely leaves his apartment, so it's surprising to see him outside with the storm approaching.

"What are you doing out here, Ethan?"

"I've been thinking about something, Jake."

"You should be inside. It's not safe out here."

"You're out in it."

"I'm on my way inside now. I—" I start to tell him about Jordan and Mackenzie but stop. I don't want to be delayed any longer than necessary. "Let's go."

Ethan doesn't move. He takes another drag off the cigarette and exhales, the wind rushing the plume of smoke away. He tosses the butt into the standing water in the garage.

"I'm not a bad guy, am I, Jake?"

"A bad guy? Of course not."

"I just . . ."

I take a step toward him, my shoes getting wetter than I thought possible. "It's just what? What's wrong?"

He looks at me, his eyes a little bloodshot. "It's nothing. You're right—we should get inside. Isaac's alone in the apartment."

"He's probably freaking out."

"Yeah."

"Are you sure you're okay, Ethan?"

"It's fine. Just forget it. We'll talk later."

"Okay, all right. I have to get upstairs. And you should too."

Ethan nods, and I take that as permission to dash for the stairs, anxious to get to Jordan and Mackenzie.

For months, I've been pushing Jordan to bring Mackenzie down here. What teenager doesn't want to go to the beach? But Jordan was slow to commit. First, she didn't want to take time off work. She's a guidance counselor at our local high school. Then she claimed she didn't want to create the false hope that we were getting back together. Eventually, we arranged for Mackenzie to come visit before school started this fall. But Jordan's mother fell and went into the hospital. The whole thing broke down.

I know Mackenzie, though. I'm sure she continued to push for the trip. Teenagers can be relentless. Mackenzie is a force of nature nearly equal to a hurricane. As I pound up the stairs—and my slightly drying clothes get soaked again—I hear her voice in my head. *Mom, no, seriously. Think about how awesome it would be to surprise Dad in Florida. And then I'd become the last teenager in America to see the ocean.*

I'm betting that's how it played out. And when Kylie turned back to the coast—increasing in intensity as she rolled across South Florida—they probably determined that they had to come get me, knowing what a piece of shit the Elantra is.

I'm so anxious to see them I run up all five flights. When I arrive at the door to my apartment, my chest vibrates. I haven't responded that way to taking the stairs in months. It must be because of the adrenaline. I'm excited. Rain sprays my back, hits the exposed skin of my neck. I try the knob, and when it doesn't turn, I knock. Pound, really, with the edge of my fist. "Jordan? Kenzie?"

A muffled voice reaches me from the other side. "Dad? Is that you?"

"It is, honey. Will you please open the door?"

The chain rattles. The dead bolt slides.

When the door opens, there's Mackenzie, standing in my dingy little apartment, her mouth wide and her arms in the air like she's hosting a game show. "Surprise."

It's only in this moment that I—soaking wet—fully realize I haven't seen my daughter in person in six months.

"Come here, you."

I pull her close, as close as I can. Mackenzie squirms for a second—"Dad, you're dripping"—before giving in and hugging me back. I hold her until she says, "Yeah, I get it, Dad. You're feeling all the feels. It's nice to see you too." I let go. "And, by the way, I need to talk to you about this decor. What do they call it? Modern penitentiary?"

When I step back and take her in at arm's length, I notice something. "Are you taller?"

She shrugs. Her light blond hair is pulled back in a ponytail, and her blue eyes glisten above a freckle spray identical to the one on Jordan's face. "Maybe. It's been a while." She wipes her eyes. "Right?"

"It has. Yes. Yes." My eyes fill as well. I swallow hard. "I'm sorry you couldn't come down sooner. I wish you'd been able to visit this spring. Before hurricane season."

She lets out a tiny laugh. "It's okay, Dad. I'm here now. *We're* here now." She looks over her shoulder. "I wanted to see the ocean. Well, look, the ocean is pretty much everywhere tonight. It's like bonus ocean. What better time to visit?"

"Jake?" Jordan says from across the room. Her hair is darker than Mackenzie's, and, as strange as it is to realize, I think she's now a little shorter than our daughter. She's wearing a blue hoodie and jeans and her favorite running shoes. She looks amazing—as beautiful as the first time we saw each other, eighteen years ago.

Before I take a step toward her, I remember something I forgot to do. Something even more important than going to my wife.

I turn, go back to the door, push it shut, and flip the dead bolt.

"It's wet out there." It's the most obvious thing anyone has ever said.

But I'm not ready to tell them yet that I'm trying to keep a killer out instead of the rain.

"It's pretty liquid in here," Mackenzie says. "It smells like wet dog."

I ignore Mackenzie and lock my eyes on Jordan. "Hey."

"Hey," she says back.

That's all I need her to say to make me cross the room and open my arms.

To my relief, she accepts my embrace, and we fall against each other like two weary travelers. It feels like it's been a thousand years since I touched her. A thousand years since I touched anyone.

I squeeze her as tight as I can. She's still lean and muscular. Years of running have kept her fit as long as I've known her. She feels so good I don't want to let go.

Ever.

"You smell the same," I say into her hair.

She laughs in my ear, and it's a happy laugh, not an uncomfortable one. "So do you."

I tilt my head to the side. "Is that good? I've been out in the rain all day."

"Yes, it's good. It's . . . familiar." She pulls back, takes me in. She presses her hand against my chest, pokes me in the belly. "And, wow, you really have lost weight. You weren't kidding."

"I've had time to spare. Plus, I work outside."

"It looks good on you. *Really* good." She runs her hand along my biceps. "It's like you're ten years younger."

"Let's not get into the realm of science fiction."

Mackenzie clears her throat. "I'm still here, you know. Can you two tone it down a little?"

Mackenzie's wisecracking breaks the spell, and Jordan pulls back. Something crosses her face like a shadow. "Jake, we do need to talk about something." Her voice is low, almost like she doesn't want Mackenzie to hear, even though she clearly can in this small space. "Like, maybe now."

I want to hold on, keep her close. I don't want to ever let go. Of either one of them. But the look on Jordan's face doesn't allow me much choice. I drop her arms and take a small step back. "Why are you here? In the middle of a hurricane?"

"I—we can explain."

"It's my fault," Mackenzie says. "My ocean obsession. And my surprise obsession."

"Jake, can we—" She glances at Mackenzie before turning back to me.

"Dad, talk to her. Seriously, she's been acting very strange since we got here. Something's going on, but she won't tell me what. She's treating me like I'm six. And that's not like Mom. You do that, but she doesn't."

"What's happening?" I ask. "Did someone try to hurt you?"

"Hurt us?" Mackenzie asks. "Is that why you locked the door, Mom? What is this?"

Jordan runs both hands over her hair, lets out a long breath. "No, they didn't."

"Good."

"But we came here—to your apartment. We knocked and knocked, but you didn't answer. We figured you were here, because the Elantra was parked downstairs. It was a real Sherlock Holmes deduction on our part. But we were wrong, apparently. You weren't here, even though the car was."

"So, when I didn't answer . . ."

"Yeah . . ." Jordan touches her hair again, shivers. "You always talk about the guy who runs the building. Dallas. I know you two have become good friends. I had seen the door down on two marked MANAGER when we came up the stairs. So when you didn't answer, I went back to the second floor. But no one answered there either. And, honestly, I was starting to get a little worried . . . the storm . . . nobody answering."

Jordan's face is calm, her eyes clear. But her voice quavers a little. Jordan rarely cries. She almost always keeps her shit together.

"So you opened the door?" I say, prompting her.

"I did. And I saw . . ."

"Oh, shit, Jordan. I'm sorry." I take her in my arms again and hold her tight. I rub her back. "I'm so sorry you had to see that. That's—well, that's why I was gone. I was going to get help on the mainland. . . ."

Jordan steps back. "So the police are coming?"

"The police?" Mackenzie asks. "Okay, I'm getting tired of the whole parents-having-secrets thing. I've been pretty patient while the two of you, you know, work through whatever all of this is." She flips her hands up and down in our direction. "But now I want to know what's going on. You have to tell me."

"I didn't want you to know," Jordan says.

"Know what?"

"Just—it's going to be okay, Kenzie."

"I'll tell you," I say. "But listen, honey—you need to brace yourself. Okay? My friend Dallas—" The words catch in my throat, choking me. I have to take a moment to get it together.

"Dad?"

"Just give me a—" I hold a finger up. "My friend Dallas . . . He's dead, honey. Somebody killed him. I mean, that's what it looks like. And when Mom went into his apartment, she saw his body."

"Dad's right," Jordan says. "I didn't want you to see it, Kenzie."

"Are you kidding me?" There's real anxiety in her voice now. "No, no. You can't tell me this. This is so not cool."

"I'm going to do everything I can to protect you." I look from Mackenzie to Jordan. "To protect both of you."

"But the police are coming, right?" Jordan's voice is shot through with hope. "You went and told them."

I thought it was hard to talk about Dallas being dead. But it's even harder to tell them this.

"They're not coming, Jordan. Not anytime soon. The way that causeway looks, the way it's crumbling, I'm not sure how long it will be."

"But—" Jordan doesn't finish.

"I'm sorry to say we're on our own."

Both Mackenzie and Jordan stare at me with fear in their eyes.

"And I think the killer is still on the island with us."

FIFTEEN

"I can't believe this is happening," Jordan says.

"Me neither."

Mackenzie comes to me and puts her arms around me. "I'm sorry, Dad. I'm sorry about your friend."

Jordan puts her hand on my back. "I'm sorry too, Jake. I know how close you two were. You talked about Dallas all the time."

"I know. . . ."

"One of the reasons Mom agreed to come down here was to see your life, to meet your friends. She said you sounded different here, a lot happier than when you left Ohio—"

"Kenzie, can we just—"

"What, Mom? It's what you said. It's not bad."

"Still . . . sometimes . . . Remember what we talked about? Maybe, sometimes, don't say everything that pops into your head."

"Really? Again?"

"It's okay," I say. "There'll be plenty of time for everyone to talk about everything. Later. But right now, we have to think about other things. Like making sure the rest of us are safe."

"'The rest of us'?" Mackenzie asks.

"The other tenants."

"There are *other* tenants? We didn't see one single other person. It kind of looks like the apocalypse came early."

"There are still ten or twelve people here," I say. "They didn't have time to get off the island. Or they don't have anywhere to go."

"Why don't they have anywhere to go?" Mackenzie asks.

"They're all alone in the world. Some of them are so old they don't have any family left."

"That's awful."

"I know. It is. That's why I want to make sure they're safe. I want to make sure no one hurts them."

Mackenzie's eyes trail over to the door. "That's why you locked the door? Because you think there's a killer out there?"

"Yes."

"It looks solid," Jordan says. "We should be okay."

"Well," I say, "*we* will be. . . ."

"We can wait out the hurricane too, right?" Mackenzie says. "This building is right on the ocean, so it must be made to take hurricanes. They have hurricanes here all the time, right?"

It's been so long since I've been around Jordan and Mackenzie that I've forgotten what it's like for the three of us to discuss something in earnest. The quick interplay, the torrent of words and thoughts we throw at one another. The pure joy of being around the two people I feel most comfortable with in the world.

For a moment, I get lost in an appreciation of our togetherness— and lose sight of the seriousness of our situation.

Not only are they the two people I'm most comfortable with. They're also the two people in the world I'm most committed to protecting.

Survival instinct kicks in. Despite Mackenzie's protests about being kept in the dark, she's a pretty typical only child. A very mature, intelligent only child. Jordan and I have never hidden things from her—even about our marriage. That's why I know I can speak frankly with her.

"Most of the others don't even know about what happened to Dallas. And the thing is, Dallas would've been the one to protect them."

"So now we have to protect them," Jordan says—a statement, not a question.

"Well, I feel like *I* do."

"You want to do this for Dallas, right?" Mackenzie asks. "Like you're honoring him or something?"

"Exactly. And Dallas didn't really feel confident about this building being able to withstand a hurricane. Even a less serious one."

"So we're fucked?" Mackenzie asks with a bit of urgency in her voice.

"I'm not saying that. And could my daughter try not to talk like a trucker?"

"Sorry. I curse when I'm anxious. And I'm pretty anxious right now."

Before I can say anything else, the building groans. It sounds like the dying cry of an ancient sea beast.

"Fuck," Mackenzie says. When I give her a look, she just shrugs.

"What do we do, Jake?" asks Jordan. "Is it like a tornado? Do we go into the basement? Is there a basement?"

"No, there's not."

"Should we go up to a higher floor?" Mackenzie asks. "Or totally ditch this place?"

"We had a couple of hurricane watches last month. The safest place is usually the lowest floor. But we're so close to the water, there's going to be a storm surge. It could flood. The garage already has a few inches of water in it."

"Yeah, we know," Jordan says, lifting her soaked foot.

"And you can't go high—that's too risky. The wind hits the building the hardest up on the tenth floor. The roof could come off—or at least parts of it. And you can't go out of the building. There's going to be flying debris and rising water. Unfortunately, there's no real shelter anywhere else on the island. The best thing to do is go down to the second floor. We'll ride it out there. It's high enough that it won't flood and low enough that we won't be in too much trouble if the roof goes. The storm will pass by morning."

"Okay," Jordan says. "Okay, we can do that. Right, Kenzie?"

"Sounds like some seriously bizarre family bonding."

"So let's go," Jordan says, looking at me for a response.

"We have to get all of the other tenants down there too. Most of them live higher up—on the eighth, ninth, and tenth floors." My eyes trail up to the ceiling as if I can see to the top floor of the building. "I know who I have to start with. And I don't know how I'll be able to convince her to move."

SIXTEEN

7:28 P.M.

Before we can do anything, someone knocks on the door of the apartment.

All three of us jump. Mackenzie punctuates our sudden movement by yelping.

"Don't open the door," Jordan says.

"I won't."

"Don't open it, Dad. Seriously. In every horror movie, the person who opens the door ends up dead."

"I'm not going to open it. Not yet." I look at them, trying to figure out how to make this work. "The two of you need to get back. Go to the bedroom and shut the door. Lock it. It's kind of flimsy, but it'll hold."

"I'm not leaving you out here alone," Jordan says. She sounds determined. "Just don't open it, Jake."

I take a step toward them and speak in a low voice, just loud enough to be heard over the rain. "I need to find out who it is. What if they need help?"

"Maybe it's the cops," Mackenzie says, her eyes brightening with hope.

Her words bring me up short. Against all odds, I feel a molecule of optimism, a lightness in my chest. Did the cops drive out here? Did Sgt. Fernandez beg someone to check on us?

They wouldn't have even had to drive. They could've crossed the water in a boat.

I walk right up to the door. "Who is it?"

A muffled voice answers. At least I think it's a muffled voice. The wind moans through the spaces where the door doesn't quite fill the doorframe. Rain beats against the other side. It's hard as hell to hear anything clearly.

"Hello?"

"If they're not answering . . ."

"I think they're saying something, Jordan." I turn back to the door. "Hello? Who's there?"

I can't be sure, but I think the person on the other side is repeating one word. They say it twice, and then a third time.

My name. They're saying my name.

I unsnap the lock and grab the doorknob.

Jordan moves toward me. "Jake—no, don't."

I swing the door open, and there's Stanley on the landing. His thinning hair plastered to the top of his head by the rain. His shirt soaked. His mustache dripping water.

"Can I come in, Jake? I need to talk to you. I thought maybe you were gone. Aren't you supposed to be gone?"

"Yes, of course." I step back, wave Stanley inside the apartment.

"I tell you, Jake, it's warm out, but that rain is cold. Are hurricanes supposed to be cold?" He shivers, rubs his wet sleeves with his wet hands. "I'm kind of— Oh." He stops when he sees Jordan and Mackenzie. "Oh, I'm sorry. You have company. Oh, wait. I see. . . . Is this . . . ?" He turns back to me. "Why are they here?"

"Stanley Zimmer, this is my wife, Jordan, and my daughter, Mackenzie. They came down to surprise me, not knowing that Kylie was headed to our side of the state. This is Stanley—he lives up on seven."

Jordan and Mackenzie say hello, and Stanley nods back at them, a smile appearing below his drooping mustache. He moved in a month or so after I did. His arrival surprised me, since the building is scheduled to be torn down soon. The holding company seems to be in a great hurry to get everyone out. But Dallas told me Stanley didn't have anywhere else to go—and his cousin knew someone who knew someone who worked for the owners, so they arranged for him to move in.

It's all murky. But Stanley is a nice enough guy. Retired from a career in sales but vague about what he actually sold. Or where. He looks to be closing in on seventy.

"I'm sorry to interrupt," he says, like we're having a dinner party. "But I wanted to talk to you. I guess . . ." He peeks at Jordan and Mackenzie again. "I guess you all know about . . ." He points at the floor, indicating Dallas' dead body a few floors below us.

"They know, Stanley."

"My mom saw him."

"She did? Oh, I'm so sorry."

"It's okay, Stanley. How did you find out about Dallas?" As soon as the question leaves my mouth, I know the answer.

"Alaina told me. She said you were going to send the cops over."

I shake my head. "They're not coming."

"I figured as much," Stanley says, before letting out a deep breath. "She also said you gave her your car."

"What?" Jordan wheels toward me. "Your car, Jake?"

"You gave someone a car, Dad? You know I need a car, right?"

"Just wait." I hold my hands out to them. "It's way more complicated than that." I turn from Jordan and Mackenzie back to Stanley. "Why are you here, Stanley? What's going on?"

"Well, after Alaina told me about Dallas, I went into his apartment . . . to see him."

"Eww. Why?" Mackenzie asks.

"Dallas has a passkey that lets him into every apartment. So I wanted to see if he still had his keys on him. If he didn't, that means somebody else has them." Stanley glances at me. A sick feeling slithers through my gut. I hadn't thought of the passkey. "You know Dallas always has that passkey on him, right, Jake? On that Bears key chain?" I picture the blue and orange key chain sticking out of Dallas' jeans at the same time Stanley mentions it. "But his keys weren't there, so I was hoping . . . I was hoping you might have them."

The sick feeling grows inside me.

I reach into my pocket and pull out the single Highlander key fob I removed from Dallas' pocket. *After* he was dead.

Jordan stares at the fat black key fob. "What does this mean?"

I let Stanley answer. "It means whoever killed our Dallas has a key to every single apartment in this building."

SEVENTEEN

I swivel toward the door.

I didn't bother to lock it when Stanley came in, but even if I had, what good would it have done? Someone out there has the key to every unit.

We can barricade the door, yes, and hope whoever comes along doesn't have the strength or determination to push through whatever we use to block the entry.

But this is just one apartment. What about the others?

"So we're on our own, I guess," Stanley says. "Until . . ."

"Through the night, I'm sure," I say. "Maybe longer, since the causeway is falling apart."

"Really?" Stanley asks.

"I just drove across it."

"We all did," Jordan says.

"Let me get this straight. You were on the mainland and opted to drive over an insecure causeway to get to a barrier island? In a hurricane?" Stanley looks at all three of us like we've lost our minds. "Did you know Kylie's a Category Three now?"

"It's a long story, but yes. The causeway is nearly impassable. I almost drove into the water coming back. The waves are chewing more of it up every minute."

The color drains from Stanley's face. He starts rubbing his arms again. "Alaina . . ." He looks directly into my eyes. "She said she was going to leave the island. She said she had somewhere to go."

"Shit. She might not make it, especially in that car."

"I thought she was staying," Stanley says. "All of a sudden, she's leaving. It makes you wonder. . . ."

"Wonder what?" Jordan asks.

"Stanley, it does no good to speculate—"

He continues, as if I haven't spoken. "Alaina, she's trouble. She hasn't paid rent in nearly a year. I think she's involved with drugs, and who knows what else?"

"Stanley—"

"She calls Dallas all kinds of names behind his back. Even though he tries to help her. Have you ever noticed that when you try to help a person, things only get worse for you? That's the truth." Stanley's tone is world-weary. That of the barrier-island philosopher who's seen it all and delights in reporting his findings to the rest of us. Don't hate him—he's just the messenger. "Now she's leaving in the middle of a storm. After someone's been murdered?"

Jordan and Mackenzie exchange a look. They fully understand what Stanley is implying about Alaina. The woman I gave my vehicle.

"It wasn't Alaina," I say.

"You always had something of a soft spot for her."

"Stanley, I saw someone. Leaving the building right after Dallas was killed." I look around the room at all three of them as I speak. "I was heading to the mainland when I saw someone running away from the building. Out into the storm. I'm guessing that's the person who killed Dallas. Probably a looter. I bet he and Dallas got into it. It's possible they're hiding in one of the other buildings."

"Those are the only places *to* hide."

"If they took the keys, maybe they plan on coming back. But maybe they're scared. They probably think the cops are coming for them."

Jordan clears her throat. "What are these other buildings?"

Stanley holds up two fingers. "Two buildings exactly like this one. But they're both empty, scheduled to be demolished after the first of the year. I take walks over there when the weather's nice. I haven't seen anyone lately, but someone might have come back."

Jordan clears her throat. "So they might have to come back here? If they have a key and nowhere else decent to go during the storm?"

"That's why we need to get everyone in one place," I say. "Down on the second floor. We'll barricade the door."

Stanley looks scared. Nervous.

"What is it?" I ask.

"Well . . ."

"What?"

He lifts his hands, counting something off. "On the second floor, there's Alaina's apartment, which I bet is locked. And Dallas' apartment."

"Right."

Jordan jumps in. "Dallas' is a crime scene, Jake. We can't go there."

"Okay, so that leaves—"

"Lloyd," Stanley says in a low voice, as though he's speaking the name of an evil, ancient god.

"Right. Lloyd."

"Who is Lloyd?" Jordan asks.

"Lloyd is . . . well, he's a little eccentric."

"He's nutty," Stanley says.

"'Nutty' is a strong word, Stanley," I say. "I've only seen him twice in six months."

"That's pretty nutty." Stanley looks to Jordan and Mackenzie as if he's a lawyer offering his closing argument. "The man never leaves his apartment. And he doesn't let anyone inside, even Dallas."

"He must leave at some point," Jordan says. "Doesn't he get groceries or go to the doctor?"

"Everything is delivered," Stanley says.

"That's not odd," I say. "Especially since the pandemic. I've wondered if he's immunocompromised and has to minimize contact with others."

"Well, maybe." Stanley sounds skeptical. "I do see him leave the apartment on rare occasions, when I have trouble sleeping." Stanley pauses, his eyes growing wide. "I have bad dreams some nights. Really bad. They keep me up, and I don't want to go back to sleep."

For a moment, Stanley looks embarrassed. As if he's revealed too much. Stanley never seems to think he's revealed too much.

"That sucks," Mackenzie says. "It sounds like anxiety."

"Yes, kind of." He offers Mackenzie a small smile. "Anyway, I take walks when I can't—or won't—sleep. I travel all around the island. It's quiet. There are no cars. No people, really. But a couple of times, I've seen Lloyd driving around late at night, circling the island. It's strange. Sometimes I see him going out in the early morning too."

I'm reluctant to pile on to Stanley's "Lloyd is a freak" case, but—

"Yeah," I say, "I've seen him leaving the apartment early in the morning a couple of times. I see him when I swim really early."

"See," Stanley says with triumph, as if he's just produced the weapon that killed Dallas.

"So he keeps odd hours, Stanley. So what?"

"Plus, he's mean. He'll never let us inside his fortress."

"He doesn't have a choice," I say. "That's the safest bet for all of us, including Lloyd."

"Good luck with that," Stanley says.

"I'll talk to him," I say. "In fact, I should do that now."

"Wait." Mackenzie's voice rises to a volume louder than the rain and the wind.

We all turn to where she stands, with her hands held out from her side like she's about to fly.

"What is it, Kenzie?" Jordan asks.

"I want to know who Alaina is, Dad. And why did you give her your car?"

EIGHTEEN

Before I can address my daughter's question—which I know is actually a complaint—the lights in the apartment flicker off and on.

A second later they go off again. Someone yelps out loud. I can't tell if it's Stanley or Mackenzie. Only a moment passes before they come back on.

"The power's not going to last," Stanley says, always the bearer of glad tidings. "Too much wind."

"We should move before it goes out," I say. "It's only going to be harder in the dark."

"Dad?"

Jordan's right—our daughter needs to learn when it's not the right time to speak. I don't want ever to be the kind of father who tells his child—his daughter, especially—that she isn't allowed to speak. We raised her to speak up for herself and ask questions about the world. But sometimes it comes flying back at me during the most inopportune times. "Kenzie, can we talk about the car later?"

She lets out an exasperated gasp, and I think it's over. But then she starts muttering at the floor. "I thought I was getting the Elantra. You said I was getting the Elantra so I could drive it to school next year...."

"Kenzie—"

She looks up from the floor and speaks at a normal volume. "Instead you gave it to someone who . . . who sounds like a criminal. I mean, she might have killed that guy."

"Kenzie, enough." My voice rises above hers. "Alaina is my neighbor, my friend. She needed help, so I gave it to her. You've been lucky enough in life that you don't know what it means to *really* need help. You should be glad about that rather than worrying about what you're going to drive to school next year."

"But—"

"Enough, Kenzie." I make a slashing gesture with my hand. "Enough."

Mackenzie lowers her head. Jordan looks at me with—is it frustration or disappointment? We've been back together for such a short time, and now I'm already arguing with my daughter. I need to make this right.

I can't say it—or I won't—but I regret giving the car to Alaina, since I'm starting to wonder if her sudden departure is related to Dallas' death.

"I hear you, Kenzie, but we can't talk about this now." I turn to Jordan. "Why don't the two of you stay here? For now. Lock the door after we leave, and . . ." I look around the room. My eyes settle on the dining room table that came with the apartment. It's made of fake wood, and the top is scarred from years of abuse. But it's a heavy piece. "Push that table up against the door. And don't open it unless you know it's me." I turn to Stanley. "You're going with me."

"Why me?"

"Because you know Lloyd better than anybody else."

"I hate Lloyd." Stanley's mouth drops into a frown.

"That's proof you know him better than anyone else." I put my hand on Stanley's back and guide him to the door. When it's open, and we've steadied ourselves against the wind and rain, I gently push Stanley through before turning back to my family. "You'll wait here?"

"We will, but you have to promise me you'll be careful, Jake," Jordan says. "Please." The emotion in her voice makes me feel like we're still okay.

"I will." I point at the beat-up table. "Don't forget. Against the door."

Jordan nods. Mackenzie's eyes are on me, but she doesn't say anything.

Stanley is already heading slowly down the stairs, his right hand gripping the banister like it's a life vest. The thinning hair on the back of his head swirls in the wind.

When we reach the fourth floor, Stanley hesitates.

"Jake, please know I had no intention of causing any trouble between you and your family. I didn't realize the car was a bone of contention with your daughter."

"It's not your fault, Stanley. Forget about it."

But Stanley doesn't move on or forget things quickly. I know that about him. "It's just that I was worried about the passkey. And I wanted to keep you informed about Alaina. I figured you ought to know. I mean, I guess you're in charge here now, right?"

"I'm not in charge of anything— Hold on, Stanley."

I go by Stanley and move to the railing at the other side of the landing. The rain hits me with more force, pelting my eyes. I squint into the distance. The causeway is obscured in the rain and dark. A few of its streetlights still burn brightly, while others have been toppled by the wind.

"What do you see, Jake?"

"Look." I point in the direction of two small spots of red light barely visible in the gloom. They're moving very slowly. The Elantra, making its way across the causeway.

"There she goes," Stanley says.

My best guess is that she's a third of the way across—and just about to reach the spot where I nearly went in.

"She should stop. It's bad out there."

It's as if Alaina hears me. The taillights intensify as the brakes are applied. A faint cone from the headlights glows in the dark.

"What's she doing, Jake?"

"She stopped. She should—well, I guess she should back up. But that will be hard to do in this wind. She should just get out, I guess."

But the car inches forward, ever so slightly. I did the same thing half an hour ago. Tried to navigate my way past the gaping hole in the causeway. And I made it.

Barely.

The gap in the causeway has surely widened in the last thirty minutes as more waves have slammed into it, eating away at the asphalt and rocks like a hungry beast.

Stanley and I are soaked through. The wind shakes us, howling in our ears like a demon. Stanley steps back, moving under the overhang. He was right—the rain is cold, and I shiver.

"She stopped again," Stanley says. He talks loudly—above the wind and rain. "Maybe she wised up."

"I hope so. . . ."

The car remains still. Frozen in place.

My eyes may be playing tricks on me, but after thirty seconds the Elantra appears to move. It lists toward the driver's side, tilting like—

"Good Lord," Stanley says, his voice heavy with fear.

The Elantra teeters precariously—no doubt on the edge of the gash I almost went into only half an hour ago.

The car's brake lights come on and then go off. This happens two more times in rapid succession. The Elantra—smaller and less powerful than the Highlander—clearly can't get enough traction to extricate itself from the edge of the hole.

The brakes light up again. They stay on until the vehicle appears to move slowly forward again. *Why is she moving forward?*

A second later, the car lurches toward the gash, and plunges into the opening and off the causeway in one fluid motion. Even from this far away, we can clearly discern the outline of the car plummeting toward the Intracoastal.

Neither Stanley nor I breathe a word.

We stand there mute, watching in horror as the car sinks faster than I would've thought possible, its red taillights almost immediately disappearing into the murky water.

NINETEEN

"She's going to drown, Stanley. We have to do something."

As I turn for the stairs, Stanley grabs my arm. "Jake." His grip is surprisingly strong for that of a wiry guy close to seventy. It's like a large claw is clamping hold of me. "Jake," he says again as I tug away from him for a moment, the two of us perched on the edge of the landing, our feet dangerously close to the slick steps leading down to the next landing.

But Stanley doesn't let go. He says my name over and over.

"Jake. Listen to me, Jake—wait."

When I see I'm not going anywhere—at least not without the two of us tumbling down the stairs together—I stop resisting.

"Jake, what are you going to do?"

"I'm going to go out there—I'm going to help her."

Stanley shakes his head. "You can't do that." He lets go of my arm and points into the darkness where the Elantra used to be. "The rain is heavier. The wind is worse. If you go out there—either on foot or in a car—damn it, Jake, you'll suffer the same fate."

"We can't just let her get swept away."

"The current in the Intracoastal? It's strong. And we're coming off high tide. You've been swimming out there, right? You know what it's like."

The storm, the tide, the darkness. I don't have to answer him. Yes, I know.

"Jake, the moment that car went into the water, it was over. There's nothing you or anyone else can do. And Alaina? I saw her before she left. I don't know if she was . . . well, sober. I smelled the weed on her. She's not clearheaded. You'd have to be clearheaded and a Navy SEAL to get out of that water on a night like this."

Stanley's face is more serious than I've ever seen it. He makes more sense than I've ever heard him make. I struggle to accept the truth of his words, the reality of what we just watched happen to Alaina. On the heels of Dallas' death, it's enough to overwhelm me.

"Jake, we have to focus on the people who are still here. Right now." He points upward. "Your family is here. Everyone else who's still in the building." Stanley looks at the wet ground, the water pooling at our feet. "Did I ever tell you I served in Vietnam?"

"No, I didn't know that."

"I was just a kid." Stanley lifts his head toward the spot where we last saw the Elantra. "Over there, we had to keep going no matter what happened. Even when one of our buddies got zapped right in front of us. Maybe that's made me hard. I don't know. But I'm just trying to think of who we can still help. Who is still in this building."

My heart pounds so hard I have to place my hand on my chest. As if I need to stop it from spilling out from beneath my shirt. "I gave her the car, Stanley. If I hadn't . . ."

"What you did was try to help the kid out. So did Dallas. That's a good thing. You didn't make her drive out there. We don't know what kind of troubles she was dealing with. We've all seen how she acts. We don't know what was motivating her to go out there in this awful storm."

"You think she killed Dallas."

"What do I know about that? Maybe. Maybe not. But what I do know is, we need to focus on the here and now. The cops will sort this out when the storm is past. In the meantime . . ." He tilts his head back toward the building.

Like he said—everyone else.

The living.

"Why don't we go downstairs?" he says. "We can try Alaina's door, but it's probably locked. If it is, we'll go talk to Lloyd about using his place. He's a bastard, but he might listen to the two of us together."

His words hit home—like an arrow slamming into a bull's-eye. I risk one more look out toward the water, hoping against hope I'll see—what? A miracle? The Elantra driving out of the Intracoastal like an amphibious landing craft? Alaina emerging from the water unharmed?

But there's nothing there. As I knew there wouldn't be.

My hand goes out and clasps the railing for support. "I know you're right, Stanley." I turn and look him in the eye. "Thank you."

"Jake, we need you. Hell, we need all of us rowing in the same direction. But, like I said, you're in charge now."

I want to object again, but the truth is, Stanley is right. Now that Dallas is gone, there's no one else here to lead us. Jordan would be better at communicating than I will, but I'm the one who knows the people in this building, knows the island. I don't have much choice in the matter.

"Come on, boss. Let's go downstairs and talk to that slippery bastard."

TWENTY

Stanley checks Alaina's door first—which is locked.

Then he leads me to Lloyd's place.

We linger outside like two salesmen contemplating the best approach to a difficult customer—which, in a way, is kind of what we are.

Stanley looks at me and jerks his head at the door. My cue.

The wind picks up suddenly and pushes Stanley and me against the building with one strong gust. We both reach out, brace ourselves against the wall on either side of Lloyd's door. We can't just stand around in this weather. We might get knocked to the ground.

Lloyd surprises me by answering after one knock. He pulls the door open, chain still engaged, and looks out at both of us, his ruddy face filling the small space. Up close, he's younger than I thought—not much past sixty—despite the presence of a white beard. His face is unlined, and his vibrant eyes move from Stanley to me and then back again.

"What?"

"Lloyd," I say, "this storm looks to be bigger than anyone expected."

"Category Three," he says with a slight nod.

"We're all in the line of fire."

"So? Get inside your apartment."

He starts to push the door shut, but my foot stops him.

"Hey," he says.

"Here's the thing, Lloyd—we need to get everyone into the safest space possible before the full force of the storm lands. Together." Lloyd's eyebrows go up. "We can't use Alaina's or Dallas' apartments, and you're the only other person on this floor. So I was thinking . . . maybe we could all wait out the storm here?"

"What's wrong with Dallas' unit?" A perfectly reasonable question.

Stanley looks at me with a question on his face, as if to remind me I'm *in charge* now.

"Something happened to Dallas. He's . . . incapacitated."

Lloyd shows little reaction. "Well, I'm sorry. But you can't possibly come in here. Go bug Alaina. She's so high she won't notice ten more people crowding in her place."

"Alaina's gone." I leave it at that. "Her apartment's locked."

"I thought *you* were leaving."

"I was. But I can't go now. The causeway's washed out." I study Lloyd for a second, trying to determine if he looks like the kind of person who has a family. "And on top of that . . . my family's here now. My wife and daughter. I need to protect them. And everyone else. We all need to stick together." Lloyd grunts his disagreement, but I go on. "Your apartment is on the lowest floor, and it's in the center of the building. It's the safest place. It'll just be a few hours, Lloyd, maybe overnight. By morning the worst should have passed. We hope . . ."

Lloyd's eyes bounce between the two of us again. They linger on Stanley a little longer than on me. He shakes his head emphatically. "No."

When he tries to close the door this time, I push back with more force. Everything that's happened—the causeway, Dallas getting murdered, Mackenzie and Jordan showing up, Alaina . . . poor, poor Alaina going off that bridge—conspires to make me want to kick Lloyd's door in.

I don't. But my foot hits it with enough force to make him jump back.

"Listen, Lloyd, we're not playing around here. A hurricane is bearing down on us. People are going to get hurt. Quit thinking only of yourself and open the damn door."

His eyes flare with anger. "Who are you to ask anything of me? You're all the time sitting out here with Dallas. Right on this walkway, yukking it up. And you never once invited me to join you. Now when you need something you come knocking on my door? You can go to hell. Both of you."

He slams the door so fast—and so hard—I have to move my foot or risk its getting sheared off.

I keep talking like the door is wide-open.

"Is that what this is all about, Lloyd? An invitation to have a beer? It never once occurred to me you'd accept. What is this—eighth grade?"

"Easy, Jake. We'll just—"

I turn to Stanley. "Can you believe how selfish he's being? Doesn't he understand what's going on?"

"Maybe we can get into Alaina's place. Or we can go up to the third floor."

"He's pissed about us not inviting him to have a beer?"

Stanley remains quiet. Doesn't look me in the eye.

"What?" I ask.

"Well, you and Dallas—you know, the two of you seemed pretty tight. Like there wasn't room for anyone else to join in the fun."

"Are you serious, Stanley?"

"Hey, it's no big deal. I know I can be irritating sometimes, but the two of you . . . well, you were kind of in your own world. You had your own jokes and your own talk. You know . . . it was easy for other people to feel left out."

My mouth hangs open for a second before I respond. "Okay, Stanley. Well, I am sorry. I guess . . . well, I guess I was always telling Dallas about my problems. He listened. And gave me advice."

"We all have problems, Jake. The whole world has problems. Anyway, let's go upstairs."

My face flushes with embarrassment. Was I really so lost in my own issues that I failed to see what the people living right next to me were dealing with? Was I that clueless?

Before Stanley and I hit the stairs, something rattles behind us. I fear it's something coming loose in the wind—a railing or an awning, something about to break free and fly off into the night.

Instead, Lloyd's door opens again, revealing his ruddy face and broad shoulders. I anticipate another shot, one last dismissal before he hunkers down in his apartment for good.

But Lloyd waves his hand, indicating that he wants the two of us to come closer.

Maybe he wants to take a swing at us. Maybe I deserve it.

Stanley doesn't hesitate. He passes me, and I follow. When we get to Lloyd's door, he's stepped back, leaving it wide-open. A lone lamp burns behind him, producing a sickly yellow glow. The place smells like disinfectant. The only visible items of furniture are a hospital bed with a kitchen chair sitting next to it.

A woman lies in the bed, the covers up to her chin.

She pushes down the sheet and beckons us closer.

"Who is this, Lloyd?" Stanley asks, not bothering to hide the shock in his voice.

"My wife . . . well, not legally, but she is my wife. Her name is Catalina, and she said I should invite all of you in. And . . . the truth is, I always do what Cat says, so if you two idiots want to bring everyone in here, I guess I don't have much say in the matter."

TWENTY-ONE

Stanley and I exchange the same look.

Surprise. Confusion.

Shock.

One question races through my head. Stanley, as always, can't keep it in, giving voice to what we're both thinking. "You have a wife, Lloyd?"

Lloyd's face turns an even darker shade of red. He holds up his hands like he's getting ready to shove both of us back out the door and into the storm. "Now, don't start asking me a bunch of questions. I didn't—Catalina didn't—invite the two of you in here so you could interrogate me. Accept the offer or don't. But no questions."

"Okay—"

"Lloyd?" From the bed, Catalina's voice is surprisingly strong. She talks over me, getting Lloyd's attention. We all look her way.

"Lloyd, you can tell them. Remember—" She starts to cough, cutting her words off.

Lloyd moves to her bedside. He reaches down, gently helps her sit up, and with his other hand holds out a plastic cup of water with a straw. Catalina takes a couple of sips and then falls back against the pillows, as though the effort has exhausted her.

"Thank you, sweetheart," she says, her voice much softer.

"You're welcome."

Lloyd turns back to the two of us, his face returning to its usual mask of anger. "You're already upsetting her. So just keep your mouths shut."

"Lloyd," I say, "you don't have to tell us anything, okay?" I look directly at Catalina. "Neither one of you does. We're just grateful to have a place to go. It's very generous of both of you."

I'm ready to accept their offer and get everybody else downstairs. But Catalina's hand reaches toward her nightstand. It quivers ever so slightly, but she manages to wrap her hand around a small bell and shakes it in the air.

Catalina nods in our direction. I've known her five minutes, but even I understand what she's saying. She wants Lloyd to tell us what's going on. And why no one else knew she existed.

"Okay, okay." Lloyd turns back to us. "I'll give you two idiots the CliffsNotes. And then no more questions." He sighs. "Catalina has something called PSP. Ever heard of it?"

Stanley and I look at each other like a couple of kids in a difficult science class. We both shrug.

"That stands for 'progressive supranuclear palsy.' It's a neurological disease, kind of like Parkinson's but not really. Catalina and I met online. She's from Nicaragua. She moved here to be with me, but we couldn't get married right away." Lloyd lets out a barely audible grunt. "She was still married back home, and we were waiting for all of that to get sorted out. Then she got sick. Since she's not a citizen and not married to one, she couldn't get health care here. We spent a lot of money, but . . ." Lloyd looks back at Catalina, and she nods. "There's not much you can do for PSP. That's just a fact. You can give patients medication to make them more comfortable or decrease symptoms, but there's no cure. So we moved to Florida a couple of years ago. We wanted to spend our time together near the beach. Alone. I can take care of her. I can and I am."

"So, nobody knew Catalina was living here with you?" Stanley asks.

"Dallas knew." Lloyd nearly spits the words out. "He said it was okay. He said he'd cover for us."

"What's there to cover for?" I ask.

"He said he'd protect us from the owners. They charge disabled tenants more. They say it's because they're a fall risk."

"That's illegal," I say.

Lloyd wheels on me. "No shit. But do you know how much it costs to hire an attorney? How much time? That's the only way to fight it. Besides, Dallas said he wouldn't tell them about Catalina."

"That sounds like Dallas," Stanley says.

"I thought so too. But he double-crossed us. A few weeks ago, we got a notice that our rent was going up. And we can't afford it. Dallas must have ratted us out."

Catalina rings the bell again. This time more insistently.

"I *don't* care," Lloyd says over his shoulder. "It had to be him." Lloyd waves at us with unveiled disgust. "The rest of you can wait out the hurricane here. Bring your own food. You're not going to eat us out of house and home. But Dallas is not welcome. He's on this floor. He can stay in his own apartment and keep the hell out of ours."

Stanley and I go through our routine again, exchanging looks.

For a change, Stanley opts to stay quiet, letting me be the bearer of bad news.

"The thing is, Lloyd, Dallas isn't . . . Well, remember when I said he was incapacitated?"

"Of course. I'm not that old."

"Well, what I meant was . . . Dallas isn't alive."

"What?" Lloyd doesn't hide his irritation with this new development, and Catalina rings her bell so hard I'm afraid she'll hurt herself.

"I don't know how to tell you both this, but someone murdered Dallas. Earlier tonight. That's another reason we all need to stay together. There's a killer out there somewhere."

TWENTY-TWO

Lloyd shakes his head in disbelief.

Catalina waves at me. When I get to her bedside, she puts her hand on mine. "I'm so sorry about Dallas."

"Thank you."

She squeezes my hand with surprising strength.

When she lets go, I turn back to Lloyd. "I should probably tell you about Alaina too. Well, she drove off in my car. It's a long story. But she got washed off the causeway and into the water."

Catalina gasps.

"This storm is incredibly dangerous. Not to mention the situation with Dallas. More people could die if we don't work together. Whatever might have happened in the past, we have no choice but to put it aside and help each other. Are we all in agreement?"

Lloyd doesn't respond at first, but after a long pause he finally nods.

"Stanley and I are going to round everybody up. You two don't have to go to any trouble. People can sit quietly on the floor and read or play cards. The storm should pass in a few hours. By morning it will be clear, and with any luck the cops will be here not long after that."

When neither one of them says anything, I motion Stanley toward the door.

"Wait," Lloyd says, holding up a finger before disappearing into the bedroom. I can hear him rustling around, searching for something.

Catalina's large eyes focus on me. "I'm sorry," she says again, her voice softer, like she's running out of energy. "Alaina was a sweet girl. Sweet but troubled."

"You're right about that. I feel terrible about it. I was only trying to help."

"You and Dallas were always good to her. To everyone."

I flash back to what Lloyd said when we knocked on the door. "Maybe not good enough. Maybe we should have reached out more. To Lloyd." I turn to Stanley. "To you."

Catalina shakes her head. "Lloyd . . . He's very . . . sensitive."

"Lloyd is?" Stanley says.

"Yes, he is."

"I wish I'd known about your troubles here. I would have tried to help."

"Lloyd didn't want . . ."

"He didn't want anyone to know. He didn't want to be a burden."

"Yes . . ."

"I get it. But we're all a burden sometimes. That's what makes us human."

Lloyd reappears from the bedroom. In his hand he's holding a sleek black object that shines in the overhead lights. A split second after I see it, it hits me what it is. "What the hell, Lloyd?"

"Do either of you know how to handle something like this?" he asks as casually as if we're talking about a vacuum cleaner or a blender, even though what he's holding—based on my very limited knowledge—appears to be a Glock.

"Lloyd, let's not bother with that." I hold up my hands. "I don't know how to use one of those things."

"I do." Stanley passes me and walks right up to Lloyd. "Have you got a clip in there?"

I'm almost as surprised by what Stanley says as I was a moment ago by Lloyd coming out of his bedroom with a perfectly polished pistol.

"I do. And the safety's on."

Stanley takes the gun and examines it, opening it and closing it thoughtfully. To me he looks like he's Dirty Harry. Given his revelation about being in Vietnam, I shouldn't be surprised he knows how to handle a firearm.

He stuffs the gun into the back of his pants like he's been doing it for years. But his comfort with the gun doesn't put me at ease.

"You ready, Jake?" Stanley asks, moving toward the door.

"We don't want anyone to get hurt."

He stops next to me and slaps me on the shoulder. "That's why we have the Glock. So no one gets hurt."

The presence of the gun seems to inject Stanley with a confidence he lacked before. His posture is straighter. His gait more certain. He doesn't say anything else but instead goes right to the door and pulls it open, waiting for me to follow.

TWENTY-THREE

7:55 P.M.

Stanley and I go halfway up the next flight of stairs and stop on the small landing between floors. We're slightly protected from the wind and the rain here. But the storm still buffets us.

Stanley struggles to hold himself steady. He can't weigh more than 120 pounds.

"Okay," I yell over the rain and wind, "let's divide and conquer. How many other tenants are there? No one's left on this floor. Who else is there besides my family, and Hazel way up at the top?"

"Well, there's Nina and Kiara on the fourth floor. They'll probably be willing to move. And there's Sawyer up on six."

"And Ethan on seven. That's five apartments total."

"Right, Ethan. He's so quiet, sometimes I forget about him."

"I saw him downstairs. He was—I don't know—upset. He seemed to have something on his mind."

"That guy's mind is like a computer. Something's always rushing through it."

"True. I told him to go back to his apartment. I'm going to start with Hazel."

"You think she'll be willing to leave her apartment? She's so uptight about her things. I've heard she made quite a fuss when she had to move units."

"She had no choice then, and she has no choice now. I'll get her, and then my family. You okay to get the rest, starting with Nina and Kiara?"

He ignores my question. "Are you going to take the elevator with Hazel?" he asks. "Otherwise, it's eight flights of stairs in the wind and rain. And she's what, ninety?"

"Ninety-one. I don't know if she can do the stairs."

But I don't know if I can do the elevator. . . .

I do know Hazel won't listen to or go with anyone but me. No way she'd let Stanley talk her into anything.

"What if the power goes out while she's in that old junker?"

As if Stanley's words cast a spell, the lights flicker off. Then back on again. And then they go off. We stand in the dark, and the building makes a groaning sound, as if it too is fed up with the weak electrical grid.

"Shit," I say.

The lights flicker again, like a sick patient opening their eyes in order to take one last breath. To my surprise, when they come on this time, they grow brighter and stay on. Somehow.

"That was close," Stanley says. "You better hurry if you want to use that elevator."

"Yeah, but—"

"Unless you're going to put her on your back. I know you're in tip-top shape, but she's heavier than I am."

"Who isn't?"

Stanley lets out a little laugh.

"I'll figure it out when I get there."

"I know you're uncomfortable about me having the Glock, Jake." He reaches around and starts to remove the gun. "Would you feel better if you carried it?"

"Not a chance."

He pulls his hand back and keeps talking. "I learned a long time ago, I have to protect myself. But if you want to take it—"

"I really don't, Stanley. Just—just keep it. Okay? And be careful. We don't want anyone else getting hurt."

"Oh, I'm always careful. And don't worry, Jake. I'm like a cat. I have nine lives."

I know this is supposed to make me feel better, but I can't help but wonder how many of those lives Stanley has already used.

"I'll see you back at Lloyd's as soon as possible. Don't forget to tell everyone to bring enough food for a few days. We could be stuck awhile."

Stanley points down the walkway. "I'm going to take the stairs at the end, since that's closer to Nina and Kiara." He gives me a little salute. When he turns and walks away, the outline of the Glock is visible beneath his shirt.

He's right—I'm not crazy about him having the gun, and I hope like hell he doesn't have to use it. I'm not crazy about anyone having one. Certainly not me. I haven't held or fired one since I was a kid. And that was shooting at cans with a BB gun in my neighbors' backyard.

As I climb to Hazel, my mind cycles through the night's events. Like a damaged record, I keep getting stuck on two images. Dallas lying dead on his apartment floor. And the Elantra sliding off the causeway with poor Alaina inside.

Those images will play in my mind for years to come. Is there anything I could have done to prevent them from happening?

When I reach the fifth floor, I hesitate, making a conscious effort to shove the rest of the night out of my mind. I'll revisit those memories—often—on other days. But for now, my focus needs to be singular.

Protect those of us who are still alive.

Make it through the night.

My body wills itself in the direction of my family, a primordial urge rising somewhere deep inside me, to force my body in a different direction than my mind wants to go. I grit my teeth and keep going up the stairs. Hazel is the most vulnerable. She's the oldest. She's the one with dementia. She's on the highest floor.

Hazel first.

Then Jordan and Mackenzie.

As hard as it is, that's the way it has to be. I don't want any other images circulating in my head like the ones already there. I'm so distracted by this that I'm not paying any attention to what's going on around me.

That's why it's a complete surprise when I turn on the landing between the seventh and eighth floors and there's a man standing there, a man I've never seen before.

TWENTY-FOUR

He's half a flight up, standing on the eighth-floor landing.

Looking down at me.

Looming over me.

His dark wet hair is plastered to his head, his hands tensed in muscular anticipation. He wears a dark jacket and work boots. He's a slender guy, but his shoulders are broad.

My mind goes back to the moment when I saw a figure dash out of the parking garage and into the rain.

That person wore a dark jacket.

I take a step back. "Who are you?"

His left eye narrows, and he cocks his head. "Security."

"Who do you work for?"

He doesn't answer.

"Were you downstairs earlier?" I ask.

"I told you who I am. Who are you?"

Maybe it's impossible to ask someone who they are without it sounding like some kind of accusation. But the man's words seem accusatory.

Threatening.

"I live here," I say, "and I've never seen you before."

He starts down the stairs toward me, boots clomping on the steps.

"Name?" He's halfway to me now.

"Jake Powell."

He stops moving when I say my name. His eye narrows again.

"We've never had security here," I say.

"There's a hurricane hitting this island. And the building. The owners sent me to check on things. That's reasonable, isn't it?"

"It would be if they ever gave a shit about the building or anyone who lives here on any other day of the year. How did you even get here?"

"You're friends with Dallas, right?"

"Why do you ask?"

The man's nose wrinkles, like he's smelled something bad. "I should talk to the building manager, shouldn't I?"

"*Did* you talk to him?"

The man turns his head, looking away from me, as if he can see all around the island despite the blinding rain and wind. My back is exposed to the elements, getting soaked. "There aren't many residents left," he says. "That's my understanding. It's a collection of dead-enders."

"Did you talk to him or not?"

"Why did you ask if I was downstairs before?"

It's my turn to look away. I regret voicing the question. If this man—whoever he is—killed Dallas, then isn't it better if he doesn't know what I know? If I saw him running away, and he knows it, he has every reason to hurt me. "I was worried about the flooding—"

"There've been a few cars coming and going. Was one of them you?"

All of a sudden it feels like I'm the one getting interrogated. "I went to get help."

The man looks one way and then the other. "So . . . where's the help?"

"The police know we're here. They're sending someone as soon as they can."

"And the check's in the mail, right? You're going to hold your breath until those cops show up?"

"They'll be here." I'm well aware I sound like a child trying to will away ghosts in the night. I know as well as he does the cops aren't going to be rolling up here anytime soon.

Nobody is.

"Yeah, right."

"Why don't *you* go get help?" I ask. "If you're security and you have the owners' interests in mind, why don't you go to the mainland and send help? We sure could use it."

Rather than answer, the man comes the rest of the way down the steps, so we're on the same level. He's a few inches taller than I am but so thin he looks frail, and up close, his eyes are bloodshot, his hair streaked with a gray. "You know as well as I do we're all stuck here tonight. Maybe longer. Everybody should hunker down in their apartments and ride it out. That's what I'm doing."

"How are you doing that?"

The man stares at me, saying nothing.

"What's *your* name?" I ask.

Someone says a name out loud, but it's mine, not his. The voice echoes off the stairs and walls. Panicked.

"Jacob! Come help me."

My first thought is of Jordan and Mackenzie. But the voice is frail, scratchy. Old.

The man looks up just before I do.

Two floors above us, Hazel stands at the railing, looking down as rain drenches her clothes.

"Jacob, I need your help. Please."

My body brushes against the man's as I start past him. He grabs hold of my left arm with an iron grip.

"Wait," he says. "Just—"

I yank myself free. When he grabs for me again, I shove him away.

He loses his balance, stumbles back against the interior wall of the stairwell.

I take the opening and rush up the stairs to where Hazel stands on the landing, calling my name over and over again.

TWENTY-FIVE

Hazel stands perilously close to the top of the flight of stairs. I can't tell if she's aware of how close she is.

I look back once. No sign of the man from the stairs. The "security" guy.

Hazel's hands flutter in the air, like she's trying to dry them off. "Jacob, it is *about time*, young man."

"Are you hurt?" I reach the landing and gently guide her back to her apartment. She's still wearing her housecoat, and her glasses are now perched on top of her head, partially disappearing into her gray hair. "What happened?"

"You saw him, didn't you? You saw him. I know you did."

"Let's talk inside, Hazel."

Hazel allows herself to be led back into her apartment. I close the door behind us and throw the dead bolt. Her apartment looks exactly the same as it did a couple of hours earlier. It's hard to process, considering how much has gone wrong in such a short period of time. How much has changed.

Hazel won't sit. She paces across the middle of the room, her slippered feet occasionally knocking aside a book or crunching on one of her precious papers.

"What happened?" I ask.

"You saw him. That man down there. He was trying to get into my apartment. He came to the door and knocked so hard I thought he wanted to break it down." Hazel's eyes widen. "He knew my name, Jacob."

"Hazel, are you saying that man is . . . your stalker?"

She stops pacing, looks at me like I'm simple. "No, I am not, Jacob. I've never seen that man before in my life."

"You don't know him?" I point to the closed door as if we can see through it.

"Why on earth would you think that?"

It's disconcerting to hear Hazel say that. Does she not remember claiming she has a stalker? Is she forgetting things that much? "Then how did he know your name? And why would he bang on your door?"

"I don't know, Jacob." When she wants to, Hazel can sound as imperious as a crowned head. She's using that voice now. "I wish you'd stop asking me questions and do something. Just *do* something."

Jordan and Mackenzie are in my apartment. I know they've locked the door and blocked it with the table. But still . . .

I need to check on them. Soon.

"Well, Jacob? What are you going to do?"

"*We* are going to go down to Lloyd's apartment. It's the safest place for everyone."

Hazel gasps. "I'm not going *anywhere*."

"Hazel, we have no choice. The fact that a strange man came around here and pounded on your door proves it. Plus, the full force of the hurricane is going to hit us soon, and your apartment is way too high. There's strength in numbers. And safety on a lower floor."

Hazel ignores my arguments. She walks over and sits down on the end of the couch, in her customary position. It looks like she's starting some kind of strike. "You need to stay here with me. You stay here and keep that man from getting in, and I'll be fine."

"I can't do that, Hazel."

"Well, why not?"

"My family is here. Jordan and Mackenzie."

She looks up, a flash of curiosity in her eyes. "What are you talking about?"

"They're here. My wife and daughter. They're in my apartment." I give her a quick summary—their attempt to surprise me, the sudden turn of the hurricane. "I have to get back to them. I've been gone too long. The past six months and tonight. So—"

"Okay, then, fine. You go be with them. Send Dallas up here. He's always wanted to be my nursemaid. It's time he got his wish. He can ride out the storm with me here. In *my* home."

It hits me—she has no idea what happened to Dallas. Not Alaina either.

She knows none of it.

My eyes cut to the left. The photos of her husband and son sit on the end table. They both look back at me, imploring me not to add any more pain to Hazel's life.

But I don't have any choice.

I move slowly across the room, approaching her with caution.

She shifts her eyes to the many piles of paper near my feet. "Watch my papers."

"I will." When I get to the couch, I sit on the edge of the coffee table, facing her. It's vintage 1970s, built like a battleship.

Hazel looks scared. She reaches up, fumbles in her hair for the glasses. She takes them off and then puts them back on top of her head. "What are you doing? Why aren't you getting Dallas? Why aren't you going to your family?"

I don't want to tell her. If I could do anything else in the world, I would.

But I have no choice.

"Hazel, I have to tell you something about Dallas."

The words refuse to come. My chest tightens, and in the space that opens between us—the overwhelming silence—Hazel makes a low whimpering noise.

"No," she says. "Don't."

"I'm sorry, Hazel."

TWENTY-SIX

Hazel stares past me for a long time.

As if I'm not here. As if she's looking at the howling wind outside.

We're in a hurry, but I don't want to rush her.

Yet.

Finally, she says, "There's a box of tissues on the table over there."

I bring the box and resume my seat while she yanks two out, dabs at her nose and eyes. "He's so stubborn."

"Stubborn?"

"He's been fighting with the owners for years. *Years*, Jacob. About everything. I knew he was going to get on the wrong side of them."

"You think whoever hurt Dallas works for the owners of the building?"

"Dallas is all the time fussing at them. Telling them about code violations with the electricity and the sewage. The mold. The elevator. He's filed complaints with the government—the Fair Housing Office or whoever they are. Owners don't like that kind of thing."

"I didn't know he'd gone that far."

"Oh, yes, he has. They're trying to sell this property."

"They want to sell the land, not the building."

"Any complaint slows things down, Jacob. Gums up the works. Dallas is doing that. Nothing is finalized yet."

My forearm aches. The man on the stairs did more damage than I thought. A three-inch scratch, red and raw, crosses my wrist. He said he was security. Could he have been hired by the owners to intimidate Dallas? Did he go too far?

"The police are going to have to sort that out in the morning," I say. "Or whenever they get over here. In the meantime, we need to protect ourselves."

"Or maybe"—Hazel dabs at her eyes again, balls up the tissues, and tosses them onto the floor, where they join the mess and chaos—"it was my stalker."

"But you just said he wasn't your stalker."

"Maybe he hurt Dallas to try to intimidate me. I believe Dallas was protecting me, Jacob."

"That man on the stairs? The one I was just talking to? You said you'd never seen him before."

"I hadn't. At least, I think I hadn't."

This Abbott and Costello routine is leading nowhere. "Hazel, for now, we just need to get downstairs. This is the top floor of the building. It's not safe. The way the wind is blowing, the roof could come off." I glance up at the ceiling. "Water could come pouring in. You said it yourself—the building isn't in great shape. That's why Dallas complained about it. Now, let's get you out of here." I clap my hands together as if this will jar Hazel into action.

"My papers . . ."

"We can't take all of them, Hazel. You'll just have to—"

"Then I'm not leaving. I'll take my chances."

"Hazel, no. Look . . ."

She turns her head to the side, childishly acting as if I'm not here. It wouldn't surprise me if she threatened to hold her breath until she turned blue. My patience is quickly evaporating, so I play my last card.

"Hazel, I want you to come downstairs so you can meet Jordan and Mackenzie. I told them how important you are to me. They both want to meet you. We're all going to hide together downstairs, barricade ourselves in Lloyd's apartment. You just need to get up so we can get on the elevator and get down there before the power goes out. And before that man comes back, whoever he is."

"You hate the elevator. I know that."

"This is an emergency."

Hazel keeps her face averted. "Your family can come up and meet me here. They're young. They can climb the stairs."

The hurricane shutters rattle in the wind. The door shakes. Reminders of how bad things are—and how much worse they're going to get. Her stubbornness, which can be somewhat charming in the best of times, does nothing for me as the storm bears down on us.

As my family waits downstairs.

"Hazel, this is your last chance. I have to go."

She offers me a continued view of the side of her head. My hands go into the air and land against my thighs with a dull smack. I suddenly realize how cold it is in Hazel's apartment. The air-conditioning is blasting out of the vents. It doesn't help that everything on my body is still wet. Hazel is never going to listen to reason. I have to accept it.

I stand up and cross the room, heading to the door. I don't have a plan. I don't know if I can actually go through with leaving Hazel in these conditions. But I don't know what else to do. She's refusing to budge—as Stanley predicted—and at some point, tough decisions have to be made.

Hazel's voice stops me, prevents me from having to see if I have the courage of my convictions.

"What did you do with my gift, Jacob?"

My hand hovers above the doorknob. "Your what?"

"My going-away gift. Do you still have it?"

I pat my pockets as if I'm going to find the box on my body. "I have no idea where it is, Hazel. I might have . . ." I try to think. I had it earlier. With my luggage. And the baseball. I may have dropped Hazel's gift in Dallas' apartment. "I must have put it down. It's not the most important—"

Hazel scoots forward on the couch. She starts rocking. It's the same routine she always uses to get herself up. She grunts, and it takes everything in me not to go help her. I've tried that, and it only makes Hazel frustrated.

"Hazel, what are you doing?"

"If you lost my damn gift, I'll kill you, Jacob."

"Are you serious?"

"Dead serious, young man."

She rises from the couch a few inches, but then falls back. She starts rocking again.

I cross the room, lean down next to her. "Are you actually getting up and coming with me?"

"I'm not coming with you," she says. "I'm finding that gift. If you can't take care of it, I will."

"Why are you so worried about it? What is it? A puppy?"

"Will you just help me off this damn couch and take me down-stairs? Haven't we talked enough?"

Rather than argue, I do exactly as she says.

Anything to get her down to the second floor.

TWENTY-SEVEN

Hazel shuffles across the landing to the elevator door, my hand on her arm in case she stumbles.

She's going nowhere fast. It's clear to me now that it would be a slow, dangerous trek for her down the stairs. She'd probably never make it.

The elevator is our only real option. Even though the thought of taking it makes my stomach churn with the ferocity of the ocean.

My hand is shaking when I hit the down button. Once, twice, and three times. I know it won't make the elevator come any faster, but it gives me the illusion of control.

Hazel shivers.

"Are you okay?" I ask.

"I'm cold. And wet."

"The elevator will be dry."

"You really think that old contraption's going to work, Jacob?"

"I doubt it. Want to try our luck on the stairs? Only eight floors to Lloyd's place."

"*Pshhh.* I'm only out here because you lost my gift."

"I didn't *lose* it. I misplaced it. Temporarily."

"I *told* you to take it home. And not to look back. And yet, here you are."

"Helping you."

"*Pshhh.*"

The elevator gears and cables whine loudly enough to hear them over the wind and rain. They squeal like a dying animal. *Eight floors. One elevator ride. A few minutes of my life . . .*

Hazel shivers a second time. I wish I'd made her wear a coat, but we rushed out the door of her apartment so fast I didn't have time to think. No way I can risk going back. I might never get her out of there again.

"I'm sorry," she says. When I glance at her, her eyes trap me in their gaze. "About Dallas. I know you're close."

"Thanks. I'm sorry for you too. I know the two of you were close."

She doesn't respond. The wind whips through the landing. I shiver as well.

"I know you've lost some people in your life." I feel like I'm on thin ice. Have I gone too far?

She remains silent so long I think she's ignoring me. Then she says, "Thank you."

The elevator rattles to a stop on her floor. The door slides open with the speed of a glacier.

My heart speeds up. "Ready?" I ask.

"I feel like the poor chimpanzee they launched into space."

"We're not going into orbit. We're going downstairs." I put one hand in front of the open doors and keep the other on Hazel. "Come on."

Hazel shuffles into the elevator with me at her side. The space inside feels smaller than I remember. As if the storm has managed to shrink it a few feet. The floor is wet, and two of the four lights in the ceiling have burned out.

Every nerve in my body tingles. Each one of them exerts its own tiny will, trying to get me to turn around and exit this death trap. I do my best to fight them off, forcing my feet to stay in place.

After a deep breath, my quivering finger hits the number two.

The heavy doors close, possibly even more slowly than they opened. Now would be a good time to pray—if I believed in prayer.

We hang suspended for a long moment, the steel doors shut in front of our faces, before the car lurches into motion.

"Oh, my," Hazel says.

That's about all there is to say.

She pulls her arm free of my grip, fumbling, until her hand clasps mine. Tight. Her skin is sweaty. She holds on to me like it's for dear life.

I get it. I do.

I hadn't thought a creaky elevator ride would scare someone as tough as Hazel, but it seems to do exactly that. She starts to hum, presumably to distract herself. I distract myself by trying to decipher the tune, and just as I do—"Lonely Is a Man Without Love"—the two working bulbs above us flicker. We look up at the same time, Hazel's hand squeezing mine even tighter, and as soon as our eyes land on them with hope, they flicker out. We are surrounded by total darkness. A split second later, the elevator car jerks to a stop, clunking as loudly as a locomotive when it does. As soon as the elevator gears stop grinding, we hear it—the sound of the wind howling just outside the thick walls of the elevator shaft.

TWENTY-EIGHT

"Oh, no." Hazel's grip tightens even more. She squeezes my hand so hard it hurts. "No, no, no, no."

"Easy, now." It's blacker than the darkest night inside this thing. We can't even see each other.

"This is like being in a coffin."

"It's not that bad." But it is that bad. The wind slows outside, and the dampening of sound is like dirt being shoveled over the lid of a casket. I have the strong desire to claw and scratch my way out. I suppress my worst impulses for Hazel's sake, feeling like I'm a parent who has to calm a child. It's just like all the times I had to put on a brave face for Mackenzie when she was scared.

"Hazel, I have to push the emergency button."

"Please do."

"I need both of my hands."

She doesn't seem willing, but she finally lets go. I move forward like a blind man, reaching out with both of my hands until I make contact with the elevator's control panel. The floor buttons are flush with the panel. I hit as many of them as I can, but nothing happens. My pressing becomes more panicked, less controlled.

I work my way lower, find the raised emergency knob, hit it as hard as I can.

It makes a screeching ring, like the fire alarm in my grade school. Dallas explained once that the elevator has a backup power system that brings it back online even when everything else is out.

I wait for that to kick in.

At least everyone in the whole building now knows that someone is stuck in the elevator. And they can probably guess who.

Not that there's anything they can do about it. Dallas could—maybe—but he's gone.

In some small way, it makes me feel better to hit it again. Like whistling in the dark past the graveyard. So I do. I smack it again and again with the edge of my closed fist.

"I don't think that's helping," Hazel says. "We're going to die in here."

"No, we're not, Hazel." Even though what I'm really thinking is *Yes, we are.*

"We're going to be in here until Christmas. Why did I let you drag me into this contraption?"

"Because I wanted to save your life."

"I was safer in my apartment."

"You're actually safer inside this stupid thing if the roof comes off."

I hit the alarm one more time. "Damn it." My voice is louder than I intend, the sound bouncing off the walls and making me feel more trapped.

Maybe it was a bad idea to get into this thing. It seemed like the best option. But now that we're stuck here in the dark, it feels like the walls are closing in. Like we'll soon be squeezed into pulpy flesh.

My breathing comes faster, panic rising in my throat like a choking wad of cotton.

I suddenly feel farther away from Jordan and Mackenzie than I did when they were still in Ohio. I feel like I'll never be able to reach them.

Every step I've taken has led me farther and farther away from them. Every choice has been the wrong one.

When I left Ohio and came to Florida . . .

When I left Dallas alone in his apartment . . .

When I gave Alaina the keys . . .

When I got into the elevator . . .

"Jacob?"

"What?"

"I have to tell you something, and it's important." Hazel pauses for a long moment, letting me register her words. "If I don't get out of here . . ."

"What do you mean?"

"If I don't make it, and I might not, you have to find that gift."

"Hazel, *why* are you worrying so much about a gift?"

"I worked hard on that gift, Jacob. It's quite meaningful to me. And to Dallas. If you care about him at all . . ."

I hit all the buttons again, to no avail. Hazel's right—we could be in here a long time. Maybe the entire night. Maybe we *will* die in here.

"What does Dallas have to do with the gift?"

"If you care about him, find that gift. Promise me, Jacob. Promise me right now."

"Yeah, okay, Hazel . . ."

Something thumps in the elevator shaft. *Thump-thump-thump.* Like a person is banging somewhere.

A second later, I think I hear my name. *Jake?* It's faint, but I'm pretty sure I'm not imagining it.

"Hello?" I wait. "Hello?" I say more loudly.

No one answers, but a couple of moments later I hear the sound of more thumping along the side of the elevator shaft. Like someone is running up the stairs. Like *multiple people* are running up the stairs.

Someone yells my name again, and this time I can hear it more clearly. "Jake?" It sounds just like Stanley. Like Stanley is right outside the elevator door.

"Stanley? Is that you?"

"Jake!" The voice yells, saying one word at a time, "Are? You? Okay?"

"We're stuck!" I yell back through the elevator doors.

I can barely make out what he says next. "Well, that's obvious."

"Stanley?" I yell again.

"I'm here."

"Is everything okay?"

"Yes. Everyone . . ."

"What?"

Again he says one word at a time. "Everyone. Is. In. Lloyd's. Apartment."

"Jordan and Mackenzie?"

There's a long pause. It's dead quiet. Where did he go?

"Dad?" a voice calls out. It's Mackenzie. She's there. Right on the other side of the elevator doors. "Dad, are you okay?"

TWENTY-NINE

"Kenzie. Go to Lloyd's apartment. Please."

"Okay, Dad."

"Is Mom there?"

"I'm here, Jake."

"Go with Stanley."

Mackenzie's voice gets louder. "Are you hurt, Dad?" She sounds upset.

"I'm fine. Just stuck."

Sweat covers the back of my neck. It feels sticky and slick. Hazel breathes heavily beside me. The walls are moving again. I place one hand on the wall in front of me and the other on the wall next to me, trying to convince myself things aren't really closing in on us.

"Why did you get in there, Dad?" Kenzie yells. Just like a teenager to ask *why* at a time like this. "You hate elevators."

I swallow hard. My throat is too dry. I have to work to get the words out. "Kenzie, just go with Mom." I lean against the elevator door. "Go with Stanley. Okay?"

"Are you really okay?" Now it's Jordan who sounds upset.

"I'm fine." I'm not sure there's ever been a larger disconnect between my words and feelings. "Just go."

"Jake." It's Stanley again. "You know . . ." He hesitates. Like there's something he doesn't want to say.

"Spit it out, Stanley."

There's no time for secrets. We're yelling at each other through an elevator door while a hurricane churns toward us. Secrecy is out the window.

"Someone is here, Jake. In the building."

"I know."

"What are we going to do?"

"Go back downstairs. Just go."

"Okay."

"We're going," Jordan yells through the door.

"Good," I yell. "I'll be there soon." It's like I'm trying to convince myself.

I wait, listening. But no one says anything else. I assume they've headed back down the stairs. My throat still feels like it's stuffed with cotton, but the feeling of panic eases a little. At least they'll be safe when they get to Lloyd's place. It's the best option they have—that any of us have.

"Okay," I say, more to myself than to Hazel. "Okay."

I take a few deep breaths, my hand still pressed against the steel door in front of me.

"Are you okay, Jacob?"

"I guess."

"I'm getting hot."

"Me too. I'm sorry there isn't somewhere to sit."

"My legs are starting to hurt, but I'm not worried about that. That I can handle."

"We'll get out of here, Hazel. We will."

"I was going to say . . . Well, never mind. . . ."

I turn from the door. My eyes have adjusted enough for Hazel to be a fuzzy shape in the darkness. "What is it, Hazel?"

"It's just . . . Stanley."

"What about him?"

"I don't trust him."

"You don't trust anybody."

"That's not true." She sounds huffy. "I trust you . . . and Dallas."

"I appreciate that, but I've led you into a dead end here."

"But, Stanley," she goes on as if she didn't hear what I just said, "he's a tough case. You remember the man who was pounding on my door?"

My gut starts churning. "What about him?"

"I think—no, I know—the other day . . . I saw him talking to Stanley outside the building. I said I hadn't seen him, but I think I did."

"Stanley and the man who said your name when he pounded on your door?"

"Yes, that's right."

"Are you sure, Hazel? Because you don't always—"

"I'm not crazy, Jacob. And I'm not blind either."

"What do you know about Lloyd?"

"He's an old crank."

I keep any sarcastic comments to myself. "Is that all you know about him?"

"He keeps to himself. I wish more people would."

"Did you know he's married? I mean, kind of."

Hazel's eyes brighten. "Well, that old dog. There *really* are only two kinds of old men, Jacob. Dead and dirty."

"His wife is sick, Hazel."

"But, as I was saying, Jacob, I'm worried about Stanley and that man—"

The two bulbs flicker slowly on and off, which means the backup system is starting to work. A dead patient coming back to life. When they come on all the way, they're so bright I have to cover my eyes and squint.

The elevator follows suit, slowly lurching to life. The car shakes. I reach out to steady Hazel. We're moving again. Finally.

The button for the second floor is the only one illuminated on the control panel.

"Oh, thank God." Hazel grips my arm with one hand and raises the other to her chest. "We're saved from this death trap."

The wheels grind loudly, but at least we're moving. Slowly as ever, but moving.

The lights above the door count down our progress.

When we get to the third floor, I hold my breath. Moving from the third to the second feels like it takes one hundred years, but eventually the car comes to a stop on two, and the doors magically thud open. Rain spits inside the elevator and brushes my face.

The light from inside the elevator spills onto the landing, and Hazel and I come face-to-face with a man staring back at us.

The so-called security guy.

He's waiting for us like we're old friends.

THIRTY

I put my arm across Hazel, using it as a barrier between her and the man.

We have to get away.

I shouldn't go. It's important to be with Jordan and Mackenzie. The others. If everyone is here on the second floor—and so is this guy—I need to stay. But something primal kicks in. Fight or flight.

I hit the button for another floor—any floor—but before the doors close, the security guy throws his hand out, preventing the doors from shutting.

"Hold on," he says.

"Back off," I say.

But he stands firm, his rain-soaked hair dripping into his face.

"Whoa," the security guy says. "Easy, now. I think we got off on the wrong foot."

"That tends to happen when you grab someone for no reason." I hold up my arm, revealing the scratch on my wrist.

"Sorry about that," he says. "I just wanted to talk."

"You have a funny way of talking. And you still haven't told me: Who are you?"

"I did tell you. I work security for the building." His hand still blocks the elevator door. He presses his other hand flat against his chest. "I'm Tyler Rigdon. I work security for the Bennets. I came out here to check on the building. And now . . . Look, I'm stuck here now. I know you're friends with Dallas, and he didn't take kindly to anything or anyone involved with the Bennets. When I saw you, I was worried you would give me a hard time. I was being careful."

Earlier, this guy stood above me in the stairwell. Loomed over me like a grizzly bear. But now, in the door of the elevator, we're on even footing. He's a little taller than I am, but not much. He takes his hand off the door and leans closer to me. "I'm sorry about Dallas, by the way. I really am."

"How do you know about that?"

Before he answers, I know. Stanley.

As if he can read my mind, Stanley comes walking up. Behind him are Jordan and Mackenzie. To say my heart lifts would be to make the understatement of the decade. I could reach the tenth floor without benefit of an elevator or stairs.

I want to go to them, pull them to me, but everyone is staring at me. Hazel is behind me, saying my name.

"Jacob? Jacob?"

"What is it, Hazel?"

"I told you—that's the man, the one who pounded on my door. The one who was talking to Stanley a few days—"

"Hazel—"

"I did *knock* on your door," Tyler says. "And I did say your name. I came here to check on the tenants, and I was particularly concerned about you. . . . We were worried you might need help."

"You think I'm an invalid too."

"And, yes, I *have* talked to Stanley before," Tyler says with an exaggerated nod. "I was out here checking on things the other day, and Stanley was kind enough to answer a few of my questions."

Tyler's personality has undergone a shift from when I ran into him on the stairs. He's trying hard—*very* hard—to convince me, to convince all of us, that he intends no harm, that he's just a regular guy doing his job. Is he trying too hard? I'm not sure.

"This is all very sweet," Mackenzie says, "but it's cold out here. And wet." She shivers, a bit dramatically, it seems, and I have to resist a desire to roll my eyes. Jordan pulls her close, rubbing her arms. "Can we go inside now? I mean, really, can we?"

"I think we should," Jordan says.

"Everyone is waiting," Stanley says.

A giant gust of wind blows down the walkway, causing the building to creak loudly. It's as if it wants to encourage us to get moving.

"Jacob?" Hazel says behind me, and I know what she's thinking. *Don't do it. Don't trust that man.*

Just then, a palm frond comes flying down the landing, hitting Stanley in the backs of his legs.

"Jacob?"

I turn to Hazel. "It'll be fine. We need to stick together. It's safer."

"But, Jacob—"

"We'll talk once we're inside, Hazel."

THIRTY-ONE

8:40 P.M.

We all file into Lloyd and Catalina's apartment. The wind blows the door shut as soon as we are inside.

There isn't much room. Catalina's bed takes up most of the small space. We shuffle in and spread around the end of it. I say hello to Nina and Kiara, whom I haven't seen since the day before when we ran into one another at the only gas station on the island. That feels like a million years ago now.

Lloyd emerges from the bedroom holding a weather radio, the announcer's tinny, droning voice laying out the worsening threat from Kylie.

The storm is approaching peak intensity now as the outer bands begin to lash the coast. Anyone in the path of the storm right now is in grave danger. The next couple of hours will be the most harrowing of all. . . .

"Oh, crap," Stanley says.

"Shh." Lloyd glares at him, and Stanley shuts up.

Find shelter immediately. . . .

Stay off roads and away from flooded areas. . . .

Two hurricane lamps burn on the kitchen table, their flames casting a flicker of orange light onto the ceiling and walls. A thick candle with three wicks sits on Catalina's bedside table, its flames quivering. The air in the apartment is close and humid, slightly musty.

Lloyd sets the radio down and comes past me to bolt and chain the door. "Okay, we're all inside. Do you want to barricade the door, Jake?"

"We should—"

"Wait." It's Stanley. "Ethan isn't here yet."

"He's not?"

"He's trying to get Isaac out from under the bed."

"Isaac?" I say. "You mean the cat?"

"Ethan won't leave without him."

"Well, he can't bring a cat in here," Lloyd says. "Catalina's allergic, and she can't have anything disrupting her breathing."

The bell quickly rings out from the bed. We all turn. Catalina shakes her head, the candlelight illuminating dark circles under her eyes. She brushes her hand across her face and shakes her head with more strength.

"Looks like Cat doesn't mind the cat," Stanley says.

Lloyd growls and shakes his head in defeat.

"Well," Nina says, "maybe we should all get to know each other." She looks around the room, her eyes moving from one person to the next. "I'm not sure I've been properly introduced to all of our neighbors. Not to mention our guest." Her eyes pause for a moment on Tyler. "It looks like we're going to be spending the night here, so we might as well get to know each other."

"Maybe more," Stanley says, voice bleak.

"Okay, this will kill a little time." I point at Nina. "Why don't you start, and then everyone else can introduce themselves."

Lloyd growls again, more loudly.

We all ignore him and go ahead.

Nina clearly enjoys leading us off. "Well, okay, I'm Nina Savage. I'm originally from Saint Paul, Minnesota, but I came down here in high school—to live with my dad." My eyes go to Mackenzie. What does she think when she hears that? Does she regret coming to

Florida now that we're stuck in a hurricane with a killer on the loose? "That was about twenty years ago, and I've been here ever since. Oh, we brought a bag of stuff to eat." She bends down, lifts a bulging canvas bag. "There's peanut butter. Crackers. Granola bars. Some fruit. I thought about bringing the fish we have in the fridge, since the power was likely to go out. Now I wish I had brought it." Nina's close to my age and slender. Her cheeks flush in the dark even though she never seems shy. "Oh, and this is my wife, Kiara. Do you want to introduce yourself, hon?"

Kiara shrugs and rolls her eyes. "It looked like you were going to use all the time."

"Oh, hush."

"I'm Kiara Savage. I'm married to Nina. Obviously." She lets her gaze fall on Nina, and the two of them lock eyes. All of a sudden the room is charged with so much electricity it feels awkward to watch the two of them sharing this moment. I glance at Jordan, who shrugs back at me before Kiara finishes. "I'm from Sarasota, the other side of the state. I got laid off a few years ago. Been trying to find something permanent ever since, but I've had no luck."

"Oh, yeah," Nina says, "I got laid off too." Nina must sense the question we all have—*They were* both *laid off?*—because she explains, "We worked together. At an indie bookstore. The place was limping along before the pandemic. When COVID hit . . . they closed pretty much right away. Anyway, that's where we met. Where did you meet your wife, Lloyd?"

"That's not important right now. We're in the middle of a hurricane."

"Come on, Lloyd," Nina says. "Everyone's playing."

"No."

The bell rings.

"No," Lloyd says. "I'm not doing this."

Before Lloyd gets too angry and decides to run us all out of his apartment, I step in. "Let's leave Lloyd alone. He's doing us a big favor. I'll introduce my family next."

Jordan nods and smiles at everyone when I say her name. Mac-kenzie makes a somewhat sarcastic—I imagine—half bow, like she works at Medieval Times.

But no one cares. Everyone oohs and aahs, thrilled to finally meet my wife and daughter.

"Oh," says Kiara, "isn't she precious? She looks just like you, Jake."

"She looks like a nice cross between both of them. Very pretty."

Even in the dim candlelight, I can see Mackenzie avert her eyes.

"And to think, this whole time I thought you were making them up, Jake," Nina says with a laugh.

Before I can respond, a raspy voice emerges from the darkness. "I'm Sawyer."

Everyone cranes their neck trying to find him. Sawyer sits on a rickety-looking dining room chair. He's younger than I am but looks twenty years older. He wears blue sweatpants with a white stripe up each side and an oversized bright orange University of Florida sweat-shirt. His right arm rests on a metal cane, the kind with four prongs that touch the ground. Sawyer got injured on the job. His hip. He's been on disability as long as I've been here.

He holds up a plastic grocery bag. "I don't eat much, but I brought some . . . Well, there are some Pop-Tarts and frozen burritos. I guess we can't heat them up." He shrugs. "You don't have to worry too much about me. What I want to know is, who's that guy?"

Sawyer jerks his thumb toward Tyler, who seems to have receded into the walls, as if he doesn't want anyone to notice him.

"That's the guy I told you about, Kiara," Nina says, squinting at Tyler. "You were sneaking around here the other day. You work for the Bennets, right?"

"Yes, I do."

The mood shifts rapidly, like a school of fish darting one way and then another beneath the waves.

"The Bennets?" Lloyd says. "No, you can't be here."

"Now, hold on, Lloyd," I say. "We have to put all that aside. Tyler's stuck here like the rest of us, and he deserves to be safe just like anyone else. So he's going to stay."

"I don't like it, Jacob," Hazel says. "I don't like him. Or what he represents."

"Hazel, please."

"But I told you—"

"Hazel, enough."

Everyone grows quiet. That awkward feeling when one person snaps at another and no one quite knows what to say descends over all of us. Hazel averts her eyes, looking as hurt as a kicked puppy. I immediately regret speaking so harshly. It's the same way I felt when I talked back to my parents as a teenager and quickly wished I could take it back. I didn't have the maturity to do it then, but I do now.

"I'm sorry, Hazel. I didn't mean to snap at you. I just—" My face flushes in the dark. I'm sure no one can see, but I can feel it.

"Wait just a minute," Sawyer says. "Ethan isn't here because of Isaac. But where's Alaina? Shouldn't she be here?"

Stanley looks at me, his lips pressed tight. For a change. He's not going to say anything. He's going to let me handle it.

"That's a good question," Kiara says. "Do you want me to go look for her?"

"And what about Dallas?" Nina asks.

Now I look at Stanley. I'd assumed he told everyone what happened to Dallas when he went to round them up, but he gives me a subtle shake of his head. Then nods at me.

The ball's in my court.

All I want to do is go home. But I can't.

All these lives are in my hands.

Including the lives of my wife and daughter.

As strange as it all seems, it appears as though Stanley was right. I'm in charge.

On top of that, a killer lurks on this island. One who could very well be intent on harming all of us. A killer who may come directly after me.

A killer who may be in the room with us.

A killer one of us—even I—may have to face to save the others.

I'm in charge . . . yes . . . one of the loneliest feelings I've ever had.

PART TWO

THIRTY-TWO

8:55 P.M.

All eyes turn my way.

I'm not a leader. Or a boss. I'm just a regular guy.

This is Dallas' role. The kind of thing he excelled at.

When my dad died, I immediately felt so much older. Not because of my chronological age, but because my safety net was gone. All of a sudden I was the oldest person in my family. I was an adult. Technically I'd been an adult for years. I even had a family of my own. But it always felt like Dad was there if I needed him. Ready to jump in and tell me what to do. Ready to pick me up if my car broke down or to give me advice about insurance.

Dad stuff.

Since my mother died when I was in high school, and I don't have any siblings, I needed to make all the decisions about Dad's estate. But the whole time I felt like I was pretending. Like I was pretending to be my dad.

And that's exactly how I feel now, with everyone looking at me with expectation in their eyes. But I know the truth. This is a mistake— someone else should be standing here. But there isn't anyone else.

Just me.

Jordan and Mackenzie are both looking at me, expecting me to know what to do, how to take care of all these people I've known for months.

The building creaks and groans around us as the wind increases. The faces arrayed before me look terrified. Their eyes dart from side to side. They look up at the ceiling and down at the floor. The muscles in their jaws clench.

My fellow tenants know we're in trouble. They know the building is in bad shape. And on top of that, I have more bad news to share.

"I guess it's time I tell you all what's happened."

It feels like I've swallowed a handful of dust.

I tell them about Dallas. Those who haven't heard the news yet gasp. The fear on their faces is replaced by shock. Everyone looks around, as if searching for a culprit. A brittle tension weaves its way through the room.

"I know this is upsetting to hear. But there's no way to get off the island now, so we just need to hunker down and wait for this hurricane to pass."

The tension increases. It seems sharper, like something that could cut a person.

"Are you telling us Dallas was murdered?" Nina asks, a hand pressed to her chest. "Is that what you're saying?"

My heart clenches. I'm grateful no one can see me trembling. "It does appear that way. It was probably a looter. They may not have known anyone was here."

Lloyd speaks up. "My money's on those squatters in the other buildings. They've been a problem for months."

"Those squatters, as you call them," Kiara says, "are displaced, unhoused people. We can't just assume they're guilty of everything that goes wrong around here."

"Anything is possible," I say. "That's why it's good we're all together."

"Who would want to hurt Dallas?" Nina asks. "Everyone loved him. It had to be random. Wrong place, wrong time."

"The people who own this building would want to hurt Dallas," Sawyer says. "He was always giving them hell."

"That's—" Hazel stops herself, looks at me. "Well, I'd say that's one possibility that can't be ruled out."

Once again, every head turns toward Tyler. The air, already so close and humid that being in here was like being locked in a damp closet, grows even thicker with suspicion and fear. Every pore in the room seems to be giving off the scent of desperation.

"You still haven't told us about Alaina," Kiara says.

"She drove off," Mackenzie says. Maybe she knows me well enough to detect something on my face, because she quickly follows up. "Right, Dad? Isn't that the woman you gave the car to?"

Again, all eyes turn to me. I wish they'd look anywhere else.

"It's true that Alaina took my car and tried to leave."

"She *stole* your car?" Kiara asks.

"No. No, she didn't steal my car. I gave her the keys. Dallas gave me his car so I could drive home, and I gave mine to Alaina because she wanted to leave. She had friends, I guess, who said she could crash with them on the mainland. She really wanted to get off the island. And, you know, Alaina, she's not—she wasn't—she's had her struggles."

"A lot of that was self-inflicted," Lloyd says.

Catalina rings her bell, shakes her head. Lloyd presses his lips tight. Like he doesn't intend to speak ever again. I've never seen anyone else have that effect on Lloyd.

"So, yes, it's true that Alaina tried to drive to the mainland . . . across the causeway. . . . I wish I hadn't given her the keys. Or that I'd told her not to go . . ."

"Why?" Jordan asks. "What happened?"

"The causeway isn't safe." My eyes meet Jordan's, and now it's our turn to speak without words. As soon as her gaze catches mine, she knows. Her expression shifts from interest to horror. "The rain, the wind . . . You all know the guardrails aren't very high to begin with. And now the whole thing is starting to fall apart. There's a big chunk missing."

Kiara gasps.

"Stanley and I were on the landing, and we saw Alaina try to drive across." I pause for a long moment, take in a deep breath before

I say it. "She didn't make it. The car slid off the causeway and into the water. We saw it happen. . . ."

"Oh, my God," Nina says.

Out of the corner of my eye, I catch Catalina making the sign of the cross, her lips moving silently.

"I know this is all terrible. And I wish, more than anything, I could bring those two people back. But I can't. That's why we need to stay together and make sure the rest of us get through this safely. And we can. I know that." I look around the room, my eyes landing on each of my fellow tenants. "Really, we can."

"I don't know how we're going to—"

I cut Sawyer off. "We will. Okay?" No one responds. I wonder if I've come off too strong again. "Look, can I just have a moment alone with my family? I've barely seen them since they got here, and we've been apart for six months."

"Sure, don't mind us," Nina says. "I mean, we're all friends here."

"Actually, I was hoping . . ." I look around the room but there's nowhere to go. It's like all of us are standing in a jam-packed subway car.

Catalina rings her bell. We all turn and look.

She lifts her arm and points toward the bedroom down the hallway. "Go on. . . ." Her voice is low but clear. We all hear her.

I look at Lloyd, figuring he won't want us in his private space. But I also know I've found the one person Lloyd will consistently defer to. He nods his head, lips still tight.

"Thank you." I grab a flashlight off the coffee table and flick it on before turning to Catalina. "Thank you both. Maybe everyone else should settle in. Sit on the floor. Eat some of the snacks . . . try to remain calm."

I point the light in the direction Catalina indicated. Jordan and Mackenzie go down the hallway ahead of me, toward the apartment's lone bedroom, leaving everything and everyone else behind.

THIRTY-THREE

It's strange to be in someone else's bedroom. Their most intimate and personal space.

I close the door behind us, and for the first time in a long time, the three of us are together with a few minutes to breathe.

Jordan and Mackenzie come right to me, and we cling to one another. We're a tangle of arms and heads pressed together. I pull them tight to my body, squeezing as hard as I can and wishing I'd never had to let go. Even as the moment begins, I know it will have to end, that we'll have to release one another and deal with everything that's happening.

I try to drink in this brief moment, sear it into my memory. It's all I'll have to sustain me through the rest of the night.

"Dad?"

We're still holding one another.

"Yes, Kenzie?"

"I'm sorry I popped off about the car."

"It's fine."

"I was an asshole, wasn't I? I mean, you were trying to do something nice for somebody, and I was all caught up in how it affected me. And now she's dead."

"None of this is your fault, Mackenzie."

"It's not your fault either," Jordan says in my ear. "I can tell you feel guilty about giving her the keys. But that's not your fault. You can't control what anyone else does."

"I should have stopped her from going across the causeway. I knew how bad it was."

"We made it across. And so did you. She had someone she wanted or needed to see. I'm sorry, Jake. I'm really sorry. But it was an accident."

I give them one more squeeze before I let go. They both step back, and in the faint glow of the flashlight I see the worry on their faces.

"What do we do now?" Jordan asks.

"This isn't really the time to lie to each other. As much as I hate to admit it, there might be—probably is—a killer out there. A looter, or one of the homeless people from the other buildings."

"Unhoused people, Dad. Kiara's right. You can't blame them for no reason."

"You know what I mean. And this storm is landing. I'll tell you the real truth. This building is not in great shape. Dallas was always worried about it withstanding a hurricane, and Kylie is going to be a big one."

"Yeah," Jordan says, "this place is . . . rustic?"

Mackenzie jumps in. "It's a dump, Dad. I can't believe you live here."

"It's served its purpose. All it has to do now is serve it for one more night. Then we'll get out of here."

Neither one of them says anything, but they exchange a look. It's something I've seen many times before—my wife and daughter speaking to each other without words, sharing an insight that I can't quite figure out. I don't even mind. In fact, I love their closeness, their deep unspoken bond.

But right now, I can tell they've been talking about something they need to share. Or thinking about it, their minds linked like two computers on the same network, silently exchanging files.

"What?" I ask.

"Don't worry about it now," Jordan says. "We've got bigger problems. Obviously."

"No, I want to know. If there's something that needs to be said . . ." I look between the two of them. "Did something happen at home? Are your mom and dad okay?"

"Everybody's fine, Jake. Mom and Dad are fine. As crazy as ever but fine."

"Grandpa's totally freaking out."

"Kenzie . . ."

"He's all holed up at the lake house and refusing to leave. He thinks people are after him."

"He watches too much TV news, that's all."

"Dad, he wants to convert all his money to silver and sink it in the water at the lake so no one can find it but him. It would be like hundreds and hundreds of pounds of silver. Like a shipwreck or something."

"He won't do that, Kenzie. Grandma will kill him if he tries. No, it's not that. It's nothing like that."

"Then what?"

Something familiar grips me. A twisting pain in my chest. Not a heart attack, not a physical ailment. No, it's the pain and anxiety of worrying about our marriage, the nagging, wrenching worry I've lived with for months and months. Since long before I came to Florida. Has Jordan come to Florida not to get back together but to end it in person? Is this our last night as a family? And are we going to spend it under the relentless onslaught of Hurricane Kylie?

"Despite what Kenzie says about this building—"

"You said it too, Mom. Don't throw me under the bus."

"Despite what both of us said about this building, it really seems like you have a good life here. I was worried we'd come down here and you'd be spending your days on the beach with a bunch of beautiful bikini-clad neighbors, but everyone seems so real, so down-to-earth."

I let out a little laugh. "You were worried about that? Trust me,

Jordan—that's not happening. And even if it was, I promise no one looks as beautiful in a bikini as you do."

Jordan rolls her eyes and blushes at the same time. "Please, Jake." But as she says it, a small smile appears on her face. She loves it when I say things like that. What she doesn't know is, I really mean it.

"You have all these people who care about you—and who you obviously care for."

"Yeah, like that Hazel. She's totally harsh, but I'd kind of like her to be my grandmother."

"She'd more likely be your great-grandmother," I say, "but I get your point."

"Anyway," Jordan says, "you like it here, and when you talk about your job, you sound so excited, so happy. We're just not sure—" She pauses. Even in the dim light, I can read her. Emotion is catching in her throat and filling her eyes.

"Mom?"

"It's okay. I'm okay." She turns to me. "I'm just worried you're not going to want to come back."

"No, no, it's not like that. . . ."

The same way it feels sometimes like Jordan and Mackenzie share a brain, I know I can't hide anything from Jordan. Ever.

She's picked up on something real—my feelings about my life here in Florida. My job. My renewed sense of purpose, belonging.

I don't want to lie to her. Ever.

"I'm coming back to Ohio. To both of you. I'm already packed. Dallas gave me his car because he said it'd have a better chance of making it to Ohio than the Elantra. You're all that matters to me."

"You're coming back?" Jordan asks, and I hear her voice cracking. "But do you *want* to come back? Do you *want* to come back to that life? That job?"

"I want to come back to the two of you. *You* are my life. You are—"

Thud-thud-thud.

We all turn toward the door. "What the hell?"

"Jake?"

It's a woman's voice. Is it Nina's? Kiara's? Can't I get five seconds alone with my family after six months away from them?

I open the door. "What is it? What's wrong?"

"It's Stanley and Lloyd, Jake. You better get out here."

THIRTY-FOUR

Everyone is standing in a circle that fills the cramped space. Catalina's bell rings continuously. In the center of the group, Stanley and Lloyd are squared off. At least six inches taller, Lloyd looms over Stanley.

They look like two obnoxious teenagers ready to throw down and fight.

"Hey, hey."

The crowd parts so I can get through, but Stanley and Lloyd keep their eyes locked on each other. Tyler stands right behind Stanley, almost like it's a duel and he's Stanley's second.

"What's the problem here?" I ask. "As if we don't have enough of them already."

Lloyd turns to me. "He won't give it back."

"Give what back?"

"My gun. He won't give my gun back."

I'd forgotten all about the Glock.

"What's the matter, Stanley? Why don't you give the gun back to Lloyd?"

"Ethan hasn't shown up yet, Jake. I want to go look for him. And if I'm going to go out into the storm with a killer, then I want to be armed. And Lloyd won't let me."

"He shouldn't go out," Lloyd says. "Nobody should go out. We need to barricade that door and stay inside, where it's safe. If Ethan can't get his ass down here because he's looking for his stupid cat, then that's his problem."

I look around the room. "Ethan still isn't here?"

"He's not," Stanley says. "And I'm worried about him. He's— Well, you know Ethan. He's sensitive. He doesn't always make good decisions. I want to find him and bring him here. And I want to do it with a weapon."

"That seems reasonable, doesn't it, Lloyd?"

"No. This is my home." He points at the bed where Catalina lies. "And that's my wife. And this is the place and the person I need to protect." Lloyd steals a look at Tyler, but I don't think anyone notices but me. "I did what you asked, gave you a chance to round up everyone. Now anybody outside of this apartment is on their own. Quit pushing me, Jake. I gave an inch, and you're taking a mile. Actually, I already gave a mile, and now you want another."

"You've been very generous, Lloyd. You and Catalina both. I know that. We all know that. Right?"

I turn to the others in the room, and they all nod. They take my cue and lay it on thick. Sometimes that's just what a person like Lloyd needs. A thick layer of appreciation.

It appears to work. His features soften a bit. He takes a step back from Stanley.

The door of the apartment rattles in its frame, as if to remind us a hurricane is still blowing outside.

"Stanley, if you want, why don't we go look for Ethan? Together."

"Dad?"

"Jake, wait—"

I turn back to Jordan and Mackenzie. "We're just going to take a quick look for Ethan. He lives up on seven. That's too high. And Stanley's right. Ethan doesn't always make the best decisions. He might need help finding his cat—or deciding it would be best to stop looking for the cat and come down here where the rest of us are. We can help him do that." I turn around again. "Right, Stanley? We can do that?"

Stanley nods. "Sure, okay."

"Why doesn't Tyler go?" Sawyer is the only person still sitting, likely due to his bad hip. "He's the security guy. That makes him some kind of expert on taking care of himself. And if he was sent here by the owners to check on everything, well, that should include Ethan."

"I agree," Kiara says. "Why doesn't Tyler go?"

"The owners don't give a shit about us," Nina says. "I'm sure Tyler doesn't either."

Even before we've all turned Tyler's way, he's shaking his head. "I think it's best we all stay here. It's not that I don't care—I'm not saying that—but the best course of action is for everyone to stay together. This Ethan guy, whoever he is—he had his chance. If he knocks on the door, we can let him in. Otherwise—"

"Didn't you hear what they said?" Kiara asks. "Ethan might need help. He's . . . he's like a child."

"I think we should all stay put." Tyler glances at the window even though the blinds are down. "It's getting worse out."

"That's cold," Sawyer says.

"It sure is." Kiara places her hands on her hips and shakes her head.

Everyone starts to speak at once, and I wave my hands, shouting them down until they're quiet.

"It's okay. It's okay. We don't want to make anyone do something they don't want to do. Stanley and I will go up to Ethan's place and have a look around. We'll be as fast as possible. In the meantime, keep the door locked. When we come back with Ethan, we'll barricade the door. No one else will be able to come or go after that. That will be it."

Everyone murmurs. It sounds like the murmurs represent agreement, but I can't be sure.

I turn to Stanley. "You ready?"

"I'm ready."

"Is the safety on?" Lloyd asks.

Stanley sneers at Lloyd. "Of course it is."

"Good to hear." I pat Stanley on the shoulder. "Let's go get Ethan."

"Wait." It's Sawyer again. "You want us to lock that door after you leave? So we're safe?"

"Absolutely," I say. "My family's here too."

"But when you come back, how will we know it's you and Stanley and not the killer?"

He has a point. "I'll use a knock you can all recognize. Three slow knocks and then three quick ones. If you don't hear that, don't open the door."

Sawyer nods, satisfied.

I look behind me at Jordan and Mackenzie. Why do I always seem to be leaving them when I have no desire to do so? Why?

Words seem inadequate, so I just say, "We'll be right back."

"Be careful," Jordan says.

"We will."

Stanley and I cross the room to the door. Stanley undoes the lock and the door flies open, letting in the rain and the wind—the never-ending reminder of the growing storm.

THIRTY-FIVE

9:19 P.M.

Out on the walkway, the rain lashes us. The wind keeps us off-balance the whole time we walk, making us stumble like a couple of drunks on Bourbon Street. If only . . .

"Shitfire," Stanley says under his breath. I can barely hear him.

I yell at him over the wind. "Are we out of our minds?"

"Do you want to go back?"

I shake my head. "I couldn't forgive myself if anything happened to Ethan. Not after Alaina."

"Let's head to the stairs at the south end. Closer to Ethan."

"Okay."

But Stanley doesn't move. "I'm not trying to make trouble, Jake." He's still yelling. "Holding on to Lloyd's gun. I just want to protect myself."

"I know—"

"Besides, I am trained to use it. And I'm trained to do other things."

"It's okay, Stanley. Can we go now? The sooner we find Ethan, the sooner we get back."

Stanley heads quickly toward the south stairs. Considering his age, he's pretty spry. I worry he's going to slip and fall. But he doesn't.

When we reach the stairs Stanley starts dashing up them, but then immediately stops ahead of me. He stops so abruptly I almost run right into his back.

"What's the matter?" I yell over the wind and rain. I can see only Stanley's back. Nothing else.

Stanley steps to the side and points without a word.

Isaac sits on the seventh-floor walkway like a pudgy king. He shakes his head, trying to get water off his body, and lets out a long, plaintive meow at us.

I've been inside Ethan's apartment only once. As soon as I walked in the door, Isaac ran away and hid in the bedroom. Ethan apologized on behalf of his cat, insisted Isaac wasn't used to being around people, no matter how many times they came to the apartment.

But Isaac doesn't run away from us now. He remains on the top step, still trying to shake himself dry.

"Well, there's the damn cat," Stanley says in a loud voice before he starts moving again, passing Isaac as if he isn't there.

I stop when I reach the landing. Isaac looks up at me and meows again. He's trembling.

Stanley urges me forward. "Come on, Jake."

I yell up the stairs at Stanley. "Why is he out here? He's an indoor cat."

"How do I know?"

"It's odd, right?"

"Do you want to ask him? Let's get going."

"We can't just leave him here. Don't you want to bring him to Ethan?"

"Ethan can get him."

"Have a heart, Stanley." I bend down and try to lift Isaac with one hand. He's too fat, so I scoop him up with both hands. Isaac meows and fusses. I brace myself for a scratch or a bite, but he eventually relaxes, letting me hold him close to my body. I unzip my hoodie and slide him inside. "Okay, Isaac. You're okay now. Let's go find Ethan."

Stanley rolls his eyes. "Are you ready now? I thought you were in such a hurry to get this over with."

"I am. But . . . he's like a drowned rat."

"He *is* a drowned rat. Now, come on."

Stanley continues up the stairs. Isaac is still against my body, quickly starting to purr.

The outline of the Glock bulges beneath the fabric of Stanley's shirt. Its very presence makes me nervous, but I'm trusting Stanley—and Lloyd—to know what he's doing.

We gain the seventh-floor walkway and start down. Ethan's apartment is a third of the way along.

When we reach the door, Stanley knocks. No, he doesn't knock. In order to be heard over the wind and rain, he pounds.

"Ethan? Open up."

"Easy, Stanley. You'll scare the crap out of the poor kid."

"It's urgent, Jake. He needs to know that."

"He probably has a handle on that. Didn't you tell him we were all hiding out together?"

"I did."

"Well—did he get it?"

"He was scared, sure."

"He's a sensitive guy, Stanley." I step closer to the door, Isaac suddenly squirming in my hoodie. "Ethan?" I say at the same time as I knock. I try to do it gently. But how do you knock gently and still manage to be heard over the sound of a hurricane? "Ethan?"

Stanley grunts impatience next to me. He takes hold of the doorknob, twisting it to the right.

And Ethan's door swings wide-open.

THIRTY-SIX

The apartment smells like stale cigarette smoke.

It's like opening the door to my grandparents' house when I was a kid. I nearly gag.

Everything is completely dark. Not even a candle glows.

Stanley lifts his flashlight and clicks it on, sending a cone of light into the room from the door. We take in the stained carpet, a full ashtray on the table, a few fast-food wrappers and plastic Coke bottles. A stack of magazines and some paperback fantasy novels . . .

"He must have left, Jake."

"And gone where? Out into the storm? Ethan doesn't go outside when the weather's perfect."

"You said you saw him downstairs."

Isaac purrs against my chest again. "He was supposed to be trying to get Isaac out from under the bed. That's what you told me. Well, here's Isaac. Where's Ethan?"

"I don't know. Maybe Isaac ran away, and the kid's out looking for him."

"You did talk to him, right? You came up here, knocked on his door, and spoke to him?"

Stanley turns to me, his face indignant. "Are you calling me a liar, Jake? Why would I lie about that?"

"Then he must be here. . . ."

"If he's in there, why isn't he answering?"

"Ethan? It's Jake and Stanley. You okay, man? I have Isaac. I think he misses you."

No response. Just the purring of the cat and the howling of the wind and rain.

"I'm going in," I say to Stanley. "Shine that beam ahead so I don't fall."

Stanley taps my arm, the Glock in his outstretched hand. "Take it, Jake."

"No way, Stanley. We don't need anyone getting shot."

"I know what I'm doing."

"Just—let's just be careful. Okay?"

"You have your family to think about, Jake. They're right downstairs. Maybe we should go back down. If Ethan doesn't want to come with us . . . that's his call."

"Stanley, you're the one that wanted to come up here in the first place. Now that we're here, I'm going in. You can go back downstairs if you want, but I wish you'd stay, because I'm scared out of my fucking mind. I can't make you—"

"Okay, okay. Go ahead."

I take a deep breath. Maybe Stanley's right. Maybe I'm a fool.

Maybe Ethan is fine.

For all I know, he's downstairs with the others by now.

I think of how anxious and troubled he seemed earlier. I blew him off, focusing on my own issues. If I'd stayed to listen, would things be different now?

"I'm coming in, Ethan. Stanley's with me. And so is Isaac."

I move into the apartment, stepping like a man walking over quicksand.

Stanley hovers behind me, the flashlight beam guiding my way. It sweeps around the living room, revealing more clutter. On a large table to the right sits Ethan's workspace—two computer monitors, a tangle of cables, a printer. Dirty dishes litter the kitchen counters.

I reach the hallway leading to the bedroom. "Ethan?"

I wait, my head tilted to one side.

"Did you say something, Stanley?"

"No."

"Did you hear that?"

"I didn't hear anything besides the blood pumping in my ears."

The noise reaches me again. It's faint. Almost like a whimpering.

"Ethan? Is that you?"

"Jake, I think you're—"

"Shh. Listen."

I strain my ears and hear it again. A barely audible noise coming from the bedroom.

I rush for the bedroom door.

"Jake, wait—"

But I don't listen. I'm in the room a second later, Stanley behind me with the flashlight.

The bed is unmade, the covers strewn across the mattress. A pair of old loafers, some pants, and a pair of boxers litter the floor. I bend down, look under the bed. Stanley shines his light.

"Nothing, Jake."

But now I smell something.

Cigarettes. Someone's smoking in here. More accurately, someone's smoking in the—

I cross the room to the closet door and throw it open. I push the hanging clothes aside to reveal Ethan, sitting as far back in the corner as he can go, a cigarette dangling from his mouth, his knees pulled up to his chest like he's a child.

THIRTY-SEVEN

I crouch in front of Ethan. It's almost impossible to squeeze my body into the cramped space of the closet.

Hanging clothes brush my face, and I push them away.

Ethan winces, backs away from me like I'm radioactive. Or like I mean to do him harm.

"Easy, Ethan. It's just Stanley and me. Are you hurt?"

He doesn't respond. He takes a long drag on the cigarette, which is almost burned down to the filter.

"And look here." I open my hoodie. "It's Isaac. He's fine. We found him on the steps."

Ethan's eyes widen. He puts the cigarette out against the wall, leaving a long, dark smear of ash on the fading white paint. He reaches for the cat.

I'm more than happy to hand Isaac back.

But not as happy as Ethan, who clutches his pet tightly to his chest. Isaac's purring grows loud enough for all of us to hear.

"Ethan, did you hear me? Did something happen? Why are you hiding?"

He strokes the cat, his eyes averted from mine. It's as if he's been rendered speechless by shock.

"Let's get him out of here, Jake."

"Can you walk, Ethan? We're all in Lloyd's apartment. It's the safest place in the building. He said you can bring Isaac."

Some of the tension goes out of Ethan's body. For the first time, he looks at me. His bloodshot eyes appear haunted. I'm not sure if he's spooked about the storm, Isaac, or something else entirely.

I think back to when I saw him downstairs, lurking around the parking garage. His words come back to me. *I'm not a bad guy, am I, Jake?*

Why would someone as harmless as Ethan ask such a question?

But there's no time to sort through that now.

"Ethan, you need to get up. The storm's about to make landfall, and then it's only going to get worse. You're too high up here. Let's get you and Isaac down to Lloyd's. We're going to barricade ourselves in and ride this thing out."

Ethan stirs. He shifts his weight like he's about to stand up.

We're moving in the right direction. I stand, hold out my hand to Ethan, his clothes brushing against my back.

Just as I start to feel optimistic, Ethan sinks back against the wall, clutching Isaac even more tightly to his chest.

"What is it?" I ask.

"Maybe we should go, Jake. He's in the closet. He's with the cat. He's safe. Maybe this is what he wants. Maybe he doesn't want to leave."

"Bullshit, Stanley. He should be downstairs. For a lot of reasons. And you know what they are." I turn back to Ethan. "Come on, man. Please."

"I'm too scared."

"We're all scared, Ethan. Shit, I'm fucking terrified. That's why we need to be together. We can share the load."

"I'm scared of *him*," he says.

"Who?"

Ethan clams up, clutches Isaac so tightly the cat makes a mewling protest.

"He's crazy, Jake. Let's go. *I'm* scared of this storm."

"Who are you scared of, Ethan?" He doesn't respond, and I can't help myself. I shake him the tiniest bit. "Who?"

Ethan looks past me. I can't tell if he's trying to indicate something outside of the apartment or if he means—

"Stanley? Are you scared of Stanley?"

"That's asinine, Jake. He's out of his mind—"

Ethan shakes his head. "Not Stanley, no. I'm scared of the guy who came into the apartment. He came into the apartment when it was completely dark." Ethan looks right into my eyes. "He tried to kill me."

THIRTY-EIGHT

It takes a few minutes, but we manage to coax Ethan out of the closet.

We assure him there's no one else in the apartment, that the two of us just went through the whole place and didn't see anyone else.

Ethan sits on the edge of the unmade bed with Isaac still clutched against his chest. Isaac looks content, the exact opposite of Ethan, who somehow manages to hold on to the cat while his hands light another cigarette. The glow from our flashlights makes everyone's features look harsh and stark.

"Why don't we go downstairs, Ethan?" I ask. "You can tell us the rest of the story once we're down there."

Ethan shakes his head. "No, no, that would be too much for me, man. I don't think I can leave here."

"Are you sure someone tried to kill you?" Stanley asks. "I mean, come on."

I gaze at Stanley and he gazes back at me. We both know what happened to Dallas. I don't think Ethan even knows about that. So it's not impossible to believe that someone—maybe the same person who killed Dallas—came into Ethan's apartment and tried to hurt him.

"What happened, Ethan?" I ask.

"Stanley came by, trying to get me to go downstairs with everybody else. And I told him I couldn't leave without Isaac. He was

148   DAVID BELL

hiding under the bed. The storm was really freaking him out. The building keeps creaking. Have you heard that?"

"We have."

"It sounds pretty bad," Ethan says. "Worse than I've ever heard it. Anyway, I was down on the floor, trying to get Isaac to come out. I had just gotten my hands on him, and that's when the power went out. Complete blackout, right?"

"Sure."

"When that happened, Isaac slipped out of my hands. I got up to find my phone, to use the flashlight. When I did that, I realized— Look, I don't know what happened. Either I didn't shut the door all the way when Stanley left or maybe the wind blew it open, but someone was in the apartment with me." He takes two quick puffs on the cigarette. "I could just feel them, you know? Feel them in here with me. I'm incredibly empathic."

"Okay, so you felt someone in here with you."

"I thought maybe it was Stanley. Coming back to get me."

"It wasn't me," Stanley says.

"I know that now, but I said your name. And the guy didn't answer. Instead, he came after me. He grabbed at me, and we went to the floor. I was trying to get him off me, and we started fighting. I'm scrawny, but I can fight pretty good if I have to. I managed to get out from under him. I ran back to the bedroom and went to the closet. I should have run out the door, but I wasn't thinking straight. Anyway, it sounded like the guy rooted around for a while, like he was looking for something, and then he left." Ethan pulls Isaac even closer to his chest. "I feel terrible."

"Are you hurt?" Stanley asks.

"No. I feel terrible that I left Isaac alone out here. I should have grabbed him, but I ran away like a little baby. He must have gotten out when the guy left."

"Did you get a look at this guy?"

"It was too dark to see."

"Did he say anything?"

"Not a word. What do you think he wanted?"

"We don't know," I say. "Possibly he was a looter."

Ethan's eyes move back and forth between Stanley and me. "What are you not telling me?"

Stanley and I exchange another look.

"What is it? I know you're hiding something. I told you, I'm empathic as shit."

Ethan's too smart to let us get away with not telling him. And he's going to find out as soon as he gets downstairs anyway. Maybe this will motivate him to vacate his apartment.

"Okay, Ethan, you better prepare yourself for some bad news." I then tell him about Dallas and how maybe—probably—the same guy who came into Ethan's apartment and attacked him might have killed Dallas. "You have a lot of expensive computer equipment in here. Maybe he knew that. Let's face it—most of us don't have anything like this. At most, we have phones or TVs. Maybe a little jewelry. But your stuff looks like it might be worth a lot."

Even in the pale beam of the flashlight, Ethan's skin blanches. He swallows hard. "That guy killed Dallas. And he meant to kill me."

"Well, maybe . . . but, listen—you're okay. You were lucky. And it didn't look like anything is missing."

"That's weird, right?" Stanley asks. "You said you could hear the guy rooting around, but it doesn't look like anything is missing. I've seen your setup more than once. He didn't grab any of the computer gear."

I jump in. "Maybe he couldn't carry it. There are a lot of cables and things. It wouldn't make sense to carry all that out into a hurricane."

"Yeah," Ethan says. "I guess so. . . ."

"Why don't we get downstairs before things get worse?" I ask. "Bring Isaac with you."

Ethan nods. He looks childlike as he pushes himself off the bed and starts to move to the living room, Stanley's beam leading the way. We walk behind him. Stanley shines the light over Ethan's desk and workstation.

"Nothing's missing that I can see," Ethan says. "Some of the papers are moved around, is all."

"Let's keep going," I say.

Before we can take another step, the door of Ethan's apartment swings open. A figure fills the doorway, set off by the faint ambient light that leaks in from outside.

It's Tyler. Why he's here, I'm not sure.

Except that as soon as he sees him, Ethan says, "That's the guy. That's the guy who came in here and tried to kill me."

THIRTY-NINE

Tyler steps inside the apartment, acting as if he hasn't heard—or isn't bothered by—Ethan's accusation.

Tyler has to use both hands to push against the force of the wind and close the door, blocking out the small amount of ambient light that was spilling into the apartment.

"Jake, you've got to do something," Ethan says.

"Try to remain calm." I nod to Ethan. "I promise I won't let him hurt you." Stanley's flashlight beam catches half of Tyler's wet face, causing him to squint. "What are you doing here, Tyler? Why didn't you stay with the others?"

"I think we need to talk," he says. "Away from the others."

"What do we need to talk about?"

"Do you mind not shining that thing in my face, Stanley?"

Stanley shifts the beam of light toward the floor, where it picks up scattered scraps of paper and cat hair.

"Jake—" Ethan's voice quavers.

My arm tingles where Tyler grabbed it earlier, a reminder of our encounter on the steps. If he was willing to grab me, isn't it possible he tried to hurt Ethan?

Or killed Dallas?

"What do you want, Tyler? Why are you here?"

"I was talking to the others. I don't think they realize the gravity of the situation we're in." Tyler's voice is calm, almost professorial. His hands are large, but he moves them with grace, like he's conducting an orchestra. "It's not just the hurricane. It's Dallas too. We're really in trouble here."

"Do you think I don't know that? That's why we were all holing up together. What else do you want us to do?"

Ethan backs away from us, shuffling toward his bedroom. "I don't want him in here, Jake. . . ."

Even in the poor light, I can see Ethan's entire body trembling. He clings to Isaac like the cat is a life preserver saving him from drowning. I'm not sure I've ever seen someone as anxious as Ethan is right now. The way he huddled in the closet was alarming. Like a frightened animal.

I turn back to Tyler. "Come out with it, Tyler: Did you attack Ethan?"

"Of course not." Tyler shakes his big head dismissively. "I've got nothing against him. It's pitch-dark. How could he know who came in here? If anyone did. But someone hurt Dallas. Maybe the same person attacked this guy too."

"They didn't *hurt* Dallas," Stanley says. "They killed him."

"I know that, but—"

"Jake, please—"

"Why did you grab me on the stairs? You acted like you were going to attack me. I had to pull away from you to be able to get to Hazel. What's going on?"

"Look—" Tyler's voice finally sounds sharp. He drops his hands to his sides and takes a deep breath. When he speaks again, his voice is softer, much more controlled. "Look, I wanted you to listen—that's all. I grew frustrated when you were trying to get past me without hearing me out. I understand now you were trying to help Hazel, but I didn't see that at the time. I thought—hell, I thought you were the most competent guy here. And that together we should try to get a handle on things."

"You had a funny way of showing it."

"Look, forget all that, okay?"

"What's your big plan, then?" Stanley asks. "If you don't like how we're taking care of things, what do you propose?"

"Jake?"

"Just wait, Ethan. It's okay."

"Okay." Tyler lifts his hands, conducting his words again. "I came here in a boat. A little dinghy. It's tied up just north of the building at the water's edge. I pushed it way back into the weeds so it wouldn't float away."

"Are you suggesting we leave in a dinghy?" Stanley asks. "In the middle of a hurricane?"

"Of course not. We can't go *now*. But the storm's going to make a direct hit on this island. That means we'll be right in the middle of it. And we'll get a break when the eye goes over us. That's when we go for help. Tell the cops what's happening. Maybe get another boat to come out to the island."

"I already told the police about Dallas. They refused to send help until Kylie is through with us."

"But they'll have a clear window when the eye hits us."

"How many people can you fit in the dinghy?" Stanley asks in an almost hopeful voice. "Can we all go?"

Tyler shakes his head. "Two, maybe three. But they can get help. I don't mind doing it when things clear up."

"So what you're saying is that you're willing to go," Stanley says, "and leave us all behind?"

"You go, then." Tyler points at Stanley, then at me. "Or you. I don't care who goes. It's a chance. That's all I'm saying. Maybe the only decent one. We're stuck here. On a small island without power and without real supplies. We're trapped with a lot of scared people, a sick woman, the old lady, and a nutcase." He flips his eyes to Ethan.

"Plus Alaina," I say. "They can look for her."

"Well, I don't know about that," Tyler says. "If she went in like you said . . . that current . . ."

"They can look." My voice reveals more indignation than I'd like.

Tyler makes soothing gestures toward me. "Okay, sure. You're right. They can look for Alaina. They can help us all." I can tell he's just placating me. It doesn't matter what he thinks. Or what I think. That will be a decision the police make.

"Jake, please . . ."

The desperation in Ethan's voice is unmistakable, and it's just too much to handle. Adrenaline courses through my body, and sweat waterfalls down my chest and sides. I take a quick glance at Ethan just as he moves farther into the darkness, a frightened rabbit. He's literally disappearing.

"It's strange," I say, turning back to Tyler. "You claim the Bennets sent you here to check on the property. They couldn't give a shit about this place any other day of the year, but suddenly, in the middle of a hurricane, they sent you to check on everything. I mean, it would be in their best interest if this whole place fell apart, wouldn't it? They're going to tear everything down anyway. Maybe it would be easier if the hurricane did that for them. Hell, they might even get some insurance money out of the deal. So you'll have to forgive me if I'm not buying any of it."

Tyler sighs. "Look, I just work for them, okay?"

"Just following orders? Not a great defense," I say. "Certainly won't hold up in court. Cut the shit, Tyler, and tell us why you're really here."

"You have to think about it from the Bennets' point of view. They're about to sell and make a windfall of cash. They're almost there. They *really* don't want the deal to fall apart now. So the last thing they need is a lawsuit from some aggrieved tenant. It's selfish, yes, but that's how the world works. So they sent me to make sure everyone is okay."

"Well, now someone's been killed on their property. Their own property manager. I sure hope that doesn't inconvenience them too much."

"I'm sorry about that, Jake. I really am. I just want us to work together to make sure no one else gets hurt."

I'm caught off guard by Tyler's offer. Of course I want to make sure no one else gets hurt. Of course I'll accept his help. "Yeah, okay."

It's impossible to get a fix on Tyler. I can't reconcile the mostly rational man—calmly proposing a way to get help and explaining the logical reason why the Bennets sent him here—with the truculent guy I tussled with on the stairs. The one who loomed over me. The one who grabbed me like he intended to take me to the ground.

The one Ethan is convinced attacked him.

"Okay, let's go, then," I say. "But"—I point at Tyler—"you stay the hell away from Ethan, understand? Stay away from anyone who doesn't want you near them."

"Do you want me to stand outside in the storm too?"

"Just be cool. You get me?" I don't wait for an answer, turning toward Stanley and the place where Ethan is hiding in the dark. "We really do need to get out of here. Ethan, we'll be right by you the whole time—don't worry."

Ethan responds with a low whimpering sound. . . .

"It's all right," I say. "We need to get off this high floor."

I move cautiously toward Ethan in the dark. When I make out the outline of his body, I gently place a hand on his upper arm.

He pulls away.

"We'll be right next to you the whole time, Ethan. But we all have to stick together now."

Everything hangs in the balance for a moment. I fear Ethan will refuse to leave. That he'll insist on staying in his own apartment. I hate thinking of Ethan riding out the storm alone.

After what feels like an hour, Ethan nods. "Okay." He shuffles forward. "Okay, Jake. I trust you."

"That's cool," I say. "All right, Stanley, why don't you lead us down?"

But Stanley has the flashlight beam aimed at Tyler's squinting face again. Alongside the flashlight, he holds up the gun, which is also aimed directly at Tyler's face.

Tyler's hands are raised, his head slightly turned, as if he can simply turn away from a bullet.

"I don't trust this guy one bit," Stanley says. "He's not holing up with us. No way, no how."

FORTY

"Come on, Stanley," I say. "You don't need to do this."

Stanley doesn't waver. He's rock steady. The gun is still pointed directly at Tyler.

"No, Jake. *We* do need to do this."

"What the fuck, Stanley?" Tyler looks and sounds surprisingly relaxed for a man who has a gun in his face. "This is incredibly unnecessary."

"It's not. You've been sneaking around here. Even before today. I've seen you looking around the island, checking up on all of us. Then you're here tonight, using the storm as a cover. Dallas is dead, and you attacked Ethan."

"I didn't—"

"He did," Ethan says with sudden composure. "I agree with Stanley. Thank you, Stanley. At least you're looking out for me."

"Now, hold on." I reach up and wipe a film of sweat off my forehead. My skin has grown clammy and hot. "Just wait. We don't know for sure that was Tyler. And even if it was, I don't think we should be pointing a gun at anyone. Stanley, I'd feel a lot better if you put that thing down."

"I won't, Jake. You can't tell me what to do on this one."

Tyler gives me a pleading look, as if he's counting on me for help. "Well?"

The wind rattles the hurricane shutters loudly. It feels like a warning. Then I hear something grinding. It sounds like metal rubbing against metal. I've never heard anything like this before. What the hell is it?

Ethan looks determined, his spine rigid.

I decide to ignore Tyler. "Okay, Stanley, what do you suggest we do now? And remember, we're running out of time. The storm is getting worse. Everybody's waiting for us. Can we figure this out in Lloyd's apartment?"

"No way." Stanley shakes his head without taking his eyes off Tyler. "No way he's coming into the apartment with us."

"Sheesh," Tyler says.

"We can't leave him out in the elements, Stanley."

"Says who?"

"We can't be that heartless." Ethan's words come back to me. "We're not bad people."

Stanley takes a step back. His hand, the one holding the gun, swings my way, almost like he wants to direct it at me. He stops before he gets to me, but I flinch. A second later, Stanley points the gun at Tyler again.

"We don't have evidence of any of this, Stanley." My mouth is dry. My lips stick together when I speak. "We can ride the storm out and then let the police figure everything out."

"He's going to bail on us, Jake. He'll take the boat and leave all of us to the storm, right?"

"Why don't we wait until tomorrow to ask these questions, Stanley? When all is clear."

"If we let him into the apartment, we're letting the fox into the henhouse."

"Then what do you suggest we—"

"I know." Ethan's voice is louder than I've ever heard it.

We all turn toward him, even Stanley, who still manages to keep the gun trained on Tyler.

"You have an idea?" I aim my own flashlight beam at Ethan. He looks pleased to have our attention. He doesn't even squint in the light.

"Yes, I do." Isaac yawns in Ethan's arms, the cat's jaw opening almost as wide as his head. Ethan scratches his ears. "If he's guilty, if he's the guy who attacked me and maybe even killed Dallas, wouldn't there be something on him? Some evidence, as you say? He was rifling through my desk, touching everything. Maybe he stole something from me. Or from Dallas."

"I didn't take anything from you," Tyler says. "Like I said, I wasn't even here."

"That's good, Ethan." Stanley nods. "Real good." Stanley tilts his head toward Tyler. "Jake, go check him out. See what's in his pockets while I keep him covered."

Tyler lets out a small laugh. "This is ridiculous."

"Will this make you happy, Stanley?" I ask. "If there's nothing there, can we all go back down to Lloyd's? Including Tyler?"

It takes Stanley a few seconds to answer. But eventually he nods. "Okay, sure. Okay. If he's clear."

"I won't do it unless you agree, Stanley."

He waits even longer than before, but finally he says, "Okay, yeah."

"Tyler?"

He vigorously shakes his head. "You are so full of shit, Jake. A guy has a gun pointed right at me, and you're acting like I have a choice in the matter." He raises his arms in the air. "Go ahead. Search me. You're not the only one who wants to get downstairs. The big bad wolf is out there trying to blow this place down."

"Okay, fine." I start across the room toward Tyler. "Stanley, are you sure you're being careful? I don't want my brains scattered all over Ethan's apartment."

"I got you, Jake," Stanley says.

When I reach Tyler, who still has his hands in the air, I hesitate.

It feels . . . To be honest, it feels . . . weird to be reaching into another person's pocket.

I had to do the same thing with Dallas—after he was murdered—and this doesn't feel any less strange.

I slowly slide my hand into the wet front pocket of Tyler's jeans. My fingers bring out a small, damp wad of money—about twenty-three dollars—and a crushed pack of gum.

"Are these yours, Ethan?"

"No."

I stuff them back in. Then I go to the other side. My fingers strike something metal. Keys.

It feels like a lot of keys, but when I jangle them in the air, there are only two. "A car key and a house key."

"What else is in there?" Stanley asks in an accusatory voice.

"Lint, I'm guessing."

"That's it," Tyler says.

"No." Stanley points his beam at the pocket. There's a tiny outline of something. "See that, Jake? You didn't get everything."

I'm surprised to see Stanley is right. I slide my fingers deeper into Tyler's pocket this time. It takes a second, but I finally reach something metal and canvas.

Tyler remains still, hands in the air.

I bring the object out—a thick industrial key on a Chicago Bears key chain.

FORTY-ONE

My hand trembles so much I can barely hold the key without dropping it.

Stanley illuminates the object in my hand with his flashlight, like it's a holy relic meant to be venerated. But what we're venerating is Stanley's worst suspicions come to life.

The trembling spreads from my hand throughout my entire body.

"It's the passkey," Stanley says in a loud whisper. "Dallas always kept it with him."

"Where did you get this?" I ask, shaking the key in Tyler's face.

"I found it. Downstairs. In the parking garage. It was on the ground, and I picked it up. I honestly forgot I had it."

"Do you make a habit of going around and picking up random keys?" Stanley asks.

"I thought someone might have lost it. Might need it."

Ethan takes a couple of steps forward, moving closer to Tyler and me. "I knew my door *was* locked. I thought maybe I didn't shut it tight enough, or maybe the wind blew it open, but I bet he used the passkey to get in and attack me."

"I didn't attack you. This is crazy."

Stanley's eyes land on me. "We can't let this guy into Lloyd's place with the rest of us. You see that now, right? We need to make sure he's someplace where he can't hurt anyone else."

"What do you want to do with him?" I realize I'm talking about Tyler as if he weren't standing right in front of us. "What are you suggesting?"

"I'd like to turn him out into the storm," Stanley says. "But that's too good for him. Then he'd take the boat and get out of here when the eye hits. That's exactly what he wants."

"So what, then?"

"I say we put him in one of the storage units. Down in the parking garage. Tie him up and only let him out when the cops get here."

"What?" Tyler's voice betrays his horror.

"Stanley, we can't do that. The garage might flood. It already has a few inches of standing water. If there's a big storm surge, and there's almost certain to be one, he could drown. Those storage units are like prison cells. No way we're doing that."

"Do you have a *better* idea, Jake?" Stanley asks.

The wind blows against the building with more strength. The hurricane is probably about to make landfall. We have no time to waste.

Tyler's explanation sounds as flimsy as the building we're standing in. If there's *any* chance he's guilty, we need to keep him away from everyone. And there's one easy way to do that.

"We have the passkey," I say. "That means we can get into any of the apartments. Since Dallas' place is a crime scene, let's put him in Alaina's apartment. He'll be as safe as the rest of us on the second floor."

"How are you going to keep him in there?" Stanley asks.

"I'm betting you learned how to tie a knot before they shipped you off to Vietnam."

"I see your thinking."

"This is bullshit," Tyler says. "I'm leaving. You can't do this to me—"

Stanley takes a step closer to Tyler, the gun still extended. "I can. And I will. We're giving you a chance to wait this out. You can do that, or I can shoot you. It's your choice."

I think I can see every muscle in Tyler's body tense. He clenches and unclenches his hands. It's easy to picture him lunging forward, trying to overpower Stanley—who is older and smaller—and wrestle the gun away from him.

Tyler's gaze moves from Stanley to Ethan and then lands on me. He must see the long odds against him. Stanley may be older and weaker than him, but he can't say the same about me. And there are three of us and only one of him. Not to mention we're the ones with a gun.

Tyler's body loses some of its steel.

"You're all nuts," he says.

"We might be," I say. "Stanley will have the gun trained on your back the whole time."

Tyler doesn't respond. He knows he's beat.

I motion to Stanley. "You go first. I want you right behind him. And don't take your eyes off him." I glance back at Ethan, who seems rejuvenated. "Lock the door and go straight to Lloyd's. Tell everyone what's going on. Stanley and I will be there soon." I tell him the special knock.

"Got it."

"Okay, Tyler," I say. "Let's go."

FORTY-TWO

It's not easy making the trip.

Down five flights of soaking wet stairs.

With three people so close we might as well be handcuffed.

In the middle of a hurricane.

Tyler goes first, his hands still up. Stanley walks behind, with the gun at Tyler's back. Then me. Ethan and Isaac head down the north staircase.

It's rainier and windier, and at any moment, I expect Tyler to make a break for it or Stanley to trip and fall.

But neither happens.

Tyler seems to have accepted his fate.

I'm starting to see Stanley in a new light. He moves with a lithe grace down the stairs, almost like a predatory jungle cat. He doesn't stumble or slip, never seems to lose focus. It's easy to picture him serving in combat as a much younger man—all these years later, those long-dormant instincts haven't left him.

When we reach Alaina's door, Stanley keeps the gun pointed at Tyler while I work the passkey into the lock.

"I figured you were smarter than this, Jake," Tyler says. "Why don't you tell this war hawk to back off?"

"This is the only way," I say. "Everybody will be safe this way. You included."

"You're all going to regret this nonsense."

"Shut the hell up," Stanley says, poking the gun into Tyler's back. Hard.

I step inside, shining my flashlight around the space. I've never been inside Alaina's apartment before. I almost expect to see her waiting for us. Against all logic to the contrary, my hopes rise.

Her apartment smells like spoiled food. I can't tell if it's coming from the garbage can or the refrigerator. Alaina's problems must have been even bigger than I realized. The furniture is sparse—just a single overstuffed chair and a card table with two folding chairs. There's no art on the walls, no curtains. The counters are greasy and covered with clutter. A slab of cheese sits on a dirty plate. Likely the source of the smell. The kitchen faucet drips slowly into the sink.

"Go on," I say to Tyler, pointing with my flashlight. "Sit in that kitchen chair over there."

Tyler, thrown by my harsh tone, gives me a look but doesn't say anything. He gives me the side-eye as he silently moves into the apartment.

"Watch him, Stanley. I'll find something to tie him with."

"Rope would be best."

"Do you think someone like Alaina has a bunch of rope sitting around in her apartment? She barely has furniture."

"Electrical cords, then. Clothes we can tear into strips. Anything."

I find an extension cord in the living room, unplug it, and give it to Stanley. Then I go into Alaina's bedroom. It feels like a violation to be here, to be intruding in someone's most private space. Especially that of a young woman.

But it reinforces the feeling that she's gone. I taste disappointment in my mouth, bitter as rotten fruit, when I understand Alaina's really not here.

Alaina's bedroom is furnished with an unmade twin mattress

and box spring resting directly on the floor. Her closet hangs open. There are just a few clothes on hangers. A plastic milk crate serves as a bedside table with a single framed photo on top. I shine the light on the image—a young Alaina, maybe fifteen years old, with an older woman who must be her grandmother.

It's too hard to think about that woman learning the news of Alaina's death, so I whip the light around the room. I see no other cords—and certainly no ropes—but there's a worn hoodie, a Tampa Bay Buccaneers logo on the front, sitting on the end of the bed. There's a drawstring hanging from the hood.

Stanley has wasted little time. He already has electrical cord running around Tyler's wrists and down to his feet, trussing him like a steer. Tyler grimaces and tries to squirm, but he can't move much.

"Looks like you have this under control," I say.

"Give me the drawstring." I do what he says, and Stanley goes on. "We'll have to gag him to keep him quiet."

"No way we're doing that," I say.

Tyler looks relieved. Stanley doesn't argue. He tucks the gun into his pants and continues his work, using the drawstring to further bind Tyler's hands and feet to the wooden slats of the chair.

Stanley looks to be enjoying his work. I question our decision to bring Tyler here. We could have just as easily tied him up in Lloyd's apartment.

But if he really is dangerous . . .

Maybe this *is* best for everyone.

Stanley tugs on all the bindings and, satisfied that Tyler can't move, straightens up. He pulls the gun out of his pants, even though there's no need anymore. Stanley appears to just like the feel of the weapon in his hand.

"You sure you don't want to gag him, Jake?"

"Who's going to hear him over the storm?"

"I guess so." Stanley can't conceal his disappointment.

"Are you really just going to leave me here? For hours? Through a hurricane?"

"We'll check on you."

"Oh, yeah?"

"We will," I say. "Just . . . just sit tight for now."

"I don't have much fucking choice." The professionalism Tyler demonstrated before is gone now, and I can't say that I blame him.

Stanley walks backward to the door, the gun lowered toward Tyler.

"Stanley," I say, "can you put that away?"

When we reach the door, he does, sliding it back into his pants. Before we go out, I lean close to Stanley and speak in a low voice so Tyler can't hear me.

"Does he have to be tied so tight?"

"Do you want him getting loose and hurting someone else? This is insurance."

Again I try to think of another way but come up empty. I'm willing to trade Tyler's discomfort for the safety and security of everyone else.

"Okay," I say. "But I'm coming back to check on him. We might have to loosen those ties if he's in pain."

"Yeah, sure." Stanley doesn't sound convincing. He sounds like a guy telling me what I want to hear.

"Are you ready to brave the elements?"

"You bet."

I take a quick look back at Tyler and throw the door open.

FORTY-THREE

10:44 P.M.

Stanley and I move down the walkway toward Lloyd's apartment.

I place my hand on Stanley's arm, stopping him three doors from Lloyd's place. The wind rattles the palm fronds with such force they sound like a stadium full of clapping hands. When one gets loose, it flies through the air and smacks the stucco on the outside of the building.

"Do you really think he killed Dallas?"

"That key is a pretty damning piece of evidence."

"Sure, but—"

"Do you believe that cockamamie story about finding it on the ground? We all know it was on Dallas' body."

"It always was."

"Jake, I learned something in the service. Sometimes you have to make tough decisions for the greater good. And sometimes it hurts to make them. This is one of those situations. But we're doing the best with what we have."

"Right." I nod, trying to talk myself into agreeing with him. "Right. We'll let the cops sort it all out when this is over."

"Exactly." Stanley claps me on the shoulder. "Now let's get the hell out of this mess and inside, where it's dry."

We deliver the coded knock to Lloyd's door. When Nina opens it, Mackenzie rushes across the room and throws her arms around me.

Jordan is less dramatic but not far behind. "Thank God you're back." She puts her hand in mine when she reaches me.

Everyone looks incredibly relieved to see us, especially Ethan.

"Did you take care of him?" Ethan asks. "You guys have been gone a long time."

"He's secure," I say. "And safe. In Alaina's apartment."

"Oh . . . okay, that's good. I guess."

"You guess?" I ask. "What did you want us to do to him?"

"I don't know. It's just—he's dangerous."

"His hands and feet are tied to each other, Ethan. And he's tied to a chair. I don't see how he could get out of that mess unless he's Houdini. That's really all we can do."

Everyone—and I mean everyone—starts throwing questions at us. They all want to know what happened. What we were doing and why it took so long. I feel like a politician at a press conference.

"Didn't you tell them?" I ask Ethan.

"I couldn't do it. I was afraid it would be too triggering."

"To tell them the truth?"

"The truth is *always* the hardest."

I have to force myself not to roll my eyes. "Okay, I'll tell you all what happened. Just let me get it out."

I give them a quick rundown. Going up to Ethan's place and finding Isaac on the way. Learning Ethan had been attacked—presumably by Tyler. And how when Tyler showed up in Ethan's apartment, we used the gun to control him and found Dallas' passkey in his pocket.

When I share this bit of news, everyone in the room except Ethan and Stanley gasps. If we were in a court of law, I would have just won over the jury. No doubt about it. I finish by telling them how we tied up Tyler in Alaina's apartment.

"What happened when Tyler left here?" I ask. "Why did he come looking for us?"

Lloyd speaks up right away. "He said the two of you had been gone awhile, and he was worried something happened to you. He insisted that since he was a trained security guard, he needed to be the one to check."

"We told him to wait," Nina says. "We told him you and Stanley can take care of yourselves, but he was determined. I mean, he was *really* determined to get out of here. I offered to go, but he said no."

"It's true, Dad. He was, like, low-key rabid to get out the door. Like he was late to catch a plane or something."

Stanley and I exchange a look, and Stanley says, "Or a boat." We tell them about Tyler's dinghy.

"He was trying to get away," Kiara says. "That's why he was so eager to get out of the apartment."

"That doesn't make any sense," Sawyer says from his perch on the dining room chair. "You can't go anywhere right now in a boat. It's a thousand feet to the mainland, but it might as well be five hundred miles in this weather."

"He insisted it would be possible when the eye of the storm passes over the island."

"The eye?" Jordan says. "Really? How could he possibly know how long that would last?"

"I don't know what Tyler was up to, but he didn't exactly run away. He came upstairs to Ethan's apartment. Not to mention he told us about the boat, so it's not like he was planning some secret getaway."

Jordan puts a hand on my arm. "Something happened while you were gone."

"What?"

"About ten minutes after you left, someone started pounding on the door."

"Nina wanted to let them in," Lloyd says with a shake of the head.

"In my defense, I thought it was Jake or Stanley," Nina says. "I thought they were in trouble."

"But they didn't give the secret knock," Jordan says.

"I was worried you might have forgotten," Nina says.

"Jordan is the one who stood firm on that," Lloyd says. "She held the line on opening the door. She said you would never forget something like that."

"They pounded on the door for a long time. Maybe ten minutes. I swear I thought they were never going to go away. I went right up to the door and asked them to identify themselves."

"Mom was totally badass, Dad. She didn't even hesitate to go up to that door."

"I knew it was locked."

"They could have kicked it in," Nina says. "Even with the chain up, someone can bust a door down." She looks at all of us. "My ex-husband did that once. That's how I know."

Kiara puts her arms around Nina and pulls her close.

"Whoever was out there finally ended up leaving," Jordan says. "And as far as we know, they never came back. That's why we were so relieved when you all showed up."

"I'm so glad you two remembered to tell me the secret knock. Otherwise, Isaac and I would never have gotten in."

"Did this person say anything when they were knocking?" I ask.

Each person in the room turns to someone else, as if no one wants to answer. "There's some debate about that," Jordan finally says. "Some people thought they said something. And others don't. The wind and rain are too loud to be sure what we're hearing."

Stanley jumps in. "We didn't see anyone but Tyler when we were out there."

The rainwater and sweat coating my body for hours are starting to dry, turning cold on my skin. I break out in goose bumps.

"Was it Tyler trying to get back in?" Hazel asks.

"Tyler knew the knock," I say. "He was here when we came up with it."

"Plus, he had the passkey," Stanley says.

"And he was upstairs with us," I say. "He couldn't have been down here knocking and upstairs that fast. Could he? And why would he do that?"

"What was he like when you saw him?" Lloyd asks.

"He was completely calm," I say. "Like he didn't have a care in the world. Even when Stanley put the gun on him, he kept his shit together. Right, Stanley?"

"Yes, but he was afraid. I've seen that look before. In other men's eyes."

An uneasy tension settles over the room. We're all wondering the same thing. Is someone in the building besides Tyler?

"Well," I say, "we're all here now. That's what matters. And Tyler is taken care of. So . . . let's try not to worry too much."

Everyone nods. We're all trying to convince ourselves we'll make it through the night.

I want to collapse to the floor. I want to allow my body to come down off the high alert it's been on since . . . well, ever since I first drove over the causeway after work. "Let's all just . . . take a breath."

I pull Jordan and Mackenzie into the kitchen. I've never been more relieved to be with them. I want to be alone with them, but I don't want to ask to go into the bedroom again. I want to fold them up in my arms again.

Mackenzie leans close to my ear, her hair brushing my face. "Dad," she says, her voice so low I can barely hear it, "I need to tell you something. About that guy who came to the door. I need to tell you what he said."

FORTY-FOUR

"Do you want to talk in the other room?" I ask Mackenzie as Ethan sits next to Hazel on the couch.

He places Isaac on Hazel's lap, and her face lights up. "Oh, Isaac." She rubs the cat behind the ears. "There's my boy."

Mackenzie lets her eyes wander over everyone in the small apartment. "Yes, Dad," she says, answering me. "We need privacy."

When I look at Jordan, she nods. She clearly knows what's going on.

While the three of us move toward the bedroom, Ethan tells Hazel all about the attack in his apartment. He spares no detail. Hazel continues to pet Isaac, but with her free hand she clasps Ethan's hand, focusing on his face like he's the only person in the world. I feel better knowing Hazel will have someone here to help her after I go home. Maybe she and Ethan will become close.

My shoes squish across the floor, and Lloyd rolls his eyes, not at all happy that his bedroom has morphed into our family conference room. I remind myself to thank him and Catalina again.

Mackenzie closes the bedroom door. She looks like she's about to burst. "Okay, Dad, I want to tell you this in private because I'm not sure anyone else will believe me. I mean, I think Mom does—"

"I do."

"—but I'm not sure anyone else will."

"What is it?"

"Okay." Mackenzie holds her hands toward me, palms out. It's the way she always prepares to tell us something important. She's done it since she was about three years old. Who knows where she picked it up? "So, when that guy was knocking on the door before, whoever he was, I heard something. Remember how Mom went up to the door like she was a badass and everything?"

"I remember."

"Well, I went with her, just to make sure she didn't get into any trouble. And when the dude was knocking on the door, I heard what he was saying."

"How could you hear him over the storm?"

"The wind wasn't as intense then. It kind of calmed down and got quiet for a minute. And that's why I could hear the dude on the other side. And, Dad? He was screaming. Like a maniac."

"She's right, Jake. He was pretty worked up."

"What did he say?"

"If you don't believe me, I'll be pissed." Mackenzie is glaring at me now. I know she's serious. "You have to promise to believe me."

"Kenzie, I believe you. I always do."

She looks from Jordan to me, her hands still extended. "Okay, he said something like 'Hazel, I know you're in there. Hazel, I need to talk to you.'" She makes her voice deeper when she imitates the man, but she just sounds like a teenage girl imitating a man.

I look at Jordan. "Did you hear him too?"

"I heard something like that. I'm not as sure about it as Kenzie, but I know she wouldn't say it if she wasn't sure."

"Dad, I know what I heard. I promise."

"I believe you, Kenzie." I scratch the tip of my nose. "I just don't have any idea why someone would be that anxious to talk to Hazel."

"Now that you mention it, she did say something interesting," Jordan says. "After you were gone, she told me she's being stalked. Did you know that?"

"Oh, yeah, we've *all* heard about it."

"Then isn't it possible that's the guy?" Jordan asks.

My wife is much more compassionate than I am. She stops to buy food for homeless people on the streets. She gives rides to people who need them, even when it's against her better judgment. It makes complete sense that she'd believe Hazel's story.

I want to believe it—and I hate to think of Hazel growing increasingly disconnected from reality. But I've seen change coming over her during the six months I've been here. "She's not well, Jordan. She has dementia. She's convinced some guy's following her, but do you know what she told me right before the storm hit? She told me he can control the weather too. That it's her stalker who's making the hurricane hit the island. Besides, she's ninety-one. Who would stalk her?"

"Then why was some guy yelling her name?" Mackenzie asks.

"I don't know. Maybe he didn't say it."

"Dad, you just said you believed me."

I lift my hands in futility. "I don't know, then. Maybe I'm wrong."

Jordan jumps in. "The thing is, Jake, if there really is another person besides Tyler on the island, maybe Tyler isn't really the problem. You've got that poor guy restrained. . . ."

"I know, okay? I know. And I feel sick about it. Stanley—well, he was pretty gung ho about tying Tyler up. I'm going to check on him soon. I promise."

"But then you'll have to go out in the storm," Mackenzie says, pouting like the teenager she is. "Again."

"I couldn't live with myself if I didn't check on him, Kenzie."

The building groans. This time it's louder than I've ever heard. Then it groans again, louder still.

"That's not good," I say. "That's not good at all."

FORTY-FIVE

"We need to get back out there," I say. "They'll be freaking out."

"Wait, I want to ask you something." Jordan puts her hand on my arm. She's wearing her engagement ring and wedding band. And the watch Mackenzie and I gave her for her last birthday. "What do you know about this Stanley guy?"

"Not much. He lives on the sixth floor. We say hi at the elevator. That kind of thing."

"Doesn't he creep you out?" she asks. "He was awfully determined to hold on to that gun. And he's got Tyler tied up in another apartment. You didn't really say if you were okay with that or not."

"We're safer with Tyler separated from the rest of the group. We don't know him. Or what his intentions are."

"But, Dad, tying a guy up? Who does that? And letting this Stanley guy run around with a gun? It's dangerous."

"This is all dangerous, Kenzie. Someone is dead. What do you want me to do?"

"Not tie up some defenseless dude."

"Did you see Tyler?" I look from one of them to the other. "He's hardly defenseless."

"Did you actually *see* him hurt someone?" Mackenzie asks.

"He had Dallas' key in his pocket."

Mackenzie starts to argue, but I cut her off.

"Sometimes you have to make tough decisions, Kenzie." As I say the words, I recognize how closely they echo what Stanley just said on the landing. Suddenly I feel a lot less comfortable with them.

Jordan won't let it go. "Jake, are you really okay with this guy being tied up? And left alone in another apartment?"

I sigh. "Not entirely, okay? Does that make you both feel better? But I said I'll check on him. I'm not sure what else we can do."

"It's so disturbing," Mackenzie says. "It's like . . . threatening."

"You're right," I say. "It is. But our lives are on the line here. Someone killed Dallas. Someone attacked Ethan. And a hurricane is moments away from making landfall on this very island. I just feel better keeping Tyler in another apartment, okay?"

Mackenzie wants to continue the debate, but Jordan cuts her off with a look.

"Okay," Jordan says, "we trust you."

"I don't feel great about *any* of this, but Tyler grabbed me too— on the stairs when I was trying to get to Hazel. That's not normal, Jordan."

Jordan squeezes my arm. Mackenzie looks away.

"What else do I need to know? Did anything else happen while I was gone? Did anybody say anything?"

"Not really, no," Jordan says. "Lloyd and Catalina are really sweet. Apparently, she's pretty sick. And they still opened their home to all of us."

"Lloyd's rough edges are definitely smoothed by Catalina. I didn't even know she existed until a few hours ago."

"I guess Hazel and Ethan are pretty tight," Mackenzie says, seeming to have finally let go of the whole thing with Tyler. "As soon as he came in here, she was raving about how much he helps her with her projects. What projects? I mean, no offense to old people, but Gramps is, like, seventy-five, and he doesn't do anything but watch TV. And you said Hazel's kind of . . . you know . . . out of it."

"She's a retired historian," I say. "She specialized in the history of the Treasure Coast, local stuff. Ethan's a computer guy. Maybe he's helping her on the computer. Or humoring her. I'm not sure what she's capable of anymore. She's drowning in paper. Maybe he's cataloging or scanning some of her stuff."

"Everyone here seems really nice," Jordan says.

"Except *Stanley*." Mackenzie scratches her head. "And Tyler. They're both total creeps."

Something thumps above us. It's so loud all three of us flinch.

"What was that?"

It thumps again. And again.

Then a screeching sound starts. It goes on and on, and it's really loud. It sounds like the building itself is being tortured and is crying out in excruciating pain.

I aim my light at the ceiling. Nothing. I move it around the room.

"Shit. Holy shit."

"What, Jake?" Jordan says. "What is it?"

"Look."

A stream of water is pouring from the ceiling in the back corner of Lloyd and Catalina's bedroom.

It's like the building really is falling apart.

FORTY-SIX

When I get to the other room, I point behind me.

"Lloyd, you might want to—"

He sees the look on my face and rushes past me into the bedroom. I follow along, but not before stopping in the kitchen to find a bucket and some rags.

When I return to the bedroom, Lloyd stands under the leak, catching the falling water in a plastic cup. At least the trickle has slowed.

I hand him some towels. While he tries to soak water out of the carpet, I position the bucket under the drip. The water thwacks against the plastic as steady as time. *Thwack-thwack-thwack.*

"This is a disaster," Lloyd says.

"Maybe a pipe burst upstairs."

"The water's not on upstairs. That apartment's been vacant for over a year. They shut the water off and pulled out all the pipes, sold them for parts. This leak originated somewhere else."

Jordan and Mackenzie stand by, looking helpless.

"That grinding sound—" I look at my family. No secrets. No lies. "It's the roof, isn't it? It's the roof coming loose."

"I think you're right," Lloyd says. "It was already in bad shape. A storm like this . . ."

"What can we do?" Mackenzie asks.

"Do you have a rosary?" Lloyd says. "Do you pray?"

"My parents didn't take me to church, so I have no clue what you're talking about."

"It means—well, people have been in tighter spots than this one, but not many."

"Is it safe in here if the roof is going?" Jordan asks.

"Jake was right to bring everyone down to a lower floor," Lloyd says. "It's the best place to be if—"

Boom!

It sounds like someone detonated an M-80 right over our heads.

We all duck, bending low to the floor. Mackenzie rushes to my side, huddles against my body.

Boom—boom—boom.

"What is that?" Jordan asks. "Did something blow up?"

"Is it gas?" I ask.

"It's the roof," Lloyd says. "It's starting to go. Come on."

"What can we do?"

"Get to the center of the apartment," Lloyd says. "The hallway out here."

"Why?" Mackenzie asks. "What is the hallway going to do to protect us?"

"If the building collapses, you want to be in the center. So the debris falls around you rather than on top of you."

"Oh. My. God."

Lloyd leads the way. When we get out to the other room, the booming continues. Everyone is talking all at once.

Stanley stands by the door. "It's the roof coming loose. I was in a tornado once when I was stationed in Kansas. It sounded exactly the same."

"You all need to get in the hallway. It's safer there," Lloyd says. "Right now. Go."

Everyone goes to the hall. Nina and Kiara grab bags of food. Hazel starts rocking and manages to rise to her feet with an assist from

Ethan. Pretty quickly, everyone is past Lloyd and me, squeezed together in the short hallway. The banging stops for a minute and then
resumes with greater force.

All of a sudden it's only Lloyd and me in the living room.

And Catalina.

Lloyd's standing at the foot of the hospital bed, Catalina gazing
at him with surprise in her eyes.

"Lloyd, do you—can I help you carry Catalina into the hall?"

He waves a hand at me. "No, no." He moves to the side of the bed
and sits next to Catalina. "It's okay, isn't it?" He places her hand in
his. "We've talked about this, haven't we?"

"Yes." Catalina struggles to get the words out. "We have."

Lloyd goes on. "That hallway is barely big enough for the eight
people who are already in there. I doubt we'd fit." He glances over his
shoulder at me before turning back to Catalina. "You go, Jake.
Squeeze in there as best you can."

A wave of emotion passes through me. Gone is the Lloyd who
wouldn't let us in the door a few hours ago. In his place is a person
who ushered everyone else into the safest place in his apartment.

"No, Lloyd. No." I'm adamant. "I'll get everyone out. Catalina is
more important—"

Lloyd interrupts me. "We've had to discuss things like this, Jake.
The end of the road. We're ready for it." He speaks to me but keeps
his eyes glued to Catalina. "We're going to face it together."

Something catches in my throat. Even if I knew what to say, I
wouldn't be able to say it. I feel like an intruder. I turn away from the
two of them and start for the hallway.

Catalina makes a low noise, something between a cough and a
throat clearing. I know it's directed at me, so I stop and return to the
side of the bed opposite Lloyd. I drop to one knee, and Catalina lifts
her hand, limp and fluttering like a wind-battered butterfly. I take it
in mine.

Her skin is as soft as well-worn cotton.

"Your . . . family . . ." Each word comes with great effort.

I nod. "They're amazing, aren't they?"

"Lucky . . ."

"Yes, I'm very lucky."

Her eyelids flutter and close. She's clearly exhausted by the effort of speaking.

I look across the bed to Lloyd, but he's gazing down at Catalina, pure devotion on his face.

I gently extract my hand from hers so she can rest. But before I break contact, she opens her eyes again, fixing her gaze right on me.

"Hold . . . on . . . to . . . them."

"I will," I say. "I promise."

Her eyes close again. A moment later, her breathing resumes its deep, regular pattern.

I listen. The banging has stopped. For now. The wind rattles the shutters and the door. I'm sure the roof is hanging by a thin thread.

Maybe, just maybe, it will last. . . .

I look across at Lloyd again. "Do you want me to stay with you? So you're not alone?"

"I'm not alone, Jake. Ever."

"I just mean, do you want some company?"

"I knew what you meant," he says. "Thank you, Jake, but I'm all right." He nods at Catalina's sleeping form. "We're all right. And you heard the boss. Hold tight to your family. You never know what tomorrow will bring."

"You're right about that, Lloyd. You'll be okay. As long as this place holds . . ."

"We'll be together. No matter what. Right here."

"Let me know if you need anything. And, Lloyd—"

He lifts his head a bit, listening.

"Thank you. Not just for letting us stay here. For getting everyone in the hallway too. I know what a sacrifice that was. . . . If we weren't here, you could . . . Catalina could . . ."

He doesn't say a word, but I know he hears me.

I stand to leave the two of them. And as soon as I do, the banging resumes even more loudly than before.

I drop to the floor next to Catalina's bed, as if that will protect me from disaster.

The banging continues, growing in volume each time we hear it. All I can picture is an angry god pounding on the building with a giant hammer, trying their best to beat us into the ground.

A second later, there's another screeching sound. It goes on longer than the last one. It sounds like thousands of metal sheets being torn in two. As soon as that stops it's followed by a giant whoosh. The exhaled breath of the hurricane.

We're all holding our collective breath, waiting to see what's next.

A gigantic crash sounds above us, a pounding, tumbling roar of noise. It's louder than the hurricane, louder than anything I've ever heard in my life.

Like a thousand airplanes landing on top of us.

Like a thousand bombs falling.

"Lloyd? Is that what I think it is?"

"That would be the roof. It's going. Completely, and once and for all, going."

PART THREE

FORTY-SEVEN

2:11 A.M.

The storm pounds us for what feels like days.

In reality, it's hours. Hours and hours of limbs and debris crashing against the building nonstop. The walls moan like they're being tortured.

When the noises finally start to slow, we're all left feeling shell-shocked.

In their wake, the wind continues to blow. Only it's louder now. It makes an eerie keening as it pushes against the door. Howling against the walls so hard I worry the whole building will be shaken off its foundation.

I'm down on the floor. When the crashing hit, I ducked, covering my head like I was in one of those old-time nuclear-bomb drills. *Duck and cover.* As if placing my hands over my head and flattening my body against the floor could protect me.

I remove my hands and lift my head. I blink a few times.

Lloyd stands up from the other side of the bed.

"Are you okay?" I ask.

"For now."

"Do you really think the roof blew off?"

"No doubt about it."

Stanley comes out from the hallway on all fours, his flashlight beaming up against the underside of his face. "Oh, yeah, that was the roof going. For sure."

Stanley aims the light at the ceiling. I get a grip on mine and do the same, as does Lloyd. We shine our beams around the ceiling. There's one long crack down the center.

"Was that there before?" I ask.

"Since the day we moved in," Lloyd says.

We continue to search with our crisscrossing beams. Nothing else seems out of place. No water. No cracks. No crumbling plaster.

"It looks okay, right?" I ask.

"No new damage, apparently," Stanley says. "I checked the leak in the bedroom. It's still dripping, but it's not any worse."

"Okay, so . . ." I straighten up even more. "We're okay, right? We made it through the roof coming off none the worse for wear."

"There's good news," Stanley says. "It didn't sound like it smashed the rest of the building up too bad when it came off." I'm surprised to hear Stanley say this, since it sounded awful to me. "Sometimes a building as big as this one can withstand that kind of trauma."

"I sense a 'but' coming. . . ."

"*But*," Lloyd says, "this is a problem. The roof was our protection from the elements. It was sheltering the rest of the building. With that gone . . ."

"It means we're going to be hammered on top," Stanley says. "Rain, wind, debris hitting the interior of the top floor. Which is going to compromise the structure if the wind doesn't let up. And I don't think that's happening. Not anytime soon."

"What can we do?" I ask.

"We need to see how much of the roof came off, how much is left," Stanley says.

"It's pitch-dark. What are you going to see?" Lloyd asks.

"What's the other choice? Wait around?" I ask. "Hope we're through the worst of it?"

"Oh, we're not through the worst of it," Lloyd says.

Lloyd's words are shocking. It's like he threw a bucket of cold water in my face. *We're not through the worst of it?* As if to prove him right, the building begins to creak and groan again.

Something wet hits the top of my head. I brush it off, but it's quickly followed by another drop. "Shit," I say.

"I felt it too," Stanley says. "This building is going to get awfully soggy awfully fast."

FORTY-EIGHT

The pounding and howling increase above us.

The hurricane shutters and apartment door rattle like they're about to fly away from the building.

I've never heard anything so loud in my life.

"This is landfall," Lloyd says. "It's coming ashore—and it sounds like it's right over us."

"What should we do?" I ask.

"What *can* we do?" Stanley says. "Get back in the hall and wait."

"Lloyd?"

He shakes his head. "You two go on ahead. We'll be okay."

I feel like more should be said, like I should be trying harder to convince him. But sometimes we come face-to-face with unmovable forces. Maybe they're natural or maybe they're human. Lloyd and Catalina are an unmovable force. Banded together right here in the living room of a crumbling building.

They've made up their minds, and I can't—and ultimately don't want to—sway them.

Stanley crawls back to the hallway, and I follow.

We're all packed in—cheek to cheek and thigh to thigh. Nina and Kiara scoot down, opening a space for me next to Mackenzie,

Jordan on her other side. I gladly take it. Hazel and Ethan are across from me. Sawyer grabs a bag of peanuts and starts eating.

"I eat when I get nervous," he says.

The noise above us is so loud we have to shout to be heard.

The air grows closer, ranker. There's no air-conditioning, no relief from the sticky humidity. Everyone sweats out their anxiety. We're all drenched with fear. The tight space smells like a locker room. My body has never smelled so fetid and overripe.

Everyone has been using the same bathroom. The scent of urine oozes through the door and into the hallway.

Mackenzie huddles next to me, rests her head on my shoulder. She says something I can't make out.

I lean close, whisper in her ear, "What did you say?"

She says the word "Mom," but I miss the rest. She leans closer. "I know all about . . . you know, you and Mom."

"We're okay, honey. Really."

"I mean . . ." She says something else I can't hear.

I look past her, at Jordan, who is listening to Hazel. I'm pretty sure she can't hear anything Hazel is saying, but she's humoring her.

"What?"

"You know, Mom and the guy at work . . . the affair thing."

"That's not really an affair, Kenzie."

"I know. Mom told me everything."

My cheeks flush. And not from the heat. I do love how close Jordan and Mackenzie are. But not all the time, not on those rare occasions when the lines blur between parent and friend. I'd prefer Mackenzie not know *all* the details of our lives. I'd rather not be talking to my daughter about our marriage. "It's—I don't want you to think bad of Mom. Or either of us. It's . . ."

"Complicated?"

"Yes, complicated."

"I get it, Dad. Really. I'm not taking sides." She lifts her thumb, chews on a loose piece of skin. "Like . . . well, Mom might kill me if

I tell you this, but it's relevant, okay? Promise to listen to the whole thing?"

My chest tightens. "Of course. What whole thing?"

"Well, like, that guy, the one from work—the emotional affair guy . . ." Mackenzie swings her head around, checks to make sure Jordan can't hear her. When she sees her mom occupied with Hazel, she turns back to me, leaning even closer. "I know for a fact that dude reached out to Mom again. Like a week ago or so."

"He did?" The tightness in my chest turns to burning. Hot. Irrational.

"Yeah, Mom was really upset about it. She was all, you know, distraught."

"She didn't tell me."

"Dad, some news isn't the kind you share long-distance. Even I know that."

"Okay. So, this asshole reached out again?"

"He did. The point is, Dad, that Mom gave him a hard no. Like, she really shut that down. It's like a stress test. Like that time they made Grandpa run on that treadmill to see if he'd croak?"

"An indelicate but apt analogy."

"But you and Mom didn't croak. You're still going. That's why we're down here." She looks at the ceiling. "Enjoying a hurricane together."

"You wanted to see the ocean."

"That too. But mostly it was to show you how much we love you. And how Mom wants you back and all that. And, you know, she's really sorry and shit."

The building groans, a long, low moaning sound, like it's in its death throes.

Everybody in the hall gasps and looks up.

"That's an ugly sound," Sawyer says, loudly enough for all of us to hear.

"We think the roof is gone," Stanley says, always the bearer of good news. "The top of the building is getting pummeled. This storm's probably chewing it up pretty good."

"Oh, no." Nina puts a hand to her heart.

"This is landfall," I say. "The worst part. If we can ride this out, we'll be in the eye. We just need to hang on."

Mackenzie asks, "How long does landfall last?"

"The storm starts to lose power as soon it reaches land. No more water to fuel it."

"You didn't answer me, Dad."

"I know. I'm not sure. Probably another hour or so. Something like that. But this is the worst part."

"So, what you're saying is— Gosh, that's loud."

Hazel starts waving her arms around, trying to get everyone's attention. It takes a moment, but eventually everyone turns to her.

When she speaks, her voice is surprisingly strong, managing to rise over the sound of the storm. "There is no reason for concern. I've studied the history of this island. The native people who originally lived here survived numerous storms, and they were never destroyed by the weather. They spoke invocations to protect the land, and I believe those invocations hold to this day."

"That's fascinating, Hazel," Ethan says.

"Yeah," Sawyer says, "I'd feel even better if the Indians built this building. They'd be more ethical about it than the owners."

Mackenzie says, "Is she serious, Dad?"

"I think so, yes. I mean, serious for her. But I'm not sure if she's, you know, completely attached to reality right now."

"She really freaked me out when she said she had a stalker."

"We don't know what's true and what isn't with Hazel. But, seriously, Kenzie, don't worry about Mom and me. We're both to blame for what went wrong between us, and we're figuring it out. We both love you very much."

"That's sweet," she says. "I love both of you. I'm not on anybody's side either."

"Good."

"I'm an only child. It's not like I can compare notes with a sibling."

"We only had one because we couldn't top perfection."

"Aww. That's bullshit, but sweet." She claps her hand to her mouth. "Sorry about the cursing. You know, that's one thing Mom doesn't mind as much as you. I guess things are a little looser on that front."

"When the storm's over and we're out of here, you can curse as much as you want."

She gives me a thumbs-up. "I just thought of something."

"What's that?"

"This storm . . . it's like a metaphor, right? For life? Sometimes you just have to ride things out and hope something's still standing. Kind of like what you and Mom have been doing."

"Did you learn that in English class?"

"I pay attention."

"I know all of this has affected you too."

She pats my knee. "I did miss you. There was no one to make lame jokes or kill spiders around the house."

"I know my place." I put my arm around Mackenzie and pull her to me.

Jordan looks at us, and I extend my arm, pulling her into our embrace. I hold them both close to me. I hope like hell we get out of here. I hope like hell Mackenzie gets to curse as much as she wants.

I hope we'll be all right.

Hazel waves her arms again. This time she's looking right at me.

"What is it, Hazel?"

"Jacob, I've been trying to ask you something, but you were ignoring me."

"I was talking to Kenzie, but you have my attention now. Ask away."

"I need to know if you found that gift I gave you."

FORTY-NINE

A long, loud groaning noise rises.

It's louder than the wind, louder than any other groan emitted by the building.

We all duck. I lift my arms over Mackenzie and Jordan, shielding them as best I can. I'm not sure what good it will do if the entire building comes down on top of us. But I'm grasping at anything I can.

"Dad, I'm scared."

I drop a hand to Mackenzie and squeeze her shoulder. "It's okay, honey. We all are."

"I've never been this scared."

"Neither have I."

"I think I'd be okay to never see the ocean now. I'd be cool with that."

"You'll see the ocean for real someday," Jordan says. "On a calm, sunny, beautiful day."

"I'll take just being alive for my sixteenth birthday."

"You will be," Jordan says, her voice as solid as a mountain. "You'll get it all."

Jordan has always been that rock for our family. More than I ever could. That's why her emotional affair or flirtation or whatever we decide to call it shocked me so much. If there was anything I could count on in life, it was Jordan. She was always it.

But I've had to admit my own culpability as well. My disenchantment with my job. The grief over my dad's death.

My own fears and anxieties about getting older. Watching Mackenzie grow up faster and faster, like someone turned the dial up on time, causing it to pass at three or four times the normal rate.

Everything terrified me.

And when that happened, I closed myself off from Jordan. I left her on her own. Not physically but emotionally. Can I blame her for looking for support elsewhere?

Hazel was right—do I really want to go back to the kind of job I had before? A career that left me so unfulfilled I stopped feeling things?

Do I have a choice if I want to be with my family?

The groaning stops suddenly. For now, we're left only with what we've grown used to—the howling of the wind, the rattling of the hurricane shutters and the door. The plopping of water into the bucket in the other room.

"Jacob? Jacob, are you listening?"

Speaking of Hazel . . .

"What is it, Hazel?"

Ethan translates for her. "She wants to know if you found the going-away gift she gave you."

"Are you fucking kidding me?"

Hazel's lower jaw swings open. She looks affronted like no one's ever been affronted before. "What did you say, young man?"

"Hazel, we're riding out a Category Three hurricane in a building that's falling down around us, and you're worried about a gift?"

"You have no idea what you're talking about, young man." Hazel sounds angry. *Really* angry. "Where is it?"

"I told you, I don't know. Probably in Dallas' apartment."

"Go get it."

"That's a crime scene, Hazel," Stanley says. "You can't just go poking around in there."

"You need to retrieve that gift, Jacob. Right now."

"Hazel, you're out of your—"

Something pokes me in the shoulder. I turn and catch a pleading look from Jordan. She's asking me to calm down, to show empathy for Hazel. Who may not really know what year we're in, much less fully grasp the danger of our situation.

"Okay, Hazel. Whatever you say. I'll be sure to get the gift."

"Please do. It's *very* important, Jacob."

"I'll take it home with me. I promise."

Hazel's posture visibly relaxes. Like a force greater than the hurricane had been weighing her down, and now it's lifted.

"Sheesh," I say, low enough so only Mackenzie hears me.

"Dad," she says, "I'm worried about something."

"Only one thing?"

"It's . . . Well, the roof is gone. There's water coming in everywhere. Chances are, there's water coming in all the apartments, right?"

I know where she's going.

"I don't like what you did to that dude, Dad. I don't like that you locked him up. *Tied* him up. And now the roof is leaking. I mean—you said you'd check on him. Don't you think you should? He's been in there for hours. It's been so loud. Imagine what it's like if you're all alone right now. And tied up."

FIFTY

I've been thinking the same thing. Tyler, whatever he may have done, is sitting tied to a chair in a dark apartment while a hurricane ravages the building.

He can't move. If anything fell near him—or even water dripped on him—he wouldn't be able to get out of the way.

Don't I have to treat him like a human being? Even if he is guilty of killing my friend?

"I hear you," I say. "It shouldn't be too big a deal to get down to Alaina's apartment. Even with the wind—"

"No."

Jordan's voice cuts through the room with such force I nearly jump.

When I catch her eye, she looks at me like I've completely lost my mind.

"You're not going out there. Not now," she says. "You've heard what's happening out there. And you heard what they're saying on the radio. The storm is at its worst right now. You have a family here. And all these other people. You need to stay."

"Mom, that man could get hurt. Or die."

"He's one person as opposed to all of us. And your dad matters more to us than anyone else."

"He'll probably be fine, Kenzie," I say.

But my voice lacks conviction, even to my own ears. A vise grip closes around my heart, squeezing until it feels like it's going to burst like a grape.

I'd be sick—forever—if something happened to Tyler.

I don't even know for sure if he's guilty of *anything*.

Ethan pipes in from the other side of the hall. "When the storm calms down, you can check on him, Jake. I don't like to take sides in domestic discussions, but Jordan's right. You need to stay here with us."

I'm not convinced. Not even close.

Jordan's hand grips my upper arm, overriding the pressure in my chest. She squeezes and then rubs my arm.

We lock eyes. There's a deep reserve of love expressed on her face, a deep concern for me. I'd almost forgotten what it feels like to have someone so closely and intently focused on my well-being. To matter so much to another person. We've already parted ways once—when I came down here—and I really don't want to risk being apart again.

It tears me up inside to think of anything happening to Tyler. But what is Tyler to me? A stranger. A person I'm not sure I can trust. If I have to choose, I'll choose to leave him on his own.

Like I said—he'll probably be okay.

I nod at Jordan, keep my eyes locked on hers. "Okay, you're right. I'll stay. We'll see what happens when the storm quiets."

"Are you kidding me? Both of you?"

"Kenzie. Don't."

"This is a person's life we're talking about."

"Mom's right—we're talking about other lives too," I say. "Our lives. Hazel's life. The lives of everyone here."

"You two always taught me to do the right thing. Remember when I borrowed a dollar from the Girl Scout cookie money, and you made me write a whole note and give the money back? Isn't that what you taught me? To always do the right thing?"

"You *stole* that dollar, honey," Jordan says. "And, yes, we always want you to do the right thing. But the lines can be blurry and complicated sometimes."

Mackenzie looks at Jordan and then swings her head to me. She wants to say more—and I could guess what it would be—but she wisely chooses to fold her hand.

"Yeah, I can see how the lines get blurry," she says. "I can see that very well."

There's movement to my right, at the end of the hall near the living room. Someone coming my way on all fours.

Stanley. "Jake, I couldn't help but overhear some of your discussion. About Tyler and all that."

"Yeah?"

"Look, I know I was the one who pushed you into tying him up. You weren't really on board."

"We made the decision together, Stanley. Both of us."

"I don't mind checking on him if you want. That way you can stay with your family—"

"That's nice of you, but—"

"Really, Jake. I don't mind."

Mackenzie nudges me in the side. I get the hint.

"Okay, Stanley. But maybe when the storm's eased a little."

"I don't think I should wait. I'll go now—pop my head in, see if he's okay, come right back."

"Just be careful," I say.

Everyone around me echoes the sentiment. They wish Stanley well, thanking him for checking on Tyler.

Stanley crawls back through the tangle of legs until he's out of sight.

"He'll be okay," I say to Jordan. "Right?"

She nods, squeezes my arm again. "Of course."

But I can't help thinking this is a mistake—and that I should be going in his place.

FIFTY-ONE

2:29 A.M.

I listen for the sound of Stanley going out the front door.

But I never hear it.

It should be easy to hear, given the wind and rain battering the outside of the building.

I flash back to the dispute between Lloyd and Stanley. Their fight over the gun. Stanley told me before we ever came to Lloyd's apartment that the two men don't like each other.

Are they arguing again right now?

Just then the door swooshes open, and slams shut with a loud thump.

No one has been saying much, and when I stand up to investigate, everyone looks at me with the same question in their eyes. *Where are you going?*

"I'm just going to check on Lloyd and Catalina. I'll be right back." I carefully step past the raised knees and folded bodies of my fellow tenants.

The flashlight beam guides me to the living room, where I half expect to see Lloyd and Stanley locked in mortal combat. Instead, I find the same peaceful tableau I left earlier.

Lloyd sits at Catalina's bedside, her hand clutched in his, the guttering candle casting soft orange light over both of their faces.

Lloyd turns his head toward me. "What is it, Jake?"

I glance around the room, moving my beam across the space. Water still drips from the ceiling. Did I expect to find Stanley crouched in some corner of the room, like a small child playing hide-and-seek?

"Where's Stanley?"

"Gone. I thought you knew he was leaving."

"I did. But it seemed to take him a while to get out of here."

"And you were worried he and I were having some kind of disagreement?"

"Exactly."

Lloyd gently lowers Catalina's hand to the bed. "The exact opposite happened." He stands up, reaches behind him, and pulls out the Glock. "Stanley went out of his way to give this back to me. He even apologized for being difficult earlier."

"He did?" I look to Catalina, figuring she's the most honest arbiter of any of us.

She nods, but there's strain on her face. I worry she's suffering.

"Wow, okay. Did he say anything else?"

Lloyd turns to Catalina before looking back at me. "He said he knew he could be a pain in the ass. I agreed he could be, but admitted that it takes one to know one."

A small smile appears on Catalina's face.

"He said I should hold on to the gun so I can protect the two of us and everyone else. I offered to go with him, but he was adamant that I stay."

Catalina says something much too low and weak for me to hear.

"What was that?"

". . . good . . ."

"Catalina felt strongly that I should not go."

"Jordan feels the same. So, that's it?"

"He told me if he didn't come back, I should help you take care of everybody. He told me not to worry about him. It all seemed a little melodramatic to me. He's just going down the way to Alaina's place. It's not far. . . ."

"And that's it?"

"That's pretty much it."

Catalina rings her bell, but she doesn't do it quite as robustly as earlier.

"Oh, he did sit with Catalina for a bit. I can't say I blame him. It's all I want to do." Lloyd walks past me to the door and puts the chain back in place. "He also said you still have the passkey."

I pat my pocket, feel the metal shape there. "I do."

"Jake?"

The voice comes from the hallway. When I turn, Nina and Kiara are beckoning me back to the hall. Once I settle in next to Mackenzie and Jordan, Nina asks me about Stanley.

I tell them Stanley gave the gun back to Lloyd, apologized even. I expect this news to be treated with relief.

But Nina's mouth opens. She turns to Kiara and smacks her on the shoulder. "See, I told you."

"Don't you see what's going on here, Jacob?" Hazel inserts herself into the conversation. "I've been trying to tell you. It's Stanley. He's up to something. I told you I saw him sneaking around the island with Tyler."

"It's not a crime for Stanley to talk to Tyler, Hazel. Or anyone else."

Ethan leans forward. "Jake, it's not just that. What do we really know about Stanley?"

"Well . . . not much, I guess. But I don't know a lot about any of you. Not really."

"But what do you know?" Ethan asks.

"I learned today he served in Vietnam."

Ethan looks surprised. "Are you for real? Vietnam? This only proves my point."

"What point?"

"Do you remember how Stanley ended up here?" Ethan's voice sounds more assured than I've ever heard it.

I'm reluctant to add any fuel to the fire of suspicion that is smoldering around Stanley. "I know he moved in after they'd decided to sell. What I understood from Dallas is that Stanley knew the Bennets, and that's why they let him rent an apartment when no one else was allowed to move in."

"Isn't that odd?"

I can clearly see the direction he's trying to drive the conversation, but I'm hesitant to give Ethan the satisfaction. "See what? Stanley moved in late, and he knows the owners in some capacity."

"What are they trying to say, Dad?"

Nina answers her before I can. "Stanley knows the owners. He shows up here a few months ago, moves in even though they're trying to get rid of the rest of us. Hell, they probably hope we'll get blown away in the storm. And now Stanley's with Tyler."

"Are you serious?" I ask. "Are you going to blame Stanley for the JFK assassination next? Ethan, you were there. Stanley pulled a gun on Tyler. He's the one who insisted we keep him away from everyone else. He's the one who wanted to tie Tyler up. He wanted to stuff a gag in Tyler's mouth, and I talked him out of it."

They all exchange looks—Nina and Kiara, Hazel and Ethan. Only Sawyer doesn't seem completely enthralled.

It's clear to me the four of them have been discussing this. And spinning their own web of conspiracy.

"What reason would Stanley have for causing all this trouble?" I ask.

Again a series of looks get exchanged.

"I don't like this kind of talk," Sawyer says. "I told them to tone it down."

"I agree," Jordan says. "If you're going to make serious allegations, you need to have proof. Real, solid proof."

"Okay, let's look at the facts," Ethan says. "Who's been hurt today?"

"Dallas," Sawyer says. "He's not hurt. He's dead."

"And we all know how Dallas felt about the Bennets. He went to bat for us, always pushing them to take better care of the building, threatening to go to the housing authority. The Bennets don't want anyone making trouble with this sale. Any bad attention could scare off buyers."

"So you're saying Stanley and Tyler killed Dallas to shut him up?"

"Dad, you kind of said the same thing when Stanley first came to the door."

I can't push back too hard. What Ethan and the rest of them are proposing makes a certain amount of sense. The question looming over everything all day has been why on earth anyone would want to kill Dallas. I'd been assuming it was a random crime—a looter, a squatter—which would explain the bedroom being ransacked, but what if it wasn't?

"You *could* make a case for the owners wanting to knock off Dallas."

My fellow tenants all start to talk at the same time. I hold my hand up, cutting them off.

"I'm not saying I'm *buying* that theory. I'm just saying—it's a theory with some logic behind it. But it still leaves one big question unanswered. If the killer was after Dallas, why did someone go into Ethan's apartment and rough him up? Why did they go through his things but not take anything? What were they looking for?"

Now it's just Ethan and Hazel who exchange a look. Hazel nods at Ethan like she's the queen and he's her footman.

Ethan turns to the rest of us, clearing his throat. "We think this is about what Hazel and I have been working on."

"What you've been *working* on?" I ask, not bothering to hide the skepticism in my voice. "You two?"

"The truth is, it's pretty big. And it could ruin everything for the Bennets. The sale of the island and any property on it."

FIFTY-TWO

Neither Ethan nor Hazel offers an explanation right away. It's almost like they want us to ask.

A low, dull thumping sound reaches us from afar.

We don't have time for games. "Okay, I'll bite. What exactly have you and Hazel been working on that would make someone kill Dallas?"

"Do you hear that?" Hazel asks. "That noise?"

We all nod. "Of course."

Hazel looks up at the ceiling, her eyes roaming over every inch of the stucco above us. "He's up there. He's doing this to us."

"Who's up where?" Nina asks. "I thought the roof was gone."

Frustration and empathy battle it out inside me. I know empathy has to win, but frustration is putting up a good fight. I get it. I do. Hazel has no control over her aging mind. It's the dementia making her believe her so-called stalker is standing on top of the building, pulling the hurricane to us like Superman. The stress of this situation is enough to make anyone question reality. Hazel's mental abilities are too diminished for her to see that clearly. But our problems are so vast right now, I really don't have the patience to deal with her.

"*He* is," Hazel says. "The man responsible for everything going on."

"Stanley?" Sawyer asks. "Stanley went up to the roof?"

"Not Stanley."

My head shakes, a demonstration of the frustration I can't hide. "She's talking about her stalker. Or the guy she *thinks* is stalking her."

"Dad? Be chill, okay?"

"Apparently, he also controls the hurricane."

Hazel drops her eyes from the ceiling and fixes them directly on me. They glisten in the faint light. She's upset. My doubt has upset her.

"Well," she says, "I'm used to this from Dallas. But not you, Jacob."

Mackenzie nudges me in the side.

"Why don't you just tell us what you've been working on?" I ask.

Hazel looks away. Haughty, hurt. Her chin lifted in the air. She's not going to answer me, not even going to deign to look at me.

I let out an involuntary groan. "Okay, Ethan, why don't *you* tell us what's going on?"

Ethan glances at Hazel, who still has her chin in the air. None of us can see her face straight on now. Ethan says her name, but she ignores him, so he turns back to us and shrugs.

"I don't know as much as she does, but I can try." He looks at her again, but she isn't budging. "You all know Hazel is a historian. She used to teach at the community college. She knows everything about the island." He shrugs again. "I guess she's found something that will prevent the sale of the property. She says it will get the Bennets to back off and leave us alone."

"How do you fit into all this?" Sawyer asks.

Ethan lets out a laugh. "Have you seen Hazel's apartment? She has papers. Lots and lots of papers."

"There's nothing wrong with paper," Hazel says, still not looking at us. "Better than staring mindlessly at your phone or the television all day."

"Anyway," Ethan says, "I was just helping Hazel scan some of her papers. I didn't understand them. They're old documents—maps and things. But I tried to help."

Hazel decides to rejoin the conversation. She whips her head back around, taking us all in before she speaks. "Ethan is correct. I did find out something important. *Very* important. You should have listened to me. But once people get to a certain age in this culture, we get shunted aside. Isn't that the truth?"

It's obvious no one really knows what to say. We all glance at one another and then away. Our bodies stir, feet shuffling against the carpet. Arms gently shifting position.

This is about me, so I try to make things right. "I'm sorry if I didn't take you seriously, Hazel. We're all listening now. Will you tell us what you've discovered? Maybe we can help too."

Hazel takes us all in again. She scans each and every one of us, as if she's trying to memorize something critical about our faces.

Or else she's searching for something.

When she's finished looking, she shakes her head. "It's too dangerous to talk about it here. Maybe when we get out of here—*if* we get out of here—I'll share."

I refrain from commenting. I can't take anything Hazel says too seriously. Or expect too much.

It occurs to me that Stanley has been gone for a while now. He was supposed to go straight to Alaina's apartment, stick his head in the door, and check on Tyler.

Has something gone wrong?

Did Tyler work his way loose? Did he hurt Stanley?

Or has Stanley finally taken matters into his own hands with Tyler?

"But," Ethan says, drawing me back to the moment, "if Hazel did find information preventing the sale of the building, it would explain a lot. It would explain why someone—probably Tyler—came into my apartment and attacked me before he started rifling through the things on my desk."

"And . . ." Mackenzie's voice isn't loud, but we hear it and turn her way. Her face flushes under the attention, but she doesn't avert her gaze from the group. "You may not have heard it, but when that guy was pounding on the door, he said—I swear this is true—he said Hazel's name. He said it like he knew you were in here and he needed to talk to you."

Hazel looks at me and nods toward Mackenzie. She doesn't say a word, but the look speaks volumes. *If you don't believe me, do you at least believe your own daughter?*

"Okay," I say. "Okay. It's clear none of us know what's going on. And we need to get help here so the authorities can figure it all out. Whenever that will be. But in the meantime—"

"I know exactly what you're thinking, Jake," Jordan says. "What the heck happened to Stanley?"

FIFTY-THREE

"That's what I want to know," I say.

"Maybe he got hurt," Mackenzie says. "He shouldn't have gone out in the storm. He's pretty old, isn't he?"

"Old?" Hazel scoffs. "Stanley's in his seventies. He's not old. Why, he's a spring chicken."

"Maybe it was a bad idea to send him out there alone," I say. "But it's been pretty safe to stick to that walkway."

"But that wind, Jake," Sawyer says. "It's getting worse."

"I know. . . ." I start to get up, pushing to my feet in the tight space.

"Jake, wait—" It's Jordan. She doesn't want me to leave.

"Doesn't this prove Stanley could be up to something?" Ethan asks. "Maybe he's run off."

I'm on my feet now. "Can we keep the speculating to a minimum?"

"Jake, what are you doing?" Jordan asks.

"I'm just going to stick my head out the door and see what happened to Stanley."

"There's a killer out there, Jacob." Hazel deigns to speak to me again. "It's dangerous."

"Dad, why don't you let me come with you?"

"No way. You need to stay here with everyone else. I'll just take a quick look. If I don't see anything, I'll come right back. But Stanley and I are responsible for Tyler, so I need to check on him."

"Be careful, please." Jordan grabs my calf and squeezes it.

"I will."

I make my way past the tangle of legs and feet again. Lloyd's hushed voice reaches me before I emerge from the hallway.

"That's it . . . just another second . . ."

I stop as soon as I see them.

Lloyd has Catalina rolled onto her side. He's removed her diaper and is gently cleaning her.

My gaze briefly locks with Catalina's. She sees me over Lloyd's shoulder, the candlelight illuminating her eyes.

I step back, wishing more than anything that she hadn't seen me.

I hear them finishing up.

"Almost done."

"Thank you."

"Of course."

I'm not sure I've ever witnessed such an act of pure devotion. And to come upon it in the midst of all of this chaos . . . it's overwhelming. For a moment I'm transported back to my dad's final days, his time in hospice. The nurses there showed him the most profound tenderness. Even though they didn't know him.

I take a deep breath. I've got to keep it together.

"There you go," Lloyd says on the other side of the wall. "Good as new."

The mattress squeaks and the sheets rustle.

I hesitate a long moment, then emerge from the hallway.

Catalina's in bed, the covers up to her chin. Lloyd is tying a plastic bag, which he tosses to the side. "Hello, Jake." He squirts hand sanitizer onto his palms and rubs it in. "What are you doing?"

"I'm going to look for Stanley."

Lloyd's forehead wrinkles. "In this mess?"

"He could be hurt. I'm going to see if he needs help."

Lloyd crosses his arms, continues to look skeptical. "I don't know, Jake. You may want to stay in. Stanley—well, he's his own man."

"Are you sure he didn't say anything else before he left?"

Lloyd's forehead remains wrinkled. "I don't think so. Just what I told you."

"Okay, thanks."

Catalina's hand comes out from under the sheet. It flops around clumsily on the nightstand. She knocks the bell to the floor, where it rings just once.

"Does she want to say something?"

Lloyd looks to Catalina, who wears an expectant look, like she *does* want to say something. She speaks, but her voice is so low I can't hear it.

Lloyd leans in close, his ear almost pressed to her lips.

He straightens up, shaking his head. "No, it's not that."

Catalina looks like she wants to say more, but Lloyd doesn't lean down again.

"Is everything okay?"

"It's something Stanley said before he left. He mentioned that the eye might be passing over us soon." Lloyd looks at the ceiling, as if he can see through eight floors to examine the storm directly. "The truth is, it might be calm enough for Tyler's boat to make it across to the mainland."

"Will the eye really be that calm?"

"It can be. The current will still be significant, but the storm will have eased to almost nothing." Lloyd shrugs. "A boat with an engine, even a small one, could make it. Maybe that's what Stanley has in mind."

"Is Stanley used to the water? Has he ever driven a boat?"

"No idea. It's not hard to do, but in a strong current, you'd want someone with experience. Didn't Stanley grow up in Oklahoma?"

"They have rivers and lakes there."

"Well, that's a horse of a different color. But maybe he is plotting his getaway. He did act like a man tying up loose ends. He gave back the gun. He apologized. Not like Stanley."

I nod, taking it all in. "Of course, he could be lying out there on the landing, knocked down by the wind."

"Could be. Or by the killer who did for Dallas."

My eyes trail across the room to the door. It suddenly seems a lot less appealing to go out there—and it wasn't anything I was that excited about in the first place.

"You don't have to go, Jake," Lloyd says, reading my mind. "You're not getting paid to be a hero. You're not wearing a cape."

"You're right about that. But it seems like somebody needs to do something."

"Do you want the gun?" Lloyd reaches behind him.

"No, you hang on to it. In fact"—I move closer, speak low enough that only he can hear me—"if, you know, anything happens to me . . ." I nod my head toward the hall, toward Jordan and Mackenzie.

"Sure thing. I'm good at taking care of people. I never thought I would be, but . . ."

"When you're forced to do something . . ."

"You can surprise yourself."

Lloyd holds out a hand, and we shake. Rather formally.

"Okay, then," I say. "Let's hope I can come right back. With Stanley. And then let's hope for that eye to get here."

I cross the room, undo the chain, the lock, throw the door open, and step into the angry wind.

FIFTY-FOUR

2:51 A.M.

Rain pummels my face like pellets of ice.

I struggle with the door. Lloyd has to come up behind me and shove it closed when I can't close it myself.

I press my body against the building. Where the wind can't push me any farther. And the rain reaches less of me. I use one hand to brace myself on the exterior wall, soaked with rain.

No one is on the walkway.

I shine my flashlight ahead, tracking the path from Lloyd's apartment to Alaina's. There's no sign of Stanley. The wind, despite its strength, didn't knock him to the ground.

A ripple of relief passes through me. Part of me feared finding him dead on the walkway right outside the apartment. At least there's still hope.

My thoughts cycle like the churning storm. Did the Bennets have Dallas killed? Did they target Hazel and Ethan? Is Hazel's stalker real?

My foot slips on the slick surface of the walkway, and I almost go down. My heart thrums with anxiety. I take a moment to make sure my footing is secure before I go on.

An unwanted thought drifts into my head. My mind travels back to the first moment we knocked on Lloyd's door, Stanley and I, the moment we learned about Catalina's existence. That was also when we learned the owners of the building had recently started charging Lloyd more for rent. He blamed Dallas.

Could Lloyd be responsible for Dallas' death? Lloyd has a weapon, but Dallas didn't die by gunshot. On the other hand, Lloyd isn't a small guy. He could overpower any one of us if he set his mind to it.

Is it possible his love for Catalina led to an act of violence? Are love and violence two sides of the same coin?

I know how I'd feel if someone threatened Jordan or Mackenzie. It wouldn't be pretty.

Something squawks to my left.

From the corner of my eye, I catch sight of an osprey hovering close to the walkway, thrown off course by the wind. After some frantic beating of its giant wings, which stretch nearly five feet across, the bird regains control and whooshes into the night, its screeching as loud as the wind.

Every creature, man and beast, is terrorized by the storm.

Once the bird is gone, I take in my immediate surroundings and see I'm right at Dallas' door. I press my hand against the cool surface right below the sign that reads MANAGER. It's hard to believe Dallas' body rests on the other side of this door. If only he were behind the door watching a baseball game. Planning his new life in Chicago. Drinking a Jai Alai.

I want desperately to believe that's what's happening, but I know it isn't. Reality has no interest in fulfilling wishes.

I remove my hand from the door, the rainwater running inside my collar and down my back, and continue down the walkway in search of Stanley.

Stanley was by my side all night, trying his best to help. But what do I really know about the guy?

He served in Vietnam, learned how to handle a gun there. And, as he put it, was trained in other things as well. Why did he go into Dallas' apartment after Dallas was killed? He'd never been in there before.

He pulled Lloyd's Glock on Tyler and wouldn't settle for anything less than tying the man up and abandoning him in Alaina's apartment. I had to dissuade him from sticking a gag in Tyler's mouth. Hazel says she saw Stanley and the security guy—maybe Tyler, maybe someone else—together in the days leading up to Dallas' death.

Was Hazel imagining things? Or did that really happen?

And if it did, was it just small talk she saw? Or the hatching of a nefarious plan?

Now Stanley is gone—having departed like a man leaving on a long trip, saying farewell to the life he once knew.

When I get closer to Alaina's door, I hear a slapping sound. Something hitting the building over and over again. My fingers search my pocket for the passkey.

But I don't need it.

When I get to Alaina's door, it's hanging wide-open, the wind blowing the door back and forth on its hinges like an out-of-control windshield wiper.

FIFTY-FIVE

I take two steps back.

I need to get Lloyd. The gun. I shouldn't go inside without the gun. But I force myself to stop and think this through.

The wind picks up, pushing against my back like one of those industrial fans on full power. I'm not sure I could make it back to Lloyd's even if I tried. At least not without expending a lot of energy.

The most plausible explanation is that the door is open because Stanley is inside, doing exactly what he's supposed to be doing: checking on Tyler.

Or maybe Stanley isn't inside the apartment, but the wind simply blew the door open.

Of course, other possibilities exist.

Someone has broken into the apartment, though I'm not sure what they'd want from Alaina, who was so broke she hadn't paid her rent in months. She apparently had nothing to her name, not even a functional car.

But a looter wouldn't know that.

I can stand out here in the wind and the rain. Or I can go in and find out what's going on.

"Stanley?" I shout as loudly as I can. "Tyler?"

I creep forward, take a few tentative steps. Like a fool, I brought nothing to protect myself with except the flashlight. What did I think I was going to do? Gong someone over the head with it? Shine it in their eyes?

I edge my body around the doorjamb. "Stanley? Tyler?"

No response.

Tyler wasn't far inside the door.

But he's not saying anything. Not even cursing me.

It dawns on me what's happened. And I can't believe I didn't see it coming. Tyler worked his way loose from the restraints. He managed to get loose and ran—likely toward the dinghy—and Stanley went after him. For what purpose, I don't know. The chances of getting hurt running around in the storm are even greater than the chances of getting hurt while piloting a dinghy across the Intracoastal during a hurricane.

But Tyler seems like a desperate man.

Made more desperate when we tied him up.

"I'm coming in," I say even though I doubt anyone is inside.

I swing my body around the doorjamb, flashlight leading the way.

It picks up murky shapes. An overstuffed chair. Discarded fast-food wrappers. Clothes.

Tyler in his chair.

His chin resting against his chest.

The beam of light exposes the carnage. Blood clotted in Tyler's thick dark hair. Blood running down the side of his face. Blood dripping off the end of his chin and onto his lap.

Tyler's skin is ashen and waxy. He's not moving, not at all.

"Shit," I say out loud. "Shit, shit, shit."

I spring forward, not bothering to see if Tyler's assailant—*Stanley?*—is still in the room. I reach for Tyler's wrist, press my fingers above the bindings that rendered him defenseless. For the second time tonight I check for the pulse of a battered human being.

Nothing. Absolutely nothing.

My hand touches his neck.

Nothing at all.

"Good God."

I helped tie this man up, left him here. And someone came along and killed him while he was completely defenseless.

A strangled cry of rage and helplessness pours out of my mouth. "Fuck!"

I've failed in so many ways tonight, failed to keep the people around me safe.

My cry is so loud, so visceral, that even above the storm I hear it echo off the walls of the small apartment, bouncing down the hallway to the bedroom and back to me.

It lingers in my ears.

"I'm sorry, Tyler," I say to my lifeless audience. "Shit, I am so, so sorry."

My cry reverberates again, but it sounds more like a choking cough.

I freeze in place next to Tyler's body. Listen.

I hear screaming wind. Driving rain. Crashing waves.

And then . . . I hear it again. An anguished cough—like someone is choking—comes from the bedroom.

"Stanley?"

Why would Stanley still be here?

Did he *just* kill Tyler? Tyler's body was warm to the touch.

It hasn't been long, not long at all.

"Stanley?"

I aim the beam down the hallway to the open bedroom door.

Listening.

I hear the same noise again. The cough that sounds more like choking.

"Stanley? Is that you? Are you okay?"

An unseen force compels me forward. I care less about my own preservation than about learning what's going on. And keeping the others safe.

I can't lose anyone else.

As I approach the open bedroom door, an odor reaches me. Something you wouldn't normally smell inside an apartment. Something muddy and dank. Earthy.

But not just earth—

"Stanley? Hello? Who's there?"

Something almost like—

The beam illuminates a figure on the bed, covers pulled up to their chin. Clothes lie scattered on the floor. Wet, soaking, muddy clothes.

The beam finds a face. It's young. Pale. A woman's.

Her eyes pressed tight. She doesn't seem aware of the light on her.

She coughs violently, a body racked by spasm.

Holy shit.

"Alaina?"

FIFTY-SIX

I place my hand against her forehead.

Clammy.

She turns her head away from me, but her eyes remain closed.

I scan her face, her head. She's dirty, her hair wet and matted against her sickly pale flesh. But there are no obvious signs of injury. No cuts or bruises.

The rest of her body is covered by a beat-up *Little Mermaid* comforter, so I can't see if anything else is wrong. I'm not even sure she's dressed.

"Alaina? Can you hear me?"

"Mm-hmm . . ."

"Alaina?"

"Mm-hmm." She turns her head back my way. Her eyelids flutter open. Then she squints against the brightness of the flashlight. "Who . . ."

I flip the light away. "It's me, Alaina. It's Jake. What happened?"

"Jake . . . I don't know. . . ."

"Alaina, we saw you try to drive across the causeway. The car went into the water. How did you get out?"

She remains silent a long time. Her eyes, brown and bloodshot, look glassy. I worry she's lapsed into a semiconscious state again. Or has suffered a concussion.

But then the eyes open wide, as if she's just remembered something.

"Oh, Jake." Tears spill onto her cheeks. "The car . . . your car . . . Oh, I'm so sorry. . . ." She pleads until the coughing starts again.

"You don't need to apologize, Alaina. I don't care about the stupid car. I care about you. I'm just so fucking glad you're okay. You have no idea. Stanley and I saw you go into the water. We thought you were dead. And now here you are. How did you . . . I mean . . . the current . . . Are you hurt?"

Alaina cries softly, her body shaking beneath the covers. She's always kept a steely wall up. This is the most emotion I've ever seen from her, which tells me how truly terrifying it must have been to go into the dark swirling depths of the Intracoastal in my shitty Hyundai. Of course it was terrifying.

"You don't have to talk about it if you don't want to." She cries a little harder now. Everything in me tells me I need to pull her into my arms. That's what I'd do with Mackenzie. But I don't with Alaina. Would she want someone she doesn't know to hold her?

I settle for putting my hand on her shoulder. It feels like cold comfort, but I'm not sure what else to do.

"I thought I was going to die." She's talking between sobs now. "I thought I *was* dead." She pulls her hand out from under the covers. It's tiny, smaller than Mackenzie's. More like a child's. She wipes her eyes. A nasty scrape nearly three inches long is slashed across the back of her hand. Her knuckles look red and raw. Mud and dirt encrust her nails. "I thought there was room to get by, but then the tires were slipping. . . . I couldn't believe it was happening. It was like a nightmare."

"I'm sorry, Alaina. I'm so, so sorry." The same words I said to Tyler. I swivel my head, instinctively looking behind me. Down the hallway and toward the rest of the apartment, where Tyler's dead body remains beaten and tied in the chair. Is there anyone else here? "Can you tell me—"

"The water just . . . it poured over the windshield. Like the blackest night. Like I was sinking in ink . . . And then it came into the car. Fast . . . I could feel the car moving in the current like a boat. . . . I actually thought, *I'm going to be swept out to the ocean. . . . I'll be floating in the ocean in this crappy car. . . .* But do you know what saved me?"

"What?"

"The driver's-side door—did you know the latch doesn't really work?"

I nod my head. "Yes, I do know that."

Alaina appears more awake, more energetic now. The coughing has stopped, the crying slowed. Maybe telling the tale has invigorated her. "I waited until the pressure started to equalize, until the water was over the door, and I pushed."

"How did you know to do that?"

"I saw a YouTube video about it once. I always expect disaster. Anyway, I pushed *hard* . . . and the door opened. Water poured in for a minute, but then I got out."

I've been holding my breath, listening. "How did you get to shore?"

"I was lucky. The driver's side was on the island side. I just started swimming. I swam and swam. I fought against the current. Jake, I kept thinking something was going to come up out of the water and get me. Or some giant piece of debris would come floating by . . . but I swam and I swam. . . . I think it took, like, four hours."

"It must have felt that way."

"All of a sudden, I saw the shore ahead of me. Then my feet touched the bottom. I literally dragged myself out of the water." She pulls her other hand out from the covers and holds them both up for me to see. The left looks worse than the right. Scraped, bloody. The nails ragged and torn. Like she's been in a brawl. A true fight for her life. "When I got up onshore, the wind was blowing so hard it literally knocked me over. I just stayed there, lying on the sand. The rain felt like ice on my face. But I was so relieved. . . . I don't know how long I lay there. I was soaking. . . ."

"What did you do?"

"I finally got up. . . . I didn't know where to go. So I just came home. Can you believe the keys were still in my pocket? I just came in here . . . took my clothes off . . . and collapsed in the dark. . . . I think I was kind of out of it. . . ."

"Did you see anyone? When you came into the apartment. Did you see Stanley?"

"Stanley . . . Why would he be in my apartment?"

"You didn't see *anyone*? Not even—not even the guy in the other room?"

"No. What guy?"

I look behind me again and then back at her. "Alaina, listen to me." Her eyes grow bigger. "We need to make sure the apartment is safe before we do anything else."

FIFTY-SEVEN

Alaina tries to sit up.

I reach out, attempt to steady her as she rises.

She hesitates, lifts her battered hand to her forehead.

"Maybe you shouldn't—"

"No. I'm okay. I think."

She remains still for a moment. I keep my hands extended in case she wavers or falls, but she doesn't.

"I can do it myself." She tosses the covers back. She's wearing a purple bathrobe.

I step back while she swings her bare feet off the bed and onto the floor. She hesitates again, rubbing her forehead and brushing the hair out of her face.

"Do you have clothes to put on?"

"Of course. This is my apartment." She must be feeling better. She hasn't lost her sassiness. "You said a man was in my apartment? Who? Why do we have to see if it's safe?" She scratches her head. "And did you say Stanley was in here? *Stanley?*"

"Get dressed, okay? I'm going to check the apartment. There have been a lot of—well, a lot of looters around. I'll check the apartment, and then we can figure out what to do. Okay?"

Alaina sits on the edge of the bed, her feet flat on the floor. Her hands rest in her lap. She rubs the belt of the robe between her thumb and index finger. "This is about Dallas, right? You think whoever killed him is still running around. Right?"

"Yes. Someone attacked Ethan too. In his apartment. And someone tried to get into Lloyd's apartment. We're all hiding there together."

"Lloyd's?" Her lip curls. "Why are you there?"

"Can you just get dressed? I need to make sure no one else is here. At this point, I'm guessing not, but who knows?"

But Alaina doesn't move. She remains on the edge of the bed, the belt getting worked over between her fingers. She stares into the distance, as if she's seeing something far away.

"Are you feeling light-headed?"

She shakes her head. "You know, I do kind of remember something when I came inside. I think . . ."

"What's that?"

"I think . . ." She drops the belt, looks right at me. "I think—maybe Stanley was in here when I came in. I think somebody was." She starts nodding, as if the memories are sharpening in her mind. "Yeah, when I came in, I stumbled into the living room. I fell . . . went down to one knee. I didn't think I could get up, and I just wanted to roll over and go to sleep on the floor. I was still in all those wet clothes. I was freezing. The water and the rain felt really fucking cold."

"So, what happened?"

"I was about to black out. To pass out on the floor. If I'd stayed on the floor in those wet clothes all night, I guess I might have gotten pneumonia or something. But someone helped me up. They put their arm around me and brought me to the bedroom." She shivers. "Do you think . . . Did I undress myself . . . or . . . ?"

"Do you think Stanley helped you?"

Alaina shudders. "Oh, God." She lifts her hand to her mouth like she's going to vomit. "He's such a creep. He's always sneaking around, trying to talk to me. Do you think he took my clothes off?"

"Do you?"

"I'm not sure. . . . I wouldn't have let him anywhere near me if I could help it. He was talking about something. . . ."

"What did he say? Do you remember?"

"I don't know. None of this makes sense. . . ."

"You need to get dressed." I step through the door, reach back to pull it shut. "I'll leave you alone."

"Jake?"

"Yeah?"

"I think he was saying something about getting on a boat. Does that make any sense to you?"

FIFTY-EIGHT

While Alaina gets dressed in her bedroom, I check the rest of the apartment.

Nothing in the bathroom. The small laundry closet—totally empty.

In the living room, I play the beam over Tyler's body, trying to see what I can learn. An impromptu amateur-hour crime-scene investigation.

Multiple gashes mark his head. Someone hit him with something. Something hard and blunt. A flashlight? Stanley was carrying one all night.

Tyler's hands remain tied but are clenched into fists, as if they froze in that position when he died. Tyler was a sitting duck. Whoever found him here had the easiest time in the world beating him to death. It must have been like pummeling a scarecrow or a mannequin.

The enormity of Tyler's death—and my role in it—falls over me, descending like a blackout.

Guilt and regret sear through me, moving from my back to my chest like a burning stake driven through my body. Bile chokes the back of my throat.

If I'd stayed with Dallas, he might still be alive. If I'd stood up to Stanley, Tyler might too.

All I really accomplished was keeping a gag out of Tyler's mouth. Maybe Tyler berated the killer as he died.

This guilt will stay with me my whole life. I know it. It doesn't matter if Stanley is the real killer. I still bear some of the responsibility.

Alaina thinks Stanley helped her to bed. Maybe even undressed her.

But she was also in such a state of distress, she didn't even notice Tyler's body. How can she be certain it was Stanley and not someone else?

No doubt Stanley had something against Tyler. He suspected him of spying for the owners. He also believed Tyler was the one who attacked Ethan, and possibly Dallas. Did Stanley finish Tyler off and flee the island in the dinghy? Why not leave him tied up until the cops showed?

Unless Tyler knew something Stanley didn't want everyone else to know. But what?

The bedroom door clicks open. I move to the hallway to prepare Alaina for what she's about to see.

Tyler. All the blood.

If she really hasn't seen him yet.

"Alaina, hold up."

"What's wrong?"

"Just hold up a minute."

She's wearing leggings, sneakers, and a heavy sweatshirt. She's washed her hands and scrubbed some of the dirt out from under her nails. Her hair is dry, and she smells like fruit. It's a shocking transformation.

"Do you know a man named Tyler?" I ask.

"Who?"

"Tyler. He works security for the building owners."

"We have security here? Sure couldn't tell."

"Do you know him?"

"I don't think so. Is that the man you said might be in the apartment?"

"He *is* in the apartment."

Alaina tries to look past me to the living room. "What's going on, Jake? I don't need to be bullshitted."

"Did he ever try to collect rent from you? Or threaten eviction?"

Alaina turns back to me, her eyes flashing. "Oh, no. Don't start that shit. That's between me and Dallas. I don't need every old gossip in this building talking about me making fucking rent. Fuck that, Jake."

"You don't know the guy?"

"Why are you asking me this?"

"You don't remember much. It seems like it's all a blur to you. So maybe—maybe you do know him."

Alaina places both of her hands on my left arm. With surprising strength, she pushes me aside.

I let her go and trail her to the living room.

Alaina stares down at Tyler's battered body. She doesn't show much reaction. No shock or disgust.

No turning away. It makes me wonder what else she's seen in her short life.

I wait a few moments before I ask, "Do you know him?"

"Hard to tell with all the blood and shit, but I think I've seen him. On the island."

"With Stanley?"

She turns my way. "Stanley? No. Alone, I guess."

"And he never asked you for rent or anything like that? Because you don't seem that upset about him being here, in your apartment . . . like that."

Her eyes bore into me. Unwavering. "Jake, I've seen some shit in my life." She points toward the Intracoastal. "I almost died, for fuck's sake. Do you think this guy's dead body is going to bother me? He can't bite."

I'd thought Alaina was dead. And I'd thought she died because I handed her my car keys.

Thank God she's okay.

"Why are you asking me all these questions, Jake? Do you think I'm the bad guy here?"

FIFTY-NINE

"I don't know, Alaina. I really don't. But Stanley is nowhere to be found. That doesn't look good."

"No, it doesn't."

"You might as well come down to Lloyd's with the rest of us."

"No doubt. I have no desire in hell to be alone with all this shit going on." But Alaina makes no move to leave the apartment. She remains in place, still staring down at Tyler's body.

Maybe, despite her bravado, she's in shock. Or maybe she's feeling the lingering effects of the accident. She places a hand on her forehead, starts to wobble.

I step closer, reach to steady her. "Do you need to sit?"

"No, I'm okay, I think. Yeah, I am. I'm okay."

"Do you feel sick? Is the blood bothering you?"

"No, no, it's not that."

"Did you hit your head when you went off the bridge?"

"No." Her voice comes out sharp, angry. "I told you it's none of those things, Jake." She lets out a sigh. "Can I ask you something? Who all is down in Lloyd's apartment?"

"Everybody left in the building. Except Dallas, of course. And Stanley, I guess. Wherever he went."

"Ethan?"

"Yeah, he's there. Why?"

She sighs again. Resignation seeps out of her body. She keeps a hand on her forehead, but it feels like it's there so she doesn't have to look at me.

"We should get out of here, Alaina—this is a crime scene."

"Jake, I think I can share this with you. . . . I trust you, okay? You know—hell, everybody in this building knows— What I am saying is, everybody in this building knows everybody else's shit. All. The. Time. It's fucking annoying. I've had substance abuse issues. You knew that about me, right?" She lowers her hand, cuts her eyes my way.

I nod. "Yes, I've heard that. But, Alaina, I don't—"

"I quit. I really did. I haven't been taking anything for about a month. I've been going to meetings and everything."

"Okay, good."

"That's where I wanted to go tonight . . . when you gave me the car. I wanted to go to a meeting. I wanted to find one in town."

"In a hurricane? Wouldn't they cancel all that?"

"I don't know." She pulls away from me and walks over to the couch. She plops down so hard it's as if gravity sucks her into the cushions. "I wasn't thinking clearly. Not at all."

"I'm sorry I gave you the keys."

She's shaking her head, and her hair, knotted on top of her head, bobs around. "It's not your fault. I wanted to go. I needed to go. I was desperate. See . . . Ethan . . . me and him, we . . ."

"Oh. I didn't know that. Maybe everybody else did, but I didn't."

"We tried to keep it, you know, low-key."

"I didn't know Ethan left his apartment."

"He doesn't. I usually went there. Well, that doesn't matter."

"I get it, and I don't want you to feel uncomfortable, Alaina, but given everything going on, it's best that we're all together. You can stay on the other side of the room. It should be fine."

Her head continues to shake. "It's not because of the sex, Jake. I don't care about that. I'm not a prude."

"Okay. Then what?"

Alaina examines one of her hands. She turns it one way and then the other, studying the marks like she hasn't really seen them yet. "Ethan does that IT job, remotely. But he also does something on the side." She blows on the back of her right hand like it's burning. "He deals, you know? Low-key, but he deals. Did you know that?"

I did not know that. And I'm more than a little surprised. All of a sudden I feel as old as an out-of-touch grandfather. "No, I didn't."

"I don't care. It should all be legal anyway. But I can't handle it. I can't even handle alcohol."

"Did Dallas know about Ethan?"

Alaina examines her other hand. And continues to not look at me. "He didn't. I don't think. Not until this morning. Ethan came by my place, and he wanted me to try something. A new product. We kind of got into it. An argument. Dallas heard us. He sent Ethan up to his apartment. And Dallas told Ethan he was going to report him to the owners, maybe the police. I've never really seen Dallas that way. He's usually pretty chill. Or he was, I guess."

"He didn't say anything to me about it."

"Maybe he didn't want to bother you before you left."

"So Ethan tried to get you to use again, and you had a fight. Did you do it?"

"I didn't. But I was so worried about it all day, just totally stressed. That's why I wanted to get to a meeting."

My mind replays the events of the day . . . seeing Ethan downstairs, smoking in the garage. I remember exactly what he said to me—*I'm not a bad guy, am I, Jake?*

I couldn't begin to guess what he was talking about at the time. But now it makes sense. Was he talking about trying to knock Alaina off the wagon?

That wasn't long before Dallas ended up dead. Maybe an hour or so. Dallas, who had threatened to evict Ethan or call the police on him for dealing . . .

Is it possible the person who attacked Ethan was looking for drugs? Maybe the assault had nothing to do with Tyler?

Ethan's down the hall in the apartment with everyone else, including my family, while I stand here talking to Alaina.

"Come on," I say. "You need to get up. We need to join the others." I walk over, extend my hand. "Come on."

"Are you worried about Ethan too?"

"Let's just go back. It's safer if we're all together."

Alaina takes my hand and pulls herself off the couch. "You think Ethan killed Dallas, don't you?"

"I don't think anything except that we need to do whatever we can to stay safe."

"Maybe he killed Dallas . . . and this guy."

I start for the door, trying my best to ignore her.

SIXTY

3:23 A.M.

Outside on the walkway, something's different.

I brace myself to be slapped back by the wind, but it doesn't happen. The wind still blows, but not nearly as hard as it has the rest of the night.

The rain still falls in sheets too, but it doesn't blow onto the walkway anymore.

"Why are you stopping?" Alaina asks.

"The storm. It's slowing, right?"

"I mean, just a little."

"It's already made landfall. We could be getting close to the eye passing over us."

"It's still windy as shit. I'm going." She moves past me before I can stop her.

"Hold on." I catch up to her. "Let me go in first. As soon as you walk in, everyone will think they're seeing a ghost."

"They are, Jake. I should have died."

"Do you have any idea how relieved I am that you didn't?" I put my hand on her arm. "Just stay away from Ethan, okay? We'll sort it all out when the police get here."

I start walking, until I realize Alaina isn't next to me.

I look back and see her leaning against the wall like she needs it for support.

"What's the matter?"

"The police . . . do I really have to talk to them?"

"You might, if they suspect Ethan of killing Dallas."

"I can't really talk to them, Jake. They might . . . I might . . . I might get in trouble if I do."

"You mean—" I decide not to ask. She must have a warrant out on her for something. The last thing I need is to learn more about my fellow tenants. We're already knee-deep in one another's lives.

Alaina's staring at the concrete walkway. It's painted turquoise. Like the bottom of a swimming pool. The paint is chipped and peeling. She looks so young I could just as easily be standing face-to-face with one of Mackenzie's friends. I suspect she's lived a very different life than the kids Mackenzie grew up with.

"Thanks for the car," she says with a hint of sadness in her voice. "No one's ever done anything like that for me. And I acted like a shitheel when you gave me the keys."

"You're welcome. But like I said, I wish I hadn't. I should've thought about it more—I knew the causeway was in shit shape—but I didn't. And I had no idea you were so freaked out by Ethan."

"You couldn't have known. You were trying to be nice. Sometimes I'm shitty when people are nice." She's still not looking at me. She kicks at the chipped floor. "Like Dallas. I was always shitty to him. And now . . ."

"Don't beat yourself up, Alaina. You were scared. We all were. . . . Can we go now?"

I want to drag her to Lloyd's, but I know I can't. Her lack of urgency makes me anxious.

"Alaina?"

"It wasn't just Ethan and the meeting. . . . I was also rushing because of the guy I saw downstairs. He freaked me out when I was leaving."

I freeze in place. The wind picks up a little, causes me to shiver. "What guy, Alaina?"

Alaina finally raises her eyes to mine. "Just some dude. Some random creep. He was poking around in the garage, looking at the cars. He asked me if I knew who was still in the building. I figured he was one of the squatters from the other buildings. Remember how they used to hang around here? I tried to call the police when I got in the car, but there was no signal. Of course."

I point toward her apartment. "It wasn't Tyler?"

She shakes her head. "No. Even with the blood all over his face, I can tell it wasn't him. It was just some rando, Jake."

"What did he look like?"

"I don't know . . . dark jacket . . . kind of clean-cut for a squatter. He'd shaved, no facial hair. His clothes looked clean too. That's all I've got."

"And he didn't say anything else?"

"No, he just acted all entitled. Like it wasn't weird at all that he was nosing around the garage."

"Shit."

"Who do you think he is?"

"I don't know, but this is not good. Come on. Let's go to Lloyd's."

SIXTY-ONE

The apartment grows chaotic after I walk in with Alaina—back from the dead and walking among us.

Everyone asks her questions all at once, and Alaina takes her time giving them a play-by-play of her escape. She's treated like an astronaut returning from a dangerous voyage to the moon. As she should be. I'm still astonished she made it out alive. She must be made of iron underneath her tiny frame.

"Can I ask you something, dear?" Hazel says.

"What's that?"

"Didn't you tell me that you have Native American ancestry? From these parts? Was it your father? Or was it someone else?"

"My grandfather. Why do you ask?"

"That's why you made it out alive, dear. The island protected you. The Native spirits."

Alaina looks like she wants to roll her eyes, but she doesn't.

Ethan stays back, but he hangs on Alaina's every word, watches her every move.

When everyone returns to the hallway—joined by Alaina—I slip back to the living room to catch Lloyd alone. He's at his post by Catalina's bedside, holding her hand, and looks up when I come in, offering his flat-mouthed version of a smile.

"That's a nice miracle to see," he says.

"It is." I pull up a chair next to him. His eyebrows rise. He knows I want to talk. "But there's something else at play."

Lloyd remains quiet. Waiting for me to go on.

I catch him up: Tyler's battered body. Alaina's story about someone helping her get undressed. Stanley AWOL, maybe making a try for the dinghy.

"The storm is letting up," I say. "We're going to be in the eye soon. Which means someone could potentially cross the water and get help. Or at least get some of us off this island and away from danger."

"How many do you think could fit in the dinghy?"

"I'd guess just two or three. Probably has an outboard motor. It will be a rough ride, but a person who knows how to control a boat like that could make it."

"You clearly have someone in mind."

My eyes move to the hallway, where the low murmur of conversation continues. I turn back to Lloyd. "Jordan could do it. Hell, Mackenzie could too. Jordan's parents live on a lake in Ohio. They've both spent a lot of time there—Jordan since she was a kid. They can do it."

Lloyd's eyebrows go up again. "You want to send your wife and daughter out in a dinghy on the Intracoastal? During a hurricane? Are you sure about that?"

"I'm going with them."

The eyebrows rise higher, which I didn't think was possible.

"Look, Lloyd. . . ." I let out a sigh so loud and long it sounds for a moment like we're sitting in a wind tunnel. "I think we're in real trouble here. The building is—well, it's not that sturdy. . . ."

Lloyd glances at the ceiling. "It's definitely on its last legs. It's used up eight and a half lives." He lowers his head, stares right into my eyes. "Maybe eight and three-quarters."

"I agree. Plus, someone—and I'm not sure who—is running around hurting people. They got Dallas. They attacked Ethan. They killed Tyler."

"It's Stanley."

"Could be. But Alaina says she saw another man downstairs. Not Stanley, not Tyler." Lloyd doesn't argue. "We're fighting a war on two fronts. Maybe three."

"When the eye reaches us, you'll only have about forty-five minutes or so. You want to strike while the iron's hot."

"If we can get over to the mainland, the police might be able to send someone before the storm kicks into gear again. Maybe a boat big enough to evacuate all of us. Maybe someone to protect us. And find the killer."

Lloyd turns his head to Catalina. "I'll be right here." He leans down and kisses her on the cheek. "But some of the others may object to your plan. They may not want you to leave without them."

"If someone else wants to step up . . ."

"No, it should be you." He nods toward the hallway. "I'm not sure I trust anyone else."

"Plus, Stanley's out there. Or whoever else."

"Is it possible he already took the dinghy?"

"Unlikely. The weather's been too bad. But the window's almost open. We need to move."

"I told you he was a snake in the grass."

Catalina manages to lift her hand enough to give Lloyd a gentle slap on the arm.

"Yeah," I say. "I'm not sure about that myself. We'll have to see."

When I stand up, Lloyd says my name like it's an order: "Jake." His hand reaches around toward his back. "If you're going out there, you don't know what you're walking into. . . ."

"No, thanks, Lloyd. I'm willing to take my chances."

SIXTY-TWO

The group in the hallway carries on a conversation somewhere between an argument and a dorm room bull session.

The air in the apartment has become repulsive. It's worse than a locker room. It's a garbage dump. Everyone wears a sheen of sweat. Everyone smells.

"Were you going to share this with us, Jake?" Sawyer has a tight grip on his cane. He looks put out. "About Stanley disappearing and Tyler being dead?"

"Murdered," Kiara says, voice low.

"Right. Murdered. Were you going to share that with us?"

"Of course. But it seems like you found out on your own."

"Everyone deserves to know," Alaina says.

"I agree. But we can't overreact. We don't know what Stanley's involvement is in any of this. Alaina must have told you she saw another man downstairs, one who wasn't Stanley or Tyler."

"No, she didn't tell us that," Nina says.

"I hadn't gotten to it yet," Alaina says.

"Well, she did. And I saw a man earlier—it might be the same guy. So we really don't know what we're dealing with. Stanley could be in trouble himself."

Sawyer taps his cane against the floor. "Or he's on his way to the mainland. If he is, he'll be long gone before we can tell anyone what he's done."

"I doubt he's doing that. The water's been too rough . . . until now."

"But why run off?" Sawyer asks. "Doesn't that look like a guilty man?"

It's a very good question, and I don't have an answer. So I tell them about my plan to take advantage of the eye by using the dinghy to get to the mainland.

Mackenzie's mouth falls open. She looks at Jordan, who appears only slightly less thrilled.

"Isn't that dangerous?" Kiara asks.

"It is. But it's hard to tell which is more dangerous—staying here and doing nothing or trying to get help."

"You're more daring than I thought, Jacob," Hazel says. "Or maybe you're dense."

"Thanks for the vote of confidence, Hazel. But I'm willing to take my chances."

"*If* the boat is still there," Ethan says, "and *if* the eye lasts long enough."

"That's right," I say. "But, in a way, it's not really my decision to make. I think Jordan should be the one to drive the dinghy."

Every head in the hallway swings from me to Jordan. She doesn't flinch from the sudden attention. She smirks, as if she knew all along I was leading up to this. She probably did. Neither Mackenzie nor I have ever been able to get anything past her.

"Why Jordan?" Alaina asks.

"Mom knows how to handle a boat better than anybody. She grew up on a lake, fishing with her dad. I've seen her take a fishing boat into the tightest coves. She's better at it than Grandpa."

"That's right," I say. "Unless someone else thinks they can handle the boat better than Jordan. I'm not opposed to that."

Each person in that hallway looks around, searching one another's faces for another volunteer. The building groans again. A sick cry from a dying beast.

"And that's why we need to move quickly," I say. "Does anybody else want to steer the boat? Or is it Jordan?"

No one speaks up except Sawyer. "I used to be able to do that. When I fished. But I don't think I could get in a boat now. I struggle to get into a car."

"Don't look at us," Nina says, grabbing Kiara's hand.

The other heads shake.

Ethan says, "I could maybe do it—I mean, I've handled a boat before. But with the hurricane . . . and after what I've just been through . . . my anxiety is through the roof."

"If there is a roof," Sawyer says, but no one laughs.

A quiet moment draws out, and then Alaina says, "I'd like to go." I catch her sneaking a look at Ethan. "I have friends in town. They might be able to help. And a meeting would help. How many can fit in the boat?"

"Three," I say. "Maybe four if two people are small. Like you and Kenzie."

"Wait a minute," Ethan says. "You're leaving, Jake? You can't. We'll be sitting ducks with a killer running around outside. Maybe more than one killer."

"I'll be here."

A voice comes from behind me. It's Lloyd's. He holds the Glock in front of his chest like an assassin. The sight of him makes me shudder a little, even though I knew all along he had the gun.

"No one's getting through that door," he says. "No one's getting at Cat if I have anything to say about it. If Jake takes the dinghy, which I think he should, we'll lock things up tight and wait."

No one says anything after that. I'm not sure there is anything that could be said. Lloyd's statement feels like the end of something. A period at the end of this sentence.

SIXTY-THREE

5:15 A.M.

I'm impatient, checking the weather dozens of times in the next couple of hours.

Finally, I stick my head out Lloyd's door and see the rain is no longer falling in sheets. An enormous weight settles inside my chest, a heavy pressure not unlike the storm hovering overhead.

It's time for us to go.

When I close the door, Lloyd's watching me. He can tell. He walks over to me, his hand extended. "Good luck, boss. I'll keep an eye on things here as best I can."

"I'm sure you can handle it."

"I guess it's pointless to offer you the gun again. You'll just say no, right?"

"You know me well by now."

"I'm only trying to be generous. I really want to keep it for myself."

"It's yours."

We shake.

Catalina's bell rings. Lloyd starts for her, but she manages to lift her hand, beckoning me closer.

When I get to her side, she points in the direction of her head. It takes me a moment to figure out that she wants me to reach under her pillow.

I find a rosary there. The off-white beads appear to be carved from either ivory or bone. The crucifix shows a writhing Christ in tarnished silver. It looks ancient and valuable.

"I can't take this."

She makes a shooing gesture toward me.

"Lloyd?"

He shrugs. "I've never won an argument with her. You won't either."

I say to her, "What if this ends up on the bottom of the Intracoastal? It's yours."

She makes the shooing gesture again. "I know . . . not your beliefs . . . but I believe . . ."

A small amount of relief settles over me, an easing of the heavy weight that accumulated in my chest when the rain slowed. I gather the rosary into my hand, close it in my fist. The smooth beads feel good against my skin.

"Okay, I'll keep it. I was actually raised Catholic. I just kind of gave up on it."

Catalina nods.

I bend down, kiss her on the cheek. "I hope Lloyd doesn't mind."

I place the rosary in the pocket of my jeans and get Alaina, Jordan, and Mackenzie from the hall. They each hold a flashlight. They're ready. Eyes wide.

"It looks like we have our window."

Even though the storm has slowed, the building lets out a long, low creaking sound above us. Like a giant door swinging open on rusty hinges.

We all look up.

"The water might be safer than this place," Alaina says.

"Are you sure you want to do this, Alaina? After what you just went through? Maybe it's best—"

"Why are you asking me this now, Jake?"

"No one *has* to go. Not if you don't want to." I look at all of them, especially Mackenzie and Jordan. "If you want to call this off . . ."

Jordan shakes her head. "Someone has to go for help." She lowers her voice so only the four of us can hear. "I'm not so sure about this building either." She grabs my hand, squeezes it. "We can't afford not to try."

Mackenzie leans forward. "You and Mom always tell me to do the right thing, Dad. I mean, like, over and over again. Maybe we should put that into practice when we have the chance."

But how do we know this is the right thing?

"Yeah, okay."

I have my doubts about Alaina. Does she really not remember all of what happened? Is there something she's not telling us?

"Alaina," I say, "are you sure you're okay going on the water again?"

"I'm fine, Jake. What are you trying to say?" Her eyes bore into mine. For someone so young, she sure can summon a lot of intensity.

"No, it's fine. Let's get going."

We say good-bye to the others. I promise to send help as soon as we can. An unsettled feeling hovers in the air. No one is quite sure what to say or do. My flashlight catches Hazel's face. Her eyes are full of tears. She wipes at them with both hands. Seeing her this way nearly kills me. It almost makes me want to stay. Almost.

"Hazel, we'll be okay."

Her sniffles are long and loud. "That gift—it's just going to go to waste. After all my work."

I'm not sure whether to laugh or to be angry. I remind myself she's an old lady. An old lady who's losing her mind. "Hazel, I'll get the gift when I come back."

"*If* you come back . . . *if* any of us are here . . ."

"Hazel, please." I stop myself from losing my temper. "We'll see you all later."

I turn to my little band of travelers, and we all head for the door, the rosary beads in my pocket offering me surprising comfort.

SIXTY-FOUR

Before we take a single step, the door to Lloyd's apartment snaps shut behind us. It sounds like a gunshot. A final statement.

The rain has lessened even more. It comes down steadily but not heavily. The wind blows, but for the first time in a day, it doesn't knock me off-balance when I step outside. The sky doesn't seem nearly as oppressive and black either.

There's no doubt—the eye is passing over us. And we're about an hour from sunrise. That means that when the sun comes up, we'll be out of time.

We move toward the north stairs. Twice I hesitate. Once when we pass Dallas' door and again at Alaina's. Two people are gone. And Stanley's missing in action.

By the time we reach the stairs, I realize I'm feeling less vigilant, less alert.

My body has been taut as a wire all night. Every muscle and tendon clenched.

A body can do that for only so long. I'm starting to slip, lose some of the edge I took on when this shitstorm started.

I stop. "Look, if there's any trouble, just run back to Lloyd's. Forget about me."

"We won't forget—"

"No, really. Just do it. That's the only way."

"But, Dad—"

"Kenzie, just do whatever Dad says, okay?"

For one of the few times in her life, my daughter stops arguing.

The encounter with Tyler comes back to me on the stairs. I take the steps slowly. Water drips everywhere, like we're in a cave. It runs through the gutters and downspouts, streams down the stairs alongside us. When—*if*—this is all over, I'd be happy to never see or hear rain again. Or not for a long, long time.

In the garage, the storm drains are completely overwhelmed and backed up. We have no choice but to walk through a pool of water to reach the sodden grass fifteen feet away.

I shine the flashlight around, illuminating every dark corner. Garbage and other debris float on the surface. Except for the gurgling of the water slowly moving into the drains, it's quiet. Quiet enough that I can hear the waves rising and falling against the shore, the eternal push and pull of the tides that flow in the waterway between us and the mainland.

We slosh through the water. It rises above the tops of our shoes. My feet have been wet since I first stepped out of the Elantra yesterday, though it might as well have been a hundred years ago. The water smells like dead fish and mud. The air has cooled in the wake of the storm.

"This is just . . . it's just . . . so wet," Mackenzie says.

Other than Mackenzie stating the obvious, we are quiet.

We reach the grass, which is covered with water as well. Not as much as the garage floor, but still a lot. The storm surge has overtaken the island. Everything is submerged.

The rain continues to fall, washing our backs and heads. I search the shore with the flashlight beam.

"Tyler said the dinghy was north of the building, in a thick clump of weeds. We just need to find that."

"What if it floated away in the storm?" Mackenzie asks.

"What if Stanley took it?" Alaina asks.

"You know what they say? If the worst can happen, it will."

"Do you really believe that?" Jordan asks.

"If I believed that, I'd still be inside. I'd have never come to Florida. And I wouldn't be trying to fix things with you."

"That's more of an answer than I bargained for," Jordan says. "I already knew you didn't believe that."

The beam picks up a clump of weeds and grass about four feet tall and eight feet wide. It's getting whipped around by the wind. Tyler had better have tied that dinghy tight to something as solid as time, or it's long gone.

The closer we get to the water, the stronger the wind gets. Waves crest the edge of the island, the water flowing around and past us, occasionally rising to the level of my shins before falling again. My hand holding the flashlight shakes. I remind myself to maintain my balance, to take my time and not fall. To do everything in my power not to get swept into the Intracoastal and dragged out to the Atlantic.

I may be at my physical best, but I'm not as young as Alaina. I might not survive something like that.

When we reach the clump of weeds and grass, I part them with my free hand. The wind blows them around so much it's hard to see anything. I decide to step into them even though I can't be sure what the footing will be like.

My first step brings my leg into contact with something hard. I adjust the angle of the light and catch the side of the dinghy. I move the light along its length. It looks none the worse for wear. Inside sit two life vests and two paddles. The engine at the back looks to be in working order.

But there's really no way to know until someone gets in and starts it.

Behind us, our building is silhouetted in the early-morning light. It's more shadow than structure.

Even in the near dark, it's obvious the roof is gone. The top of the building is jagged, like a row of broken teeth. Stanley was right—the water and the wind have pounded the daylights out of it since the roof broke free.

And once the eye passes over, another round of massive wind and unrelenting rain will be here.

"What's the matter?" Alaina asks. "Is the boat damaged?"

"No, it looks okay. He tied it up tight."

"Then what is it, Dad?"

I keep my eyes on the building's outline. Thinking.

"I was just wondering about something, that's all." I drop my gaze from the building and lock eyes with Jordan. "Something we might want to do differently."

SIXTY-FIVE

"What is it?" Jordan asks. "The sky already looks like it's getting darker. We don't have time to second-guess things."

"Plus, did I mention it's wet?" Mackenzie says.

My eyes go back to the building. Now I'm seeing the people inside.

Lloyd, and Catalina in the hospital bed.

Hazel.

Kiara and Nina.

Ethan.

Sawyer.

Are they all going to die?

Can it be prevented?

"Oh, shit." Jordan shakes her head. "I see where this is going."

"I'm sorry," I say. "I think you have to go without me. Go get help. I'll stay here and help the others until someone gets here. I don't see any other way."

"No, no, no, Dad. We're not doing this without you. Not after everything we've all been through."

"Kenzie . . ."

"No, Mom. Listen." She points at me as she speaks to Jordan. "I haven't seen Dad for six months. *Six months.* And neither have you. And we drove all the way down here to bring him back. Because we want him back. With us. With both of us. All together. We didn't come all the way down here to leave him on this stinking island, which will probably be underwater in about five minutes. We didn't . . ."

Mackenzie descends into sobs. Her body shakes as Jordan pulls her close and runs her hand over Mackenzie's hair.

"Shhh. I know. Shhh."

"Tell . . . him . . . he has . . . to go . . . with us."

"I wish I could, but I can't. He has to do what he thinks is right."

Mackenzie pulls back, looks at Jordan like she's never seen her before and couldn't possibly understand her. "What are you talking about? After . . ." Mackenzie turns to me. "Dad, I've had to watch Mom moping around for months. She tries to hide it, but I can tell. I had to see how sad she was *every day*, how much she—"

"Kenzie, enough—"

"No, Dad. Mom's been miserable without you. Even though you irritate me sometimes, honestly, so have I. We didn't come all this way to blow it now."

Alaina clears her throat. "I hate to interrupt this tender scene, but we probably should get going."

"We'll stay," Jordan says. "Alaina can drive the boat—"

"Yes," Mackenzie says. "Fine."

"No, no." I step toward them, my shoes squishing in the wet grass. "You *have* to go. You *have* to find us help. *Any* kind of help. And that's not even the real reason I want you to go. More than anything else, I want you to go because I want you to stay safe. I couldn't stand it if anything happened to you." I turn from Mackenzie to Jordan. "*Either* of you." The weight returns to my chest. Heavier than ever. Some of the pressure migrates to my shoulders, threatening to push me down into the mess of weeds. "It's the only way I can be sure you'll be safe."

Mackenzie shakes her head, and a hand covers her eyes. She sniffles. "This is just so unbelievable. Just so . . . I don't know . . ."

I go to her, put my arms around her. "Kenzie, you'll see me soon. I promise."

"You said that when you left Ohio *six months ago*."

If Mackenzie had taken a sharpened blade of steel and driven it into my chest, it wouldn't hurt any worse than her words.

If anything would make me reconsider my choice to stay, it would be the chance to make my daughter happy. To erase the difficulties of the past six months and restore everything to the way it used to be with the three of us.

But that is impossible.

"Kenzie . . ." I kiss the top of her head. "You're going with Mom. And I'll see you again. I promise."

I squeeze her as tightly as I can and then turn to Jordan.

I swallow hard. The wind picks up, blows hair across her face.

"You're going to keep that promise, right?" she says.

"I am."

She shakes her head, brushes the hair away.

"You're so worried about me," I say, "but you're the one crossing the Intracoastal in a hurricane."

"The eye of a hurricane."

"Are you sure you feel good about this? Does it look too rough? If you have doubts, *any* doubts at all, I don't want you to go."

Jordan examines the water, her eyes squinting into the distance, before turning back to me. "I've handled rougher. The tide isn't bad at all."

"It's not . . . but later this morning it will rise significantly."

"We won't be on the water long enough for that." Jordan sounds so confident, so sure of herself. This is why I fell in love with her. She can handle almost anything thrown her way. "We'll be on the mainland in fifteen minutes. And besides, these people need help."

"If you're sure . . ."

She answers by pressing her lips to mine. I get so lost in her kiss I can't tell if it lasts two seconds or two minutes.

She pulls gently away, letting me know it's time to go.

I reach into my pocket, find Catalina's rosary, place it in Jordan's hand.

"Did you become a believer?"

"No. But I'm willing to hedge my bets."

"Okay," she says, tucking it into her pocket. "It can't hurt."

She takes Mackenzie by the arm and helps her climb into the dinghy. Jordan follows her, carefully balancing the boat as she pulls herself back to the stern.

Alaina steps forward, but I put my hand out, blocking her way. "Stop."

She whips her head in my direction, eyes flashing.

"You're not going, Alaina."

"What?"

"You can't go. Not with my family. It's too much of a risk."

"What are you talking about?"

"You know what I'm talking about. I don't know what happened in your apartment. To Tyler. I'm not even sure how you pulled that Houdini act in the water. So I can't send you out there alone with my wife and daughter."

"Fuck you, Jake. I knew you'd—"

"You can say whatever you want to me. That's fine. But I'm not letting you go with them."

Jordan puts her hand on the tiller as I untie the dinghy from the mooring. The rain sluices across my face, mingling with my tears. I half expect Alaina to make a move. To smack me over the head or shove me into the water. But she remains still, standing next to me with her mouth open.

I give the dinghy a gentle shove. Jordan tilts the motor into the water and squeezes the primer bulb. She turns on the choke and starts the engine.

It sputters and dies. She tries again, with the same result.

A foolish wish swells inside me—the engine won't start. They won't be able to leave. Maybe it's waterlogged or out of gas or defective. They'll have to stay, and there won't be any reason for us to be apart.

But the engine catches on the third try. It revs to life, churning the water so hard Alaina and I back up. With an expert hand, Jordan guides the dinghy and angles the prow toward the mainland.

Mackenzie offers me the most sullen wave I've ever seen.

Jordan waves as well, her chin high, her eyes confident.

The dinghy cuts through the choppy water, leaving Alaina and me behind.

I watch them until they disappear from sight.

"You're such an asshole, Jake."

"Maybe. And maybe I'm wrong to worry. But if so, I'm an asshole who just got the two people most important to me out of danger."

SIXTY-SIX

6:01 A.M.

The weight is even heavier now. So heavy I could sit down in this water and not get up again.

I'm scared for them. Scared they won't make it.

Scared I've done the wrong thing.

But in my gut I feel it's the right move.

It's the least bad choice.

When we get back onshore, Alaina turns to me. "Do you really think I'm a murderer, Jake?" Her wet hair is plastered to her head. Her big eyes take me in.

"I don't know. Probably not, but I couldn't risk it. You seem awfully determined to get off this island. Now and earlier. When you took the car."

"I told you why."

I nod. "I appreciate it if you were going to a meeting. I do. But there are still unanswered questions, and I'm not willing to take that risk with Jordan and Kenzie. I would've taken you with me if I were going, but I couldn't risk you going with them alone."

Alaina holds her hand out near my chest. "Do you really need to know why I wanted to leave? It wasn't an AA meeting."

I wait for her to continue.

"You're such a fucker, Jake." She wipes her eyes. "Dallas didn't tell you?"

"Tell me what?"

"You're a fucker."

"We already established that."

"I was going to see my daughter."

I study her face for signs that she's lying, but she looks deadly serious. "I didn't know you had a daughter."

"Nobody does, except Dallas. Or he did, anyway. She went into foster care a couple of years ago. Because I was so messed up. I couldn't take care of her. Okay? Now I have a chance to see her again. If I stay clean. That's why I haven't been paying rent. I've been setting money aside in case I get her back. You know, to get a nicer place. And a car. All that regular-people shit."

Regular-people shit. Like what I have waiting for me back in Ohio.

"I get to visit her sometimes. Supervised visits. That's where I was trying to go. Last night."

"I'm sorry, Alaina." I feel genuinely shitty. "If I'd known . . ."

"When I fell into the water . . . she was all I could think of. I needed to get out of there. For her." She points in the direction of the dinghy. "You understand, right?"

"I do."

"So no, I didn't kill anybody. And no, I haven't been using. I even stopped drinking." She wipes her eyes again.

"Dallas never said anything to me about it. He knows how to keep a secret."

"I guess. . . ."

"What's her name? Your daughter?"

"India. I've never been there. I don't even know anything about it. But I thought it was a pretty name."

"It is."

Alaina looks down at the wet sand. "Are we going to die, Jake?"

"I don't know. But you definitely used up one of your lives last night."

She shakes her head. "If you only knew how many lives I've used up. I want things to be different now. I don't want to be the same person anymore. You know?"

"I do. I really do. Come on. Let's get inside."

Alaina's shoulders sag, but she summons the energy to walk over the soggy grass, back toward the roofless building. The storm will be picking up again soon. We're far from being out of the woods.

As we get closer, the lightening sky allows us to see the damage more clearly. Not only is the roof gone, but a large chunk of the top of the building is missing as well. It looks like a giant monster came by and took a bite.

The building is weaker than I thought.

Pieces of the roof are scattered all over the grounds. Wooden support beams cracked like twigs. Metal sheets mangled like tin cans. Canvas awnings torn like paper napkins.

"Shit," Alaina says. "What a fucking mess."

"Kylie is helping them tear the building down."

We're halfway to the parking garage when Alaina freezes in her tracks. "Wait."

"What?"

She's staring into the dark. "Something's moving in there. An animal or something."

"Are you sure?"

"Is it an alligator?"

"Let's make a run for—"

If it's an alligator, it's one that can talk. The voice is faint, but I clearly hear someone say my name.

"Did you hear that?" I ask.

It starts again. "Jake . . . Jake . . ."

"Someone's here."

I jog over to the parking garage, Alaina right behind me. We splash through the water. I slow down, try not to slip on the wet pavement.

The voice comes from beneath a large sheet of metal roofing on the far side of the garage. It's big enough to cover a person.

I lean down and shine the flashlight underneath, only to see Stanley there, trapped under its weight. With Alaina's help, I push the sheet off him. I play the beam over his body. He looks like hell—his face is incredibly pale, and there's a tremendous gash on his forehead that looks like it's been bleeding for a while.

I drop to my knees. "Oh, shit, Stanley."

"I was . . . coming back . . ."

Alaina crouches down next to Stanley's head, studies his gash.

"Coming back? From where?"

"Roof . . . blew off . . . couldn't get . . . out of . . . the way . . ."

"Okay, Stanley. Don't worry. You don't have to explain. Let's get you inside."

"Jake . . . I'm sorry."

"Sorry for what?"

His eyes flutter shut.

"Stanley?"

No response.

"Stanley, are you with us?"

"He's lost a lot of blood, Jake." Alaina has her hands under his head like she's a paramedic. "Like, *way* too much blood."

"Stanley, stay with me."

His breathing grows shallow. I check his pulse. It's barely there.

"Come on, Stanley."

His lips move, but no words come out. He keeps working his lips.

"Do you want to say something, Stanley?" I lean as close as I can. My ear is almost against his mouth. "What are you apologizing for?"

"Security . . . the owners . . . he's here . . ."

"Tyler?"

"New . . . owners . . . he's here . . . I . . . I . . . helped . . ."

"You helped him? The security guy for the new owners? And he's here on the island?"

"Wants . . . Dallas . . . Hazel . . ."

"Hazel? What does he want with Hazel, Stanley?"

His lips move, but there's nothing. No sound at all.

"What the hell, Stanley? What are you trying to tell me?"

A gurgling sound comes from his mouth, like his throat is filling with fluid. His head falls sharply to the side, dropping into the soggy grass.

"Stanley? Damn it, Stanley. Wake up right now."

But it's too late. He's gone. He bled out. Right here on the wet ground. With the rain pouring on top of him.

"Fuck," I say. "Fuck, fuck, fuck."

SIXTY-SEVEN

As we climb the steps to Lloyd's apartment—well aware that yet again everyone is going to get a surprise when we return—I try to make sense of Stanley's words.

He apologized. *Why did he apologize?* He said he was working with—*helping*, he said—a security guy hired by the new owners. Not the sellers who sent Tyler to check on the property. The *buyers*. The developers who intend to tear down our building and fill the island with luxury condos that'll sell for one and a half million dollars.

They sent a guy. And Stanley was helping him.

But why apologize for that?

And what did this security guy want from Dallas and Hazel?

Alaina must see the questions on my face. "Why would the new owners send someone to talk to Dallas? Or Hazel?"

I pause on the landing between the first and second floors. "I have no idea. The sale hasn't gone through yet, but it's close. But why would the new owners care what happens during the hurricane? If they're just going to tear these buildings down? Hell, they're probably rooting for Kylie to take them out. It would probably save them time. And money."

"But they don't want anyone to die, right?"

"Maybe not. But they're not going to lose any sleep over it either.

Who are we to them? We're just strangers. If one of us dies during the hurricane, it won't be any different to them than if someone on the mainland died."

"So, who is he? This other security guy?"

"I saw someone downstairs. And so did you. That must have been him."

"And do you think . . . do you think he's the one who killed Dallas?"

"Maybe. Maybe Dallas knew something that could scotch the deal. And maybe Tyler knew who killed Dallas, so he was silenced too."

Alaina makes a face. "Do you think he's the one who helped me?"

"I'm betting that was Stanley. For all I know, Stanley was protecting you. Maybe he put you to bed so this guy wouldn't see you. Maybe he thought you witnessed something. . . ."

Her look of disgust softens. "You think *Stanley* was protecting me?"

"Maybe. I think he cared more than we realized. He seemed kind of remorseful out there."

"People are always full of regret when they're dying, Jake."

I can't argue with that.

"But what would he want with Hazel? She's batshit crazy."

"She's not crazy, Alaina. She's old. She has dementia."

"Like I said . . ." She shrugs. "Batshit."

I ignore her comment. "Ethan was helping Hazel, and he got attacked in his apartment. Could those two things be connected?"

The building lets out a long groan, and then something makes a screeching sound above our heads. We both look up just as a giant chunk of stucco falls from the top of the building. It plummets to the ground, splatting on the grass not far from where Stanley's body still lies.

"Shit," Alaina says. "This place is *literally* falling down around us."

As she says it, the wind picks up. The rain comes down harder.

The eye will soon be past us.

I look directly into Alaina's face. I need someone to hear what I'm about to say. "I don't know if we can stay in this building. I don't know if it's safe."

SIXTY-EIGHT

6:16 A.M.

I use the secret knock.

But no one answers.

I try again, pressing my ear to the door.

It's nearly impossible to hear anything over the increasing sound of the wind and rain. I press my ear closer and think I hear rustling behind the door.

"Maybe they can't hear the knocking?" Alaina says.

I knock again, pounding the code as hard as I can.

The chain rattles against the other side of the door. Then the lock tumbles. The door swings in. Lloyd stands on the other side, with the Glock pointed out through the small open space between the door and the wall. He's ready to shoot my face off.

I step back, hold my hands up. "Whoa—it's just us."

Lloyd blinks, studying me like I'm a long-lost relative he's not sure he recognizes. "What happened? Was the dinghy gone?"

"Can we come in? The rain's picking up."

He looks past us and nods, stepping back to let us inside.

Everyone from the hallway gawks at us, their mouths half-open in shock.

Once the door is closed, I tell them Alaina and I decided to come back without Jordan and Mackenzie.

"You sent them across the water alone?" Kiara asks. "Your wife and child?"

"Shh," Nina says.

"Jordan can handle that boat better than I ever could. She wouldn't have tried it if she didn't think she could make it."

"But we won't know for sure until—"

"Shh," Nina says.

"No, Kiara, we won't. But it was the least bad option. Sometimes that's the only choice we have."

"You came back to help?" Sawyer says. "That's admirable."

"Why is Alaina here?" Nina asks, ignoring Sawyer. "I thought she wanted to leave."

I decide to let Alaina speak for herself. I fully expect her to tell the truth—to blame me for keeping her from seeing her child. She has every right to, I suppose. Instead, Alaina looks at me and lies to everyone else. "I got scared. After what happened before . . . I couldn't do it. If I freaked out while we were crossing in the dinghy, it could be bad. So I came back with Jake."

It sounds perfectly reasonable, and everyone nods, accepting her story.

I'm grateful for the lie.

"You both look a bit worse for wear," Lloyd says. "Anything else happen outside?"

There's no point in hiding the truth. Not after everything we've all been through. "We found Stanley."

"Where was he?" Ethan asks. "In the dinghy?"

"No, we heard him when we got back. He was calling for help. He was trapped under a piece of metal roofing on the grass out front. Crushed, really. He got hit when it flew off the roof." I pause before delivering the final blow. "He died not long after we found him."

A murmur of shock moves through the room. I don't think Stanley was anyone's favorite person, but it's still overwhelming to learn someone's been killed. Someone you know. Even when at least two other people have died.

Been murdered, actually.

"So he wasn't up to something?" Sawyer asks. "He just ran into some bad luck? Literally."

"Not exactly." I look back to the door. "Did anyone else come to the door while we were gone?"

"No," Lloyd says. "Except for the storm, it was quiet."

I consider not revealing in front of the whole group what Stanley told me, but what would be the point? It's like trying to keep a secret in a family. If one person knows, we all do.

"Stanley told me the new owners sent a guy to the island." I let my eyes land on Hazel for the first time since I got back. "And that he was here looking for Hazel."

"Hazel?" Nina says. "Really?"

"But Stanley didn't or couldn't say why." I intensify my gaze on Hazel, hoping to spur her to remember. "Hazel, do you have any idea why this guy would be looking for you?"

All heads turn her way.

For a moment, Hazel looks surprised. Then something kicks in. She lifts her chin a little, pushes her shoulders back. She's ready for her moment in the spotlight.

"I've been telling you, Jacob, telling *all of you*, that a man has been stalking me. Isn't it obvious this is who it is? He's been following me around *for weeks*." She turns her head. "Ethan, tell them what I told you. Go ahead—tell them."

Ethan looks uncomfortable with what's happening. Like someone is gradually shutting off the air supply to his brain. "Well, maybe that's your news to share."

"Tell them." I've got to hand it to Hazel. She's a force when she wants to be.

Ethan searches for a lifeline. "Well . . ." He clears his throat. "Hazel told me that this man—I guess I should say *a* man—approached her at the grocery store a few weeks ago. I think Dallas had given her a ride so she could shop."

"Go on," Hazel says.

"The man approached her when she was alone. The only person in the aisle. And he knew her name. Said he wanted to take her out to dinner and get to know her better."

"He was *stalking* me," Hazel says. "I believe he intended to propose marriage."

I feel like I must be hearing things. Did she just say "propose marriage"?

"Don't you see?" She turns in a slow circle, taking in her audience. "Don't you *all* see? He wants to marry me so he can get his hands on my things. And that's not all. He controls the weather too. That's why he's on the island with us. Causing this storm."

The feeling of disappointment in the room is palpable. Everyone deflates at once. For a moment, just a moment, it felt like we were getting closer to some answers. Instead, Hazel's words push us further away.

Hazel goes on. "But you don't have to worry. This island was protected by its Native people. They enchanted this land. It can't be harmed. And the people who are from here can't be either. That's why young Alaina survived what she did."

Hazel starts making low muttering sounds. For a second, I think her speech has become garbled, that she's having some kind of stroke.

But there's a rhythm to her speech. Actually, she's not speaking. She's chanting.

She's chanting something like a song or a prayer.

"What the hell is that?" Alaina asks. "Is she okay?"

"She's fine," Ethan says. "That's one of her incarnations."

Lloyd corrects him. "Incantations."

"Yeah, that's it. She does this sometimes. She says it protects her. And everyone on the island."

"What were you helping her with, Ethan?" I ask. "On the computer. Was it anything important?"

Hazel continues to chant, but her voice gets lower.

"I don't know what it was, Jake. To be honest, we didn't get much done, because she kept getting distracted. Every time we'd start, she'd stop what we were doing and want to look for something else. Some piece of paper in all those piles of endless paper. I don't think we ever got anywhere."

The building groans. Loudly. Something bangs and crashes outside, loudly enough for us to hear over the wind and rain.

"Jake?" Alaina has her eyes trained on the ceiling. "Remember that thing we were talking about outside? I think that's more important than this Hazel stuff."

She's right.

I look from Lloyd to Kiara to Hazel before delivering the bad news. "I hate to say this, everyone, but I think we all need to leave the building."

SIXTY-NINE

"What are you saying?" Kiara asks.

I cast my eyes upward, as if I can show them exactly what I'm talking about. I can't. But they've heard the sounds. They've seen the dripping water.

"The roof is gone. We confirmed that when we got outside. It's scattered all over the grounds. Pieces of it are everywhere. So water is hitting the top floor directly. And the wind is having its way with the building. There's a massive chunk of the top floor missing. It's a hole the size of probably three apartments."

Hazel gasps.

"Not your place, Hazel," Alaina says.

"Then, when we came up the stairs, a giant piece of stucco broke away from the top of the building and crashed into the yard."

"We heard it loud and clear." Lloyd is still holding the gun, now at his side.

"And that crash just now? That was probably more of the building coming down. Here's the thing—the eye is going over us right now. Things are relatively calm. But when the back side of this storm hits, it's going to get bad again. *Very* bad. Because the integrity of this building has already been severely compromised. The front end of

Kylie beat the crap out of this place. It may not make it through her second act."

The room descends into silence. Except for Hazel, who has resumed her chanting.

"Where can we go?" Sawyer asks. "And keep in mind"—he points his cane around the room—"not all of us are mobile."

My eyes trail across the room to Catalina. She looks peaceful, hands folded on top of the blanket, the candle casting soft light on the side of her face. I avoid looking at Lloyd.

"We can't go to one of the other two buildings," I say. "They're likely in worse shape than this one. No one's even been keeping them up. They've been gutted."

"There might be squatters there," Ethan says.

"That too. Although I'm less worried about that."

"Then where?" Alaina asks.

"There's that storage building in the middle of the island. It's made of cinder block. It should be able to take a pretty bad punch. The drawback is, it's low. It's ground level. So if the storm surge gets bad . . ."

"It'll fill up like an aquarium," Ethan says.

"Maybe not that bad. But it could get dangerous. Plus, there's not much ventilation. There's no fresh air in here either, but that place will be like a can of tuna. We'll be jammed in tight, and it will be miserably hot. We'd just have to ride it out that way."

"You think that's safer than here?" Kiara asks. "I mean . . . we're on the second floor here. And safe from the water."

Everyone looks at me. "I think we'd be safer out there. In that shed." No one looks convinced, so I just come out with it. "This building is a death trap." I pat my pocket. "I have Dallas' passkey. He told me it opens everything on the island, including the outbuildings."

"Okay," Sawyer says, "but that outbuilding is a hundred yards away. It's going to be tough, if not impossible, to get us all there."

"And it's really wet," Alaina says. "Like, *really* wet out there."

"We can help each other," I say. "Those who can move better will help those who can't. Like Hazel and Sawyer. We're talking two half flights down to the ground level, and then flatland to the outbuilding."

No one says anything else. The wind rattles the door. It's getting strong again.

Lloyd and I lock eyes.

"We won't be going with you, Jake. We'll take our chances here."

Catalina's bell rings.

Lloyd goes over to her side and bends down. She seems unable to get any words out, and the futile movement of her lips regrettably brings images of Stanley's last moments back to me.

Finally, Catalina gives up trying to speak. She lifts her hand and makes a shooing gesture toward the door, her eyes locked on Lloyd.

It's clear to all of us what she's telling him to do.

"No, ma'am. I'm sorry, but I'm staying right here with you."

She starts to shake her head, but he cuts her off again.

"You heard me. I'm staying put." To prove his point, Lloyd grabs the chair, scoots as close to the side of the bed as he can, and plops down into it. "See? You're stuck with me."

I step closer, again feeling like I'm intruding, but still compelled to speak.

"Lloyd, do you want to try to carry the bed—"

He shakes his head and runs his hand through the air in a slicing motion. "Now, Jake, you already know how this is going to go. We're staying put. But I agree you should get these other folks out of here. And that outbuilding sounds like your best bet. You're going to be packed in tight, but it's the best chance you've got."

"If you're sure." Lloyd gives me a steely look. This conversation is over for him. "Catalina?" She closes her eyes and nods. There's nothing more I can do.

I turn back to the others, who have been watching us the whole time. Nina wipes a tear from her eye, and Hazel's head shakes almost imperceptibly. "We need to go. Before the storm gets any worse. Are we ready?"

SEVENTY

6:29 A.M.

We all crowd around the door.

There's a quick discussion about the order we'll go in, like we're kids again, playing a life-and-death game of follow-the-leader.

The person in front won't just lead the way. They have to be able to protect us if the killer confronts us. Someone will have to walk in the middle with Hazel. And someone assertive needs to bring up the rear in order to keep the crowd moving. And to watch our backs.

We'll be doing all of this in the blowing wind and rain. Our feet sinking into the soggy earth. And two of us have limited mobility—ninety-one-year-old Hazel and an injured Sawyer.

Not ideal circumstances for an escape. But there will be safety in numbers.

I hope.

"I'll go first." Was I wrong not to accept Lloyd's offer of the gun? "Just follow me to the outbuilding. I'll have the key ready so we can get inside fast."

Ethan speaks up. "I'll stick with Hazel to make sure she doesn't fall."

"I'm fine," Hazel says. "I don't need any help."

I ignore her. "Good idea, Ethan."

Nina gestures toward Kiara. "We can walk with Sawyer in case he needs help."

"I'm not a complete invalid," Sawyer says. "But I'm close."

"You'll be fine," I say. "That just leaves you, Alaina. Do you mind bringing up the rear? Make sure we don't lose anyone."

She cocks her head to one side. "And make sure we aren't followed?"

"That's the idea, yes."

"I'm not dumb, Jake. I watched a lot of Westerns with my grandma. The guy in back always gets killed first. You know, an ambush or something."

"We're not going to be ambushed," I say, even though I am in no way certain.

Before we open the door, Lloyd waves me over. I know what he's going to say before he says it.

"Jake, I really think—"

"Okay, Lloyd, you're right. Hand it over."

He pulls the Glock out of the front of his pants—always an uncomfortable-looking spot when I see it in movies—and holds it in the space between us. "You don't really know how to handle one, do you?"

"No, I don't."

"It's easy." He shows me the safety, which is currently on. "Squeeze the trigger. Aim at the middle of the body. The chest. Don't try to merely wing the guy or shoot him in the head. Just go for the body. It's the biggest target. There will be a little kick, but not too bad."

"I really hope it doesn't come to that." The gun is heavier than I expect. Holding it is like handling a venomous snake, something that could turn on me and strike at any time. "Do I have to stick it in the front of my pants like you did?"

"Put it in the back. Like Stanley."

I do as he says. Very carefully. Expecting that, at any second, I'll touch the wrong thing and send a bullet down my leg or into my back. The cold metal rests against my body like a cancerous growth.

"Are you sure you don't—"

"We've made our choice, Jake."

Lloyd claps me on the shoulder.

"All right, then." I look from him to Catalina, nodding at each of them. "Lloyd. Catalina. I hope to see you soon."

I take in my fellow tenants at the door. We look better suited to sitting around an emergency room or waiting in line at the DMV than running for our lives.

But we're about to run for our lives. Or, rather, *walk* for them.

"Okay," I say, putting my hand on the doorknob, "let's go."

SEVENTY-ONE

The wind is blowing hard again.

It knocks me back a step. I can't imagine what it will do to Hazel.

The rain hits me directly in the face. I'm so tired of this. Tired of being wet. Tired of fighting the elements. I've never wanted a hot shower and dry clothes more in my life.

But it's going to be a while before I get them. Maybe a long while.

The sun should be rising now, lighting up the eastern sky with color, but the back end of the storm has obliterated the sunrise, darkening the sky like it's still night.

"Be careful," I say loudly over my shoulder. "Stay close to the building. The wind is getting stronger. And it's dark."

My fellow tenants start to file out, moving gingerly onto the walkway. I stay near the railing, blocking the wind with my body as much as I can.

As soon as Hazel emerges, Ethan by her side, she freezes in place, pulling her sweater tight around her body. She shakes her head, shivers. "Oh, Jacob, I'm going back inside. I don't want to do this."

"Come on, Hazel," Ethan says. "I'll help you."

"You're going to make it, Hazel," I say. "We'll be with you the whole way."

"Why does Lloyd get to stay inside?"

"He's with Catalina. You're with us. Be glad you can still walk. Not everybody can."

She purses her lips, no doubt irritated by my gentle scolding. But she moves forward, her hand locked on Ethan's arm. Sawyer comes out with his cane, Nina and Kiara on either side of him. "It takes *two* ladies to handle me, Jake."

"That's right," Kiara says. "You're *exactly* what we're looking for."

When Alaina emerges, I nod at her. She pulls the door shut while I rush past everyone to the stairway.

The only things I'm more sick of than being wet—my clothes sticking to me like a second skin I can't remove—are the blind trips down the staircase. Where I expect to find someone waiting to kill me at every turn.

This time, I slide the Glock out from the back of my pants. I even go so far as to flick off the safety.

"Do you know what you're doing, Jake?" Ethan asks behind me.

"Not a clue."

"Just aim in front of you, okay?"

I turn the corner around the edge of the stairwell. There's no one there.

It didn't even occur to me to lift the gun. It hangs by my side, useless. If a killer had been there, ready to pounce, he could've taken me before I fired a shot.

My breath is coming in great gulps, my shoulders rising and falling like I'm sobbing. I start down to the next landing, stepping carefully on the wet stairs. My mind trips back to saying good-bye to Jordan and Mackenzie, the tears that poured over my face. I'm not sure when I last cried. When my dad died? Was that it?

Maybe I'm lucky. If I get out of here—and find Jordan and Mackenzie—I'll never again take a day of happiness for granted.

When I reach the landing between the garage and the second floor, I do the same thing I did at the top of the stairs—spin around the wall like I'm in a spy movie. This time, I have the gun raised, finger near but not on the trigger.

Again there's no one there.

I wave the rest of the group forward. Hazel takes one step at a time, placing both feet on a step before moving on to the next one. This isn't going to be quick, but what did I expect?

I run down to the garage, scouting ahead.

The storm surge has hit the island again. The floor of the garage is still covered with a couple of inches of water. We'll all be sloshing through here. Hazel will be thrilled.

My eyes roam over the cars, water rising against the tires. Before today, it was always easy to leave. To jump into a car and go wherever we wanted.

That's what happened when I left Ohio. I climbed into the car and headed south without thinking much about it. That was six months ago. *Six months!* What was I thinking? What I wouldn't give to get those months back. I only wish I could.

But if I'd never left, would Jordan and I have figured things out? Would we know for sure how desperately we want to be together?

And now that we've figured things out, will we be able to put them into practice? She and Mackenzie must have made it to the mainland by now. I need to survive the next few hours so I can get out of here and go find them.

Hazel and Ethan finally reach the bottom of the stairs. Hazel stops on the last step, surveying the floor of the garage like someone preparing to jump off a high diving board. "My shoes are going to get wet."

"Everything's going to get wet, Hazel," Ethan says. "I'm sorry."

She dangles her foot in the air, then pulls it back. I worry that she's never going to take the metaphorical leap.

She turns to Ethan. "I wish we'd gotten more work done on my project."

"We tried, Hazel. We did. You told me you wanted to stop for a while. Remember?"

Hazel nods. "I do." She studies Ethan, examining his face like she's never seen him before.

The others come down the stairs, bottlenecking behind them.

"Hazel?" I say. "Do you want to take my hand? It's true you're going to get wet, but I've been wet all night. It will be worth it. We'll be safer in the shed."

She looks at me directly. "You never did get my gift, did you?"

"No, I didn't."

She turns haughty again, chin lifted.

Hazel raises her foot and splashes down onto the garage floor before I can help. She brings her other foot down a split second later, suddenly moving with the energy and steadiness of someone forty years younger.

The logjam breaks, and the others wade into the pooling water.

I grab Hazel's hand to help her maneuver. She yanks on my arm, pulling me closer, and speaks low enough that only I can hear. "I never know who I can trust. *Never.*"

SEVENTY-TWO

When we step out of the shelter of the parking garage and into the grass, the wind whips us even harder, cutting across the island like a scythe.

Ethan holds tight to Hazel on one side, and I brace her on the other. I can't help her while I'm holding the flashlight and the gun, so I put the safety on and tuck the Glock into my pants at the small of my back. I can't imagine whipping it out if there's an emergency, but this seems like the only way to proceed. The rain smashes into our faces, probing us like thousands of tiny needles.

I lean close to Hazel's ear. "It's not far."

"It might as well be a million miles."

"I won't let you fall."

I take a glance back. Kiara and Nina each have one of Sawyer's arms, their bodies bent forward to fight the wind.

Water sloshes over our shoes as high as our ankles, then recedes slightly, giving us a break.

I aim my flashlight beam forward, showing us the way, and pray the batteries hold until we reach the shed. The light picks up debris from the roof, and I know we'll soon be seeing what Alaina and I saw earlier.

Not what, I remind myself. *Who.*

"Keep your eyes straight ahead," I say, hoping everyone can hear me.

But it's no use. The light catches Stanley's bloody head. His unseeing eyes staring up into the darkened sky. The rain falling against his face.

"Oh, my," Hazel says. "Poor Stanley."

"I know."

"I never liked him," she says.

I risk a look back while all heads turn toward Stanley's body. The reactions range from shock and horror (Nina and Kiara) to near indifference (Sawyer and Alaina).

"Not too much farther." I can't tell if I intend these words for Hazel and Ethan. Or maybe I'm talking to myself, trying to keep my own tired body going.

I tell myself this is the last stop. *Get to the shed. Lock ourselves in. Wait for the storm to pass once and for all. And then everything will be all right.*

But it's hard to believe. If I've learned anything in the last thirteen hours, it's this: The road never seems to end. Once one challenge passes, the next one is there waiting. Lurking around the corner.

There's no such thing as an easy road, no sure path.

The water starts to rise again. A few second later, it goes even higher, coming up to the middle of our shins.

"Shit," Ethan says next to me. "Are we going to get completely flooded?"

Hazel loses her balance, and we both tighten our grip on her arms.

"Just go on without me," she says. "I'm tired. Leave me here to die in the water."

"Come on, Hazel," I say. "This isn't boot camp. You can do it. The shed isn't much farther."

The water is just below my knees now. Maybe I miscalculated. Maybe this is a mistake. Maybe we should have stayed in the building, taking our chances with Lloyd and Catalina. I'm worried Ethan is right—that we're about to get swept away by the storm surge.

If only the water would stop rising.

It's as if someone hears my wish.

The water stops rising and almost immediately starts to recede.

This is a break. For now. I try not to think about what might happen if we lock ourselves in the shed and the water continues to rise. We might not get off the island alive.

What if I've led all these people into a trap?

I turn back to the others, play the cheerleader. "Not much farther, everyone. We're almost there."

"Jake. Wait."

Ethan stops moving. Hazel stops. We all stop.

I freeze in place. "What's wrong? We need to keep going."

"Something's out there," he says, pointing toward the outbuilding. "I saw it."

The wind eases. The water is back down to our ankles. It feels safe to release my grip on Hazel's arm. I reach behind me, draw the gun out, its grip slick and cold in my hand.

My heart expands to twice its normal size, threatens to burst out of my rib cage. It has to be the security man who works for the owners. He's spotted our slow procession across the grounds. He's ready to take us all down while we're exposed and vulnerable.

Ethan and I both aim our flashlights in the direction of the movement.

I lift the gun, extend it into the dark morning. My hand quivers so much I don't think I can squeeze the trigger even if I have to. I certainly don't think I could hit anything.

"What is it?" Nina asks. "Should we run back?"

"Not all of us can do that," Sawyer says.

We move the beams around, searching for the target.

All of a sudden I see it too. A movement in the grass. Low to the ground.

"What the . . ."

It enters the beam. Round and dark green, it's larger than a manhole cover. As it approaches us, the head turns, revealing an inky black eye that blinks in the light.

"Holy shit," Ethan says. "A loggerhead turtle. Will you look at that thing? It's beautiful."

The turtle ignores us, dragging itself through the shallow water with its flippers.

"It must be disoriented by the storm," Sawyer says.

"Or she's taking a shortcut across the island," Nina says.

We all fall silent, watching until the turtle lumbers past us and out of sight.

"That's a good omen," Hazel says. "The Native people who lived here saw turtles as symbols of long life."

"I'll take any good omens I can get." I put the gun back in my pants, relieved. "Come on," I say, taking Hazel's arm again. "Let's get out of here."

SEVENTY-THREE

In just a few minutes, we get our first glimpse of the shed.

It's smaller than I remembered. Almost not tall enough for an adult to stand up inside. Almost.

The wet cinder blocks glisten in the weak light. The metal door is painted a dark green and splotched with rust. There are no windows, but a lone slatted vent sits above the door, allowing minimal air to circulate.

At least it looks solid. Almost like a prison cell block.

I release my grip on Hazel's arm, Ethan holding her steady.

When I approach the door, I dig in my pocket to find the passkey.

It's not there.

It's gone.

I panic—my heart starts to race.

Did it fall out while we were wading through all that water? What are we going to do?

But then my fingers locate the key at the bottom of my pocket. My heart rate slows ever so slightly.

I clutch the flashlight under my arm and stick the key into the lock. It's rusted and dirty. Will it even turn? Will the key snap off in the lock? To my surprise, the lock turns with little effort, and I'm able to shove the heavy door open.

"Thank God," Ethan says.

Stale, musty air hits my face. It feels like the place hasn't been opened in years.

A cobweb hits me in the cheek. I brush it away while I aim the flashlight into all corners of the small building. Cobwebs cover every inch, hanging from the ceilings and decorating the corners like a haunted house.

The floor is littered with crumbling cardboard boxes, lawn equipment, three folding chairs, and a garden hose.

"Well?" Ethan asks.

"It's okay. The floor is wet, but not as much as the ground outside. The door must create a pretty good seal. That helps. I think we can all fit." I step back. "Go on in. There are even a couple of chairs for Hazel and Sawyer."

Hazel stands in the doorway. She looks like a nervous filly at the starting gate. "I don't know, Jake."

"Go inside, Hazel. We're all getting wet. And running out of time. That guy could be along at any moment."

Ethan gives her a gentle tug, and they step through the door. The trio of Nina, Kiara, and Sawyer follow without any hesitation.

Next is Alaina. "I didn't see anyone following us. Not even a turtle."

I stop in the doorway and look back in the direction of our apartment building.

I'd be lying if I said I could see it in the dark. Maybe an outline, but even that would be difficult at this distance and with the cloud cover and ceaseless rain. I hope the building makes it through the storm. I hope Lloyd and Catalina stay safe. Who knows? Maybe it will all work out.

I take one last deep breath of fresh air before I draw the door shut, closing us all inside the little concrete box.

SEVENTY-FOUR

7:07 A.M.

It's tight and close.

The air is more dank than I imagined. Far worse than in the hallway in Lloyd's apartment.

We open two folding chairs, for Hazel and Sawyer. The rest of us stand, shoulder to shoulder, butt cheek to butt cheek.

"We should turn off our flashlights," I say. "Save the batteries."

Everyone does what I ask, snapping off their flashlights. It's darker than dark. Darker than any place I've ever been in. Darker than a cave we once toured during a family trip to Kentucky when I was a kid.

No one says a word.

Rain pelts the shed, muffled by the thick walls and steel door.

"I hate to ask, Jake," Sawyer says, "but do you think your family made it to shore by now?"

"They would have had to. It's been almost two hours."

"So they could be sending help soon."

I sigh. I don't like to think about the situation we're in any more than I have to. "Not right away. The water's going to be rough until the storm calms down."

"How long will that be?" Nina asks.

"I'm guessing an hour or so. Maybe two. By then it will be full daylight. Or darn close to it."

"How will they find us?" Ethan asks.

"Lloyd will tell them where we went," Kiara says.

"What if the building's fallen on top of him and Catalina?" Nina asks.

"Jesus," I say, "can we all just shut up? Please? For just a minute, can we all shut up?"

An uneasy, awkward silence settles over the space. People shuffle their feet on the wet floor. Something scurries up one of the walls. Most likely a lizard wondering why we've all invaded its private lair.

I stand by the door, my head leaning against the cold wall. I try to visualize the trip Jordan and Mackenzie took across the water. I picture Jordan's steady hand on the tiller, Mackenzie behind her, holding on to one side with both hands. The boat travels in a straight line, the most direct route possible, the prow cutting through the low chop, avoiding any unseen debris. There are no waves large enough to swamp them.

They pull up onshore and find themselves just a few hundred feet from the police station. Sgt. Fernandez is still on duty. She remembers them from before. She remembers me. She wraps them in blankets, offers them warm drinks and something to eat.

Fernandez summons help. The Coast Guard or a police boat. The storm is winding down, so it's a quick, easy trip.

Lloyd tells them where to find us. We emerge from the shed, blinking in the morning light. Like small children on a holiday morning.

We are saved.

They give us towels and blankets. We return to the mainland by boat. Jordan and Mackenzie are waiting onshore.

I take them both in my arms and vow to never, ever leave them again.

It's a dream, a fantasy, but I will it to be real.

"Sorry, Jake," Nina says.

"No, I'm sorry. It's just—I'm sorry."

Quiet settles over us again. Leaving us with nothing to do but wait.

The minutes pass slowly. They drip by like hours.

"Something moved," Hazel says, breaking the silence. "By my feet." Her voice sounds louder in this closed, quiet space.

"Probably a lizard," Ethan says. "Harmless."

"No, no, it's still there," she says.

Maybe she's imagining things again. I think this, but don't say it.

"Now I feel it too," Kiara says. "How many lizards are in here? And how big are they?"

"Could it be a snake?" Nina asks. "Is it slithering around us?"

"It's not a snake," Sawyer says. "No snake would be in here."

Sawyer's full of shit, but I keep my mouth shut, let them work it out on their own.

"I know what I feel," Hazel says.

I want to dismiss her. I want to believe they're all imagining things. That the stress of the long night has taken its toll. That they're feeling things where there's nothing to feel.

Except—now I feel it too.

And I have a terrible sense about what it really is.

I flick my flashlight on, shine it at the floor.

Water. Lots of water. It's coming under the door and swirling around our feet.

SEVENTY-FIVE

The water rises slowly.

After ten minutes, it's up to the laces of my shoes. Ten minutes later, my ankles.

Now it's coming through either side of the door, where the metal meets the jamb. About a foot off the ground.

"It can't get much higher, can it?" Sawyer asks.

"If the whole island floods—" Nina says.

"But that's not possible," Sawyer says. "The whole island can't flood. I mean—then it wouldn't be an island anymore."

"Hazel?" Ethan says. "You know about this, right?"

Hazel remains uncharacteristically silent. Almost like she hasn't heard her name being spoken. I've never really known her to shrink from the chance to speak. Like any college professor, she's always happy to share her wisdom.

"Hazel? Did you hear me? What do you know about the island flooding?"

Sawyer flicks his flashlight on. The water swirls over our feet. It's picked up an oily sheen that looks like a rainbow in the dark.

"Well"—Hazel pats her hair like she's overdue for a trip to the beauty salon—"there is a history of the island flooding. Of total submersion. It's incredibly rare, but it happens."

"How rare?" Kiara asks. "Like, once-in-five-hundred-years rare? Or once-in-fifty-years rare?"

"Oh," Hazel says, "the Native people recorded quite a few large storms and floods. They show up in some of the ancient drawings they left behind. As recently as the early twentieth century, a large hurricane hit and flooded the island completely. It was uninhabitable for a decade or so before the water receded."

"This island has been underwater more than once?" Nina asks.

"Oh, yes, dear." Hazel says this as though it's a curious fact about a distant world, not something that could doom us all in the next thirty minutes. "I don't understand why anyone would want to build here at all. With the climate changing, the waters are just going to rise, the beaches erode. But . . . I guess oceanfront property is one thing they aren't making any more of. . . ."

"So this whole island could end up underwater?" Nina asks with real panic in her voice. "But I don't know how to swim." Even in the dark, I can tell she's shaking her head. "Why are we out here with the sea turtles when we could be on the second floor, where the water's less likely to reach?"

"I think," Ethan says. "Well, I know . . . Jake . . . I guess Jake wanted us to come out here."

The conversation stops for a moment.

The air feels sticky. I'm drenched with sweat. Except around my feet and ankles, which are covered with water. Slowly rising water.

"If we have to, we'll go back," I say.

"Back?" Ethan asks. "We were lucky to get here with just a few inches of water on the ground. I don't think all of us could make it back without being swept away. Maybe none of us could."

"More of us should have gone in that boat," Nina says.

"Shhh." Kiara's voice is harsh.

"It's true. Maybe more of us should have left."

"You had a chance, and you didn't take it," Sawyer says. "Don't start trying to rewrite history now."

"I didn't know this could happen," Nina says. "I didn't have all the information. I thought we'd be okay out here. And now—"

"Just cool it."

The voice surprises me. Like something that burst out of the walls. The sound bounces off the cinder blocks and ricochets between us, shutting down all talk.

I turn toward the speaker. Even in the dark, I can see the outline of Alaina's body. She holds a hand in the air, index finger extended, like she's about to lecture a bunch of schoolchildren.

"You all need to shut up." Alaina's voice is surprisingly loud, especially coming from such a small body. "Jake's doing his best, and you all need to appreciate that. We're still alive, and if we want to stay that way, we need to shut up. I haven't seen anyone else coming up with any great ideas. And Sawyer's right. You had a chance to get on that dinghy, but you didn't take it. Probably because you were afraid. Like I was. So just deal."

Everyone grows really quiet again. The rain sounds like thousands of darts hitting the metal door. The wind rattles it in its frame.

Water continues to flow inside. By now it's risen to the level of my shins. Alaina's defense is appreciated, but I'm running out of ideas.

We all are.

But Alaina isn't finished.

"This thing isn't going to fill with water. The worst of the storm surge has probably already passed. We just need to ride this out. Okay?"

No one says another word.

There's no way to know if Alaina is right. She might be saying whatever she has to say to keep everybody calm. Even if that's so, I appreciate it.

I look down.

The water is approaching my knees.

SEVENTY-SIX

When the water passes my knees, I become convinced I've done everything wrong.

I never should have led the group out here.

I never should have left Lloyd and Catalina alone.

I never should have let Jordan and Mackenzie go.

I never should have come to Florida at all.

The weight of anxiety returns to my chest. It rises like the water, threatening to cut off all the air.

If the water keeps rising, we'll have no choice but to leave. Outside, we'll be exposed to the elements. The water may be even higher. The current rougher.

Not to mention the wind and rain.

Did I miscalculate? I thought the storm was close to being over, but maybe it isn't. Maybe it still has a long way to go. Maybe it will kill us.

Everyone in the shed remains quiet. Either because Alaina shamed them or because the same realization hitting me is landing on each of them.

They're wondering if this shed is the last place they'll ever see. A watery coffin.

"I'm going out." I'm facing the door, my back to the group. But I speak loudly enough to be heard. "I'll risk it. Maybe I can find a boat or some floating debris we can hang on to. Maybe help has arrived, and I can flag them down."

"No, Jake," Alaina says. "Just stay here. It's too dangerous."

"Not with this water rising so fast, Jake," Sawyer says. "It could . . . you could . . . get swept away. Like a twig."

Hazel starts chanting again.

But this time, it doesn't annoy me. It brings me comfort. It might be the last sound I ever hear. And at this point, I'm willing to try anything.

Hazel goes on for a few minutes. Until Ethan leans down to her.

"Hazel, maybe you should stand up. You and Sawyer. We can help you."

She keeps chanting, ignoring Ethan, acting like none of us are here.

I close my eyes, listen to the sound of her voice. I don't know what any of her chanting means, but the more I listen, the more it makes a strange kind of sense. I start to really hear the rhythm, the beats. I feel them. I hum along with Hazel. Who knows? Maybe it will help. Maybe Jordan and Mackenzie can hear us, all the way across the water. The sound of our voices will act as a beacon, leading them to the shed, leading them to rescue us.

"Hey, look. . . ."

I ignore the voice and keep muttering along with Hazel.

"Do you see that?"

I keep going until I realize Hazel has stopped. I'm the only one making noises now. I've lost myself in the sound. Almost like a meditation.

"Look, look." It's Sawyer. I don't think I've ever before heard excitement in his voice.

"I see it too," Alaina says with an almost undetectable optimism.

Nina doesn't bother to hide her joy. "Me too."

I turn around to face the others. They all have their flashlights pointed at the water. It takes a moment for me to understand. But then I see it too. "Holy shit."

Is it an illusion? Is it just what I want to see? But we're all seeing the same thing.

"The water's going down," Sawyer says. "It's fucking going down."

The waterline is now below my knees, slowly approaching my mid-shin.

"Oh, my God, we're going to be okay," Kiara says.

The pressure in my chest eases, receding with the water.

"We may not be saved," I say. "Not yet. But this gives us a chance to get out of here."

SEVENTY-SEVEN

7:43 A.M.

The water level falls to just above the soles of our shoes.

It's grown even hotter and more humid.

Stiflingly hot. Sweat sticks to my body like motor oil.

It's hard to breathe, the air as thick as cottage cheese.

We've waited as long as possible. I press my ear to the door. The wind still blows, but it sounds lighter. Rain splats against the door, but it doesn't drum incessantly, as it did earlier.

The storm should be moving past us soon. Things should be starting to clear.

"We need to open the door," I say. "We need to see how things look."

"Why don't we wait?" Nina asks. "You sent for help. Someone will come."

"It's sickeningly hot in here," I say. "We can all feel it. And it's not doing any of us any good."

"That's true," Ethan says.

"Besides . . ." I try to form the words, but they turn to dust in my mouth. I can't force them out. I swallow, trying to summon the moisture I need to speak. "Besides, we don't know for sure if Jordan and Mackenzie made it across. If they didn't, we don't know how long we'll have to wait. One cop over there knows Dallas was killed, but they're going to be occupied with a lot of other problems. I think it's best if I look and see."

"What are you going to do?" Alaina asks.

"I have no idea. Maybe there's another dinghy. Maybe someone will sail by. I'll just have to see."

"Do you want me to go with you?" Alaina asks.

"No, stay here with everyone else. Watch the door. Lock it after me. We'll use the same knock. If I'm not back in a little while . . . well, just keep waiting."

No one offers any objections. And no one else offers to join me.

I'd almost rather be alone.

When the lock is undone and my hand is on the knob, I try to think of anything else to say. But there's nothing. I'm on my own now.

When I pull the door open, I immediately feel the change. The storm has cooled the air and lowered the humidity. A light rain falls, splatting softly in the standing water on the ground. The sky has brightened on the horizon, a band of light gray visible where the clouds break.

I want to feel hopeful, but I can't quite get there yet.

As I close the door behind me, Alaina's is the last face I see. She mouths the words *Good luck.*

The door clunks shut, and I'm alone on the lawn, facing the building we all used to live in.

In the half-light, I can see it still stands, though even more of the top of the building has been destroyed. I feel a measure of relief. Lloyd and Catalina are okay.

For now.

As I squish over the grass, my eyes scan left and right, watching for any sign of trouble. I'm waiting for someone to jump out from behind a palm tree, wielding a gun or a club.

The Glock remains at my back, a heavy presence against my soaked skin.

I doubt I could shoot another human being. If confronted by a deranged killer, I'd be willing to fight, but not with the gun. That might mean I'm doomed no matter what. But I have to accept my own limitations.

The wind still blows, but compared to what it was before, it feels almost pleasant now. Almost like a lovely fall day—except for all the destruction and death.

I step through debris like I'm navigating a minefield. Stanley's body lies uncovered, his eyes staring at the clearing sky. He looks small and vulnerable, exposed. I know he can't be hurt, but somehow it seems undignified and disrespectful to leave him there like that. An unburied body.

I don't have time to bury him, but I grab the sheet of metal from the roof, one side jagged like it's been cut with a giant knife, and slide it toward him. It takes a moment—and I have to be careful not to slice my own hand wide-open—but I get it over his body.

I have no idea if Stanley cares—wherever he might be—but somehow it makes me feel better.

"Okay." I wipe my hands together, brushing dirt and twigs off them.

I look up at the building. Lloyd's door remains closed.

I'll check on them in a minute, but first, I'm going to the water's edge to see what I find.

SEVENTY-EIGHT

I veer to the left of the building, heading for the clump of weeds where we found Tyler's dinghy.

The Intracoastal is as gray as the lightening sky. It's still choppy, topped by whitecaps, and the steady drone of the tide makes a *slap-slap-slap* against the shore. A lone gull soars overhead, venturing out in search of food. The wind blows hard enough up there to send him careening off course. He flaps hard to regain control.

At the water's edge, I stare across to the mainland. A few lights shine in the vicinity of the police station, but everything else remains dark.

I scan the water both ways. Up the shore and down.

Nothing.

No sign of a boat. No emergency vehicles, no Coast Guard. Just swelling gray water as far as the eye can see.

Despite my being prepared to see nothing, my heart sinks like a stone. It's a foolish organ, incapable of listening to reason.

I wanted more than anything to have some news of Jordan or Mackenzie. To know they made it safely across, regardless of what might happen to the rest of us.

A part of me wants to jump in the water and swim across. I'm capable. I've made the swim many times. But given the rough conditions and the large amount of debris floating on the waves, it would be a fool's game. I could end up dead while my family waits safely on the other side.

I turn away from the water. I don't want to stand here too long with my back to the island. Not knowing who might come up behind me.

I actually look forward to climbing the stairs to Lloyd's apartment. Seeing him and Catalina again.

But before I move, someone calls my name.

From above.

Lloyd stands on the far end of the landing two floors above me. It's as if he read my mind.

He yells my name again. This time it's sharper, more urgent. My mind cycles through possibilities. Has something happened to Catalina?

Has someone threatened them? Is someone closing in on me?

Lloyd points in the direction of the mainland. No, not the mainland. The water.

He's pointing at the water.

I spin around, hoping to see a boat coming our way, something I missed or something that has appeared from the mist like the Flying Dutchman.

But I still don't see anything. Does he mean for me to notice something on the mainland? More lights? A fire?

"Lloyd, I don't—"

But then I do.

Halfway across the channel, in the middle of the Intracoastal. The upturned hull bobbing in the water. Blending into the gray waves. The lifeless propeller sticking up in the air.

The dinghy. The one I sent Jordan and Mackenzie in.

Overturned in the water. Floating.

And no sign of them anywhere.

PART FOUR

SEVENTY-NINE

Lloyd appears next to me.

I'm not sure how long he's been here. For a moment, I've forgotten who he is or where he came from. I'm so wrapped up in my own terror and grief.

But here he is, next to me, his hand gripping my upper arm, tethering me to reality.

We're standing waist-deep in the Intracoastal. When I saw the capsized dinghy, I jumped in, apparently thinking I could swim out to them. Find them. Save them.

If Lloyd hadn't grabbed me, it would've been bad. Very, very bad.

"Come on, Jake," he says to me in a soothing voice. Like he's talking to a scared animal. "Come on. Back to shore."

Lloyd's grip is like a clamp. His fingers mash my muscles and tendons so hard they hurt. I might try to resist if it weren't so apparent he's not going to let go.

At all.

The dark, foamy water of the Intracoastal swirls around my legs. The pull of the current is strong here. Capable of sucking someone out to sea if they let their guard down.

"I have to find them."

"Come on back now, Jake. You can't do any good in here. Not when you're this upset and the water's this rough."

My body goes limp. Maybe I'm not as capable as I thought. Lloyd moves me effortlessly toward the shore, pulling me backward. When he finally lets go I sink to my knees, staring at the water.

"They're gone, Lloyd. I never should have sent them. It was too dark, too dangerous. . . ."

"You don't know what happened, Jake."

"Then why is the dinghy upside down?"

Lloyd scrambles for an answer. "Maybe someone picked them up."

"No one's out here."

"Someone might have been. A police patrol. The Coast Guard."

"Look at that current. They couldn't . . ."

"Are they good swimmers?"

"Yes, they're both excellent swimmers. Like fish."

"And tough?"

"Yes."

"Then they'd have a puncher's chance. Hell, they've put up with you all these years. Maybe they can handle this kind of water."

I squeeze my eyes shut. Red and green starbursts appear on my eyelids. Tears come, burning on my cheeks.

Lloyd's hands are on me again, one on each side of my torso. He yanks me forward, pulling me to my feet like I'm a child.

"I need your help, Jake," he says. "That's why I came out on the landing in the first place."

"What do you want?"

"Your help, I said. It's Catalina. . . ."

The mention of his wife's name snaps me out of my own grief for the moment. "What happened? Is she hurt?"

"No, she's fine. We weathered the storm."

"Then you're safe. . . . Just wait for help, the power to come back on . . ."

Lloyd shakes his head. "No, look." He nods toward the building. The morning sky has lightened more. It's still the color of concrete, but it's a lighter shade of gray, easier to see. I examine the place Lloyd has indicated.

I hadn't noticed before, but now I see it.

Not only is more of the top of the building gone, but a large fissure splits the stucco, running from the top of the building almost all the way to the ground. It gapes like an open wound. The building looks like it's about to crack apart and collapse.

"Holy shit . . ."

"She—we thought—well, we decided to, you know, die together. If the building fell or the storm got us, I was ready to go with her. I thought she was ready to go too. But Catalina changed her mind when the sun started to come out. Once we'd really made it through the night. Now she wants to get out and live as long as she can. And I can't move her alone, Jake. Will you help me?"

I'm heading that way before he even finishes the question.

EIGHTY

As we climb the stairs, I try not to fixate on thoughts of Jordan and Mackenzie.

But how can I not?

I imagine them making it to shore. Or being rescued.

I picture them swimming to shore through the dark, choppy water.

Lloyd passes me on the second-floor walkway. He opens the apartment door, and I follow him inside.

It's still musty and humid. Not nearly as bad as the shed.

Catalina remains in the same position, still underneath the covers. A big smile overtakes her face when she sees me. But how are we going to get her out of the apartment and down the stairs?

Lloyd leans close to Catalina and speaks so low I can't hear him.

Given the look on her face, I gather he's telling her about the dinghy. Catalina turns to me. She lifts one arm, beckoning me closer.

She enfolds me in a weak hug.

"They will be okay," she says. "I can feel it."

I wish her words brought me some measure of comfort, but they don't. I appreciate her gesture, but it brings me no relief.

I straighten up. "Why don't we try to get you out of here?"

Catalina's expression grows puzzled. She looks at me and then at Lloyd. "What . . ."

It dawns on me what's going on.

Lloyd's cheeks flush, an unusual look on a man his age. "Well, I decided something. I think we ought to get out of here."

Catalina struggles to say something. She manages only one word, little more than a sound. "But . . ."

"I know what we said. But . . . look, I want to spend every moment I can with you. And this building is in really bad shape now. I don't think it's going to make it. I don't think I can get you out of here myself, but when I saw Jake outside, a light went on. . . . I say we get out of here. What do you think?"

Catalina shakes her head. Her forehead creases. She lifts her hand and gestures toward herself. "How . . . I . . . don't . . ."

She's worried about her pride. That the process of getting her out of bed and down the stairs, without a stretcher or an elevator, will be so difficult and embarrassing that it isn't worth it. She was prepared to die in the building. Alongside Lloyd. Now everything is different. She isn't sure she likes it.

"But, honey . . ."

Catalina shakes her head. Slowly but firmly. "No . . ."

"But, honey—"

"No. This . . . is . . . our . . . home."

Lloyd takes a step back, his face still colored red. He looks like a man out of options, like he can't imagine the next move he'll make.

It's none of my business. Just like during all the other intimate moments I've glimpsed between the two of them over the course of the night, it's not my place to get involved. But this time I feel I should.

"Catalina, do you know how much I wish my family were here? With me? I've wished that for six months. And I wish it even more now. I'd take any extra time with them I could. Any."

She studies me, her forehead still creased. I imagine she's summoning the energy to curse me.

"This building is fucked," I say, cutting to the chase. "There isn't much time."

The creases remain as she moves her eyes from me to Lloyd and then back again. Her hand rises from the bed, and her index finger extends in my direction. "My . . . dignity . . . Promise?"

"Yes, I promise."

She makes a shooing gesture. I think she's dismissing us, dismissing the whole idea.

But then she manages two more words: "Let's . . . go."

EIGHTY-ONE

8:24 A.M.

It takes time to get ready.

Lloyd searches the apartment, making sure there's nothing he needs to take.

"Remember when folks had to grab all their photos in a disaster?" He's talking more to himself than to me. "Now all that shit's digitized. Cat and I haven't taken a single photo that isn't saved in the cloud."

He goes back to the bedroom and returns with a soft-sided carrying case.

"Meds. She takes a lot."

Catalina watches him move, her eyes bigger than ever. She's scared.

The building makes a loud creaking noise. It's more high-pitched and desperate than before. The last cry of something about to die.

"Shit," Lloyd says. "We better go." He goes to the bed, examines his wife before glancing back at me. "What are you thinking, Jake?"

"Can we just use a sheet? Carry her in that. A wheelchair does us no good on the stairs. And there's no elevator. But we can use a sheet to get her out on the lawn."

Lloyd studies Catalina. "Is that okay with you, honey?"

Catalina nods. "I . . . trust . . . both . . ."

"Thanks," I say.

"But . . . Lloyd?" Her eyes fill with tears.

"What is it?"

Lloyd looks at me. "Her legs. She used to run. She was a track star. Now they're . . . well, everything's atrophying."

"I won't look," I say.

"It's not you. *She* doesn't want to see them. She wants me to keep them covered." Lloyd starts moving around the bed, tucking the sheet around Catalina's body. "We'll keep her in this. Then we can carry her. We can grip the elastic."

"Sounds good," I say. "The stairs will be the hard part. But it's only two flights down."

"You ready? You want to open the door?"

Outside, the day is now light enough for me to see the debris scattered on the lawn, the piece of roofing over Stanley's body. I look both ways on the landing and see no one.

My eyes trail farther across the lawn, to the shed. I can't be sure from this distance, but it looks like the door is open. Maybe they needed air. Or maybe someone needed to go to the bathroom.

I can't worry about them right now.

We'll take care of Catalina and deal with the others soon enough.

I go back to the bed, stand on the side opposite Lloyd. We lock eyes. He's placed the carrying case on the bed so we can take it. He nods my way, counts to three. We each gather fistfuls of fitted sheet, pulling it out from under the mattress.

Catalina makes the sign of the cross, her eyes closed tight.

When Lloyd gets to three, we lift.

She's surprisingly heavy. I guess even an emaciated human being is not light. She keeps her eyes closed as we shuffle toward the door, lifting the sheet high enough in the air to get around the bed.

Lloyd's face strains, the lines around his eyes and mouth becoming more pronounced. He's not a young man. But I know he'd never let go.

We both grunt as we make our way through the door, moving

cautiously so we don't bump our burden against the frame. The cool air brings relief. I'm sweating. A lot. The breeze feels good on my neck.

We shuffle down the walkway—for what I hope is the last time.

The last time past the apartment where Dallas died.

Tyler.

As we approach the stairs, my heart rate increases.

Not from the hard work of carrying Catalina, but because I fear, again, what or who might lurk around the corner. Adrenaline kicks in. My nerve endings twang like struck piano wires.

At the top of the stairs, I catch Lloyd's eye. "Let me go first."

"Be careful."

"Yes . . ." Catalina's eyes remain closed, her hands clasped on her chest.

I take a few deep breaths, make certain of my grip.

I look down the first half flight. No one's there. All clear for the moment.

I back my foot down one step, my arms and neck straining from the weight.

"Wait," Lloyd says. "I need to get a better grip."

We pause while he reconfigures himself. Then he nods at me.

But before we go again, I hear a sound. A tapping.

"What's wrong, Jake?"

"Shh."

I listen. No doubt about it. Footsteps coming up the stairs.

"Someone's coming." My voice is just above a whisper. "Should we go back?"

"We can't move very fast."

"We're sitting ducks."

"Do you have the gun?"

I do. But I can't possibly reach it.

EIGHTY-TWO

My mind toggles between two options.

Try to gently place Catalina on the ground, so I can reach for the gun.

Or hold my place between the killer and Catalina and Lloyd.

If I do that, I can protect them. Give them a chance—even a slim one—to get back to safety in the apartment.

"Lloyd, I'm going to—"

"No way, Jake. We're in this together."

A figure turns the corner, coming into view on the landing below us.

My chin drops a little.

It's Nina. "You need some help?"

Every muscle in my arms and shoulders strains. But my breath comes out in a long, relieved exhalation.

"What are you doing here?" I ask.

"I had to pee. But then I saw you all out here on the landing. I figured out what was going on." She looks behind her, down the bottom half of the stairs. "So a few of us came to help. Can I . . ." She comes up a few steps, hands outstretched.

Even though I'm still holding the sheet that supports Catalina, my stress has eased significantly. I move aside so Nina can help. She grips half of the sheet, and we move down to the landing together. When we get there, Kiara appears.

"Grab on, hon," Nina tells Kiara.

The four of us carry Catalina the rest of the way. When we get to the bottom, we rotate to ease Lloyd's load. By the time we step off the curb and into the parking garage, the floor covered with half an inch of water, I feel reinvigorated.

Alaina appears in the garage. "Do you all need help?"

"Yes," Lloyd says through slightly gritted teeth.

Alaina grabs the sheet next to him. "Where are we going?"

"As far away from this place as possible," I say. "I don't think it's long for the world. Maybe to the shed."

"Are you okay, Catalina?" Alaina shows no sign of strain at all. It's as if she's carrying a butterfly.

Catalina gives Alaina a thumbs-up.

"You're in good hands," Alaina says.

We head onto the lawn under a light rain.

"Do you mind?" Lloyd asks the rest of us.

We all nod, and Lloyd lets go, leaving the four of us to carry the sheet. He moves to Catalina's head and holds his hands over her face, protecting her from the rain.

"Is everyone okay?" I ask.

"We're all good," Alaina says. "Hot. Sweaty. Wet. But good. How about you?"

It all comes rushing back to me. The dinghy. Jordan. Mackenzie. Somehow, in the rush to get Catalina out of the building, I'd managed to forget. But Alaina's question brings it all back. Instead of responding, I stare forward, concentrating on my task.

I'm not sure I can answer.

"Jake?"

"He's fine," Lloyd says in a way that cuts off further questions.

"Is there room inside the shed?" I ask, changing the subject.

"It's not very comfortable in there," Alaina says. "The grass is soaked, though. And the rain will land on her out here."

"Hold on," Nina says. "I see something we can use. Over there." She nods to the other side of the lawn. "Can the two of you hold her?"

"Sure," Alaina says. "Jake and I can handle it."

Nina and Kiara let go. They jog across the lawn and grab a sheet of roofing material—not the one covering Stanley—and haul it back to us. They place it on the ground, close to a palm tree that somehow made it through the night.

Alaina and I scoot in that direction. Kiara and Nina help us gently set Catalina on the metal sheet, so she stays drier than she would on the lawn. Lloyd resumes his position, keeping the rain off her face.

The drizzle lands on my head and shoulders. A steady breeze whips across us.

It's safe to say we're through the worst of the hurricane.

I back away from the others, try to collect my thoughts.

Alaina comes up next to me. She speaks low enough that no one else can hear. "What happened, Jake? I can tell something happened."

I tell her what I saw. I feel my chin quivering but manage to keep it together.

Alaina places her hand on my arm. "I'm sorry, Jake. I really am. But I made it out of the water. In a sinking car. And I can't even swim that well."

"They're both good swimmers."

"See?"

"But the current out there . . . it's brutal. I stood in it. I felt it. You don't even want to know how close I came to swimming out there myself. Lloyd pulled me back. He saved me. Who's going to save them?"

"The sun's up, Jake. The police will come looking for us soon. We can find out—"

"Sure." I cut her off, grateful for the support but knowing there's nothing she can say to make me feel better.

"Jake!" Someone yells my name across the lawn. Sawyer stands in the doorway of the shed, his weight leaning on his cane. "Something's wrong with Hazel."

EIGHTY-THREE

8:46 A.M.

"She's not doing too well," Sawyer tells me when I get there. "And she's asking for you."

Inside, I find Hazel leaned back against a rusting cabinet. She fans herself with a moldy piece of cardboard, packaging for a garden hose someone purchased years earlier. Her face is covered with sweat, and her skin looks pallid.

"Oh, Jacob. Good. You're back."

"I am. How are you, Hazel?"

"I'm old."

"Are you feeling okay?"

"Did you hear me say I'm old? That means the answer is no."

I don't see any way to make her more comfortable. There's no place to lie down unless she wants to join Catalina on a piece of sheet metal on the grass.

"I'm hoping we'll get help soon," I say. "If you can hang on."

"I've been hanging on for years." Her lips look dry and cracked. Her fanning slows. "Did you see him?"

"Who?"

"The man. The stalker."

"I didn't see anyone but Lloyd and Catalina. I guess I was lucky."

"Did you get the gift?"

I sigh. "I didn't. It's not safe to go into the building, Hazel. It's about to collapse."

She stops fanning herself. Her grip on the cardboard is tight, her knuckles white. She looks past me.

Ethan and Sawyer are standing just outside the door, talking in low voices.

"What?" I ask. "What's wrong?"

Her chin lifts ever so slightly. I can't tell if it's an intentional gesture or a spasm. But she does it again. "Jacob?"

I bend down, get close to her. "What is it?"

"You need to go in and get that gift. For me. You *need* to get it."

"Oh, Hazel—"

"Jacob, I don't ask for much."

I laugh, despite myself. "Did you really just say that? To me?" I can't help myself. I have to ask. "What's the gift, Hazel? Why is it such a big deal?"

"Jacob . . ." She lowers her voice. "It's very important. To the island. That's why that man wants to get his claws on it. . . ."

"If you want me to go back into a building that's about to collapse, there's got to be a better reason than that."

Her eyes trail past me again.

This time someone's here. Inside the shed.

"Jake?"

Ethan stands just inside the door. "Can I talk to you for a minute?"

Hazel grips my arm. "Jacob . . . please . . ."

"Just a minute." I gently extract myself from her clutches. "I'll be back."

"Jacob, please."

I feel someone tugging at the back of my shirt. The gun slips out of my pants.

I turn and find myself face-to-face with the barrel of the Glock. Ethan's hands shake as he points it my way.

EIGHTY-FOUR

He steps back.

Ethan keeps the gun pointed at me with one hand. With the other, he shuts the shed door behind him.

"Ethan . . ." My insides feel watery and cold. Is that how Jordan and Mackenzie felt? "Just . . ."

"You can't go in the building. You can't get that gift."

I swallow hard. "I assume you're not saying that because you're concerned about my safety."

"Jake . . ." Hazel's voice sounds hollow, weak.

"It's about to collapse," Ethan says.

The gun still shakes in his hand, which makes me even more uneasy. As if it's possible to be more uneasy.

"Just let it fall," Ethan says. "And everything inside it. That's all you need to do."

"Why do you care so much about it? Or about me?"

"Just let it go, Jake," he says. "It's for the best."

"Do you even know how to use that?" I ask.

"Just squeeze," he says. "Don't make me do it, Jake. I will, but please don't make me."

"Don't you want to get your computer equipment?"

He shakes his head. "I'll buy more."

"I never should have trusted him, Jake. I just wanted help. . . ."

I turn my head halfway toward Hazel. "What did you find out?"

"Shut up," Ethan says. "It doesn't matter."

I speak to Hazel, my eyes still pointed toward Ethan. "I know you were researching the history of the island. Hazel, what did you find—"

"Jake, don't." He pushes the gun closer to me.

"You must have learned something that puts this whole deal in jeopardy. But what? The buyers don't care about the buildings, so what—"

"Jake . . ."

"You're asking me too many questions, Jacob," Hazel says. She fans herself with her hand. "It's hot. I feel weak. Tired."

"What did you find, Hazel?"

"I'm so—it's just so . . ." Hazel looks to the ceiling of the shed, like she can see through it. "This is my life's work . . . my husband's . . . so much work . . ."

"What is it?" I ask.

"It's in the box."

"Why didn't you just take it to the authorities? Why wrap it up like a gift?"

"I trusted you to get it out," Hazel says. "I had to be sure the right person would deliver it."

"Jake, you know this is crazy," Ethan says. "You know *she's* crazy."

"Stop," I say to Ethan. "Just stop."

"She went on and on about this. For months. She wanted me to scan the papers, but I never saw anything important. It's just nonsense. Old documents and deeds. It's crazy."

"Well, I don't trust you," Hazel says. "And as it turns out, I was right—you *were* working with him. My stalker."

"Jake, you know Hazel has lost her mind. This is the dementia talking."

"I said, stop it."

"You can't deny you've said the same thing about her, Jake. Hell, you say it almost every day."

"Is that true, Jacob? Is this how little regard you have for me? I thought we were friends. I thought you respected me."

"Oh, it's true. He said it all the time. Him and Dallas . . ."

All of a sudden I remember what he said to me in the garage. *I'm not a bad guy, am I, Jake?* "What are they giving you, Ethan? Is it just money?"

"Just money? Listen to the way you say that. You say that because you're rich."

"I'm far from rich—"

"You have a house. A family. Someone to catch you when you fall. Not me."

"My family is gone."

My words bring Ethan up short.

"What are you talking about?" he asks.

I tell him, and Hazel. The dinghy in the water. No sign of Jordan or Mackenzie.

"I'm so sorry, Jacob," Hazel says. "That's terrible."

"When we get off this island . . . I may not have anything either. I understand exactly how you feel, Ethan."

"It's not true. . . . You're lying, Jake."

"What kind of monster would I have to be to lie about something like that?" Is that the kind of person Ethan is? The kind of person who would lie about the survival of his own family? "Look, Ethan, what's your plan here? You can't shoot me and get away with it. Everybody's right outside. And there's nowhere to go until the police arrive."

"Aaron's going to get me off the island. He promised."

"That's his name? Aaron? He's the guy who works for the buyers? The guy who killed Dallas and Tyler?"

"I think he did, yes."

"Why kill Tyler? Don't they want the same thing?"

"I don't know, Jake. He's determined. They're all determined. They want everything for themselves. People go crazy for money. We all do."

"And you're helping them?"

"Just . . . just let me get what I want, Jake."

The doorknob rattles. I can't be sure if it's because of the wind or someone trying to get in.

Ethan turns his head slightly, lets the gun drop.

I take my chance. I dive forward, burying my shoulder into his chest, knocking him backward. The door swings open at just that moment, so rather than hitting the closed door, we go through it. Alaina jumps out of the way.

Ethan and I land on the wet ground. He exhales a giant breath of air as the gun flies out of his hand.

I anticipate a struggle, brace myself for having to subdue him.

I'm tired. Weary. I don't want to do this.

But I have to.

Ethan squirms beneath me, trying to buck me off his body. He manages to free one of his hands and starts swinging at my head. He connects a couple of times.

But Alaina is right there. She reaches for the Glock, but it slips out of her hand and falls back to the wet ground.

"Get it, Alaina," I say as I swing at Ethan once and then twice. I manage to connect with one of the swings. Ethan looks stunned. His eyes squint shut.

I relax a little. His eyes pop open.

He swings again, a glancing blow.

"Get the gun, Alaina!"

She manages to grab it this time.

Ethan continues to squirm, but Alaina steps close. She points the Glock right at him.

"Don't even try it, Ethan," she says. "We're done."

He looks like he wants to keep fighting. He even clenches his fist.

But then a look of defeat falls over him. His fist opens.

Ethan is finally still.

EIGHTY-FIVE

Sawyer finds some rope in the shed.

Alaina marches Ethan behind the outbuilding and holds the gun on him while Sawyer and I tie his hands and feet.

Not that there's anywhere for him to go.

"You'll put in a good word for me, won't you, Jake? With the police? I didn't hurt anybody."

"You threatened my life."

"But I didn't shoot. I don't even know *how* to shoot."

"You'll get to tell the cops whatever you want."

"Cops. They won't listen to a guy like me. I just need the money. This is all Hazel's fault."

"Hazel's fault?" Alaina asks. She looks far too comfortable holding the gun. I try not to think too much about that. "How is this Hazel's fault?"

"She went digging around when no one asked her to. Why did she do that? She interfered, stuck her nose where it didn't belong. You know how businesspeople get when they lose money. She started writing them letters. They ignored her for a long time, but she shifted gears and kept looking into it."

"So, then what?" I ask. "This Aaron guy wanted you to get whatever this stuff is from Hazel?"

"He approached me and asked if I wanted to make some money. But I couldn't find anything. None of it made sense. *Hazel* doesn't make sense. That's why Aaron took matters into his own hands."

Sawyer straightens up. "I guess we just wait now, huh, Jake? Hope the cops show up. Or at least the Coast Guard."

"Yeah . . . except . . ."

"Except," Alaina says, "that Aaron dude is still running loose. And whatever Hazel found is still in the building, right?"

"I think I left it in Dallas' apartment. I was carrying it when I found Dallas. I must have dropped it."

"Why did *you* have it?" Alaina asks.

"Hazel gave it to me. I mean, I didn't know what it was. She said it was a going-away present, but apparently it's these important documents she's been talking about."

"The cops can find it," Sawyer says. "It's a crime scene. They'll go over the whole apartment with a fine-tooth comb." He shrugs. "At least that's what they do on TV."

"Yeah, right." I turn to the building, lifting my hand to my eyes to shade them from the brightening day.

Alaina turns as well, squints. She doesn't seem overly worried about Ethan, whose head has sunk to his chest. He looks like he's about to fall asleep.

"You're worried the building's not going to make it that long," she says. "Right?"

"I am." I wipe a trickle of sweat off my cheek. "If I can just get in there for a second, go to Dallas' apartment, grab the gift, get out . . ."

"And end up under a pile of rubble," Sawyer says.

We both turn to him.

He shrugs again. "I'm just saying."

"He's right, Jake."

"Besides," Sawyer says, "it won't help us. They're tearing it all down anyway. We have to go. Hell, look at the building. *No one* can live there now."

"That's true," I say. "But I . . . I kind of believe Hazel. I think she found something."

"Jake, you can't be serious," Sawyer says.

But I'm not listening anymore. I'm already walking toward the building.

"Don't you want the gun?" Alaina asks.

I stop, look back at Ethan.

He really does appear to be sleeping. Not to mention his hands and feet are still bound. "I don't think he's going anywhere." She holds the Glock out toward me.

I hate the sight of it. The thought of it.

But . . .

EIGHTY-SIX

I cross the lawn by myself.

As I do, my eyes trail up the building, and then on to the gray, choppy water and the mainland beyond.

I cling to hope, scanning the seascape expectantly. What am I hoping to see?

A boat moving toward the island.

More lights burning.

A helicopter overhead.

Just one small sign of life.

But my surroundings are oddly silent. We're going to be on our own longer than I anticipated. And I may not know the fate of my family for a long time. It may be hours, even days.

I push those thoughts aside.

It helps to have an immediate task. Something larger than my own worries.

The water has mostly receded from the floor of the parking garage. The sewers have stopped belching everything up. The Glock rests once again at the small of my back, not as heavy as it felt before. Maybe I'm getting used to it. It's a thought that sends a shiver through my body.

I start up the stairs. I'm moving slowly. Not because I'm afraid or cautious, but because I'm dead tired. I've been up all night. I've been hot and cold at the same time. I was soaking wet for hours, and now my clothes are drying stiffly. I feel like I'm wearing a burlap bag.

A gentle onshore wind blows down the stairs. It feels refreshing. Belying the precariousness of our situation.

I make the turn at the landing and see no one. From the lawn, my fellow tenants watch me like I'm an actor on a stage. They're a motley group. Six months earlier I couldn't have dreamed this would be my life. But now we're connected in ways I couldn't have imagined when I moved here. We'll be bonded forever. Alaina still stands with her hand shading her eyes. She shrugs. I get it. She hasn't seen anything unusual. I try not to feel falsely confident or let my guard down.

It takes effort to climb. Normally I would bound up these stairs. But not now.

When I reach the second-floor walkway, my breathing is louder. But I see nothing, feeling a sudden hope.

Get to Dallas' apartment and get out. That's all I have to do.

I glance back to the lawn. Alaina is jabbing her finger in the air, pointing at something to her right and my left. Toward the other end of the walkway.

My head snaps that way. But I know before I look what I'm going to see.

A man I don't know is standing at the other end of the long expanse.

EIGHTY-SEVEN

I have no doubt it's Aaron. He looks as ragged and tired as I feel. I'm sure he's been up as long as I have.

He stares at me, unmoving. He's taller than I am, broader in the shoulders. My eyes search for a weapon, but all I see is an industrial-sized flashlight hanging from one hand.

He starts to walk my way.

A burst of adrenaline revives me, my heart galloping inside my chest.

Dallas' door is between us, closer to me than to Aaron. It's possible I could get there before him. Run in, lock the door.

But then what?

I'd be trapped inside . . . until when?

And he'd be outside with everyone else.

I move forward a few steps, hold my hands out in a pathetic attempt to calm him. "Why don't you just leave us alone?"

But he doesn't stop. He keeps coming for me.

He shakes his head. "I can't do that, Jacob." He knows my name. Of course he does. He already knows everything about us. "I need what she found. What she was working on with Ethan." He jerks his thumb toward the lawn, where Hazel still sits in the shed. "And since you came up here, I'm guessing this is where it is." He slows his pace, nods toward Dallas' door. "In the one apartment I haven't been able to get back into."

"So you *were* in there?"

He stops, laughs in an ugly way. His hand moves toward his belt, where the butt of a gun protrudes from his pants. "Can we just get on with it? I'm going to get what I want. You know that. Why make us all endure more crap than we already have?" I don't respond, and he goes on. "Do you have the key, Jacob?"

"I might."

"Just let me in."

I'm sure he has a sense of what he's looking for. But there's no way he can know it's wrapped up like a present. If I let him in, he'll likely spend a long time looking. And he might never find it. But if he finds the package, I'm no longer of any use to him. None of us are. He'll be more than happy to leave.

Or kill me and then leave.

"Okay," I say. "I have the key. If I let you in, will you leave us alone?"

"Put your hands up where I can see them."

I do as he says.

"Is the key in your front pocket?"

I nod, hands in the air.

"Reach into your pocket. Real slow. And get the key. Don't try anything stupid, okay?"

I exhale, keep my eyes on him. I lower my right hand to my jeans and—very slowly—work the tips of my fingers into the pocket. The stiff fabric resists, but I'm able to get a grip on the passkey and slide my hand back out, holding it in the air between us.

"Open the door." He raises his index finger. "With one hand. Keep the other in the air so I can see it."

I step forward and try to fit the key into the lock, but I can't stop my hand from shaking.

Truth be told, I don't want to go inside. I want the package—but I don't want to see Dallas' body again. Don't want to lay eyes on the first person we lost last night. The first of so many losses.

What I want is to stop losing people. Once and for all.

The key slides in, and I turn the lock. The door swings open. I remove the key, keeping one hand in the air, and step back.

"No, you go in and get it." He pats the butt of the gun. "Drop the key on the floor and keep your hands up."

I do as he says, the key jingling when it hits the walkway. With both my hands up, I step through the door.

Except for the band of light that comes through the open door, it's pitch-dark inside because of the hurricane shutters. Aaron is behind me, moving closer.

For the second time in a matter of minutes, the Glock is pulled out of my waistband.

"Nice piece," he says. "Clearly you weren't ready to use it."

"What you're looking for is over there. By Dal—by the body. I think you know where his body is."

"Get it." He gives me a shove in the back. Not hard enough to knock me over but hard enough to let me know he isn't up for any bullshit. "Now." When I don't move, he says, "The thing is, Jacob, I can put a bullet in the back of your head anytime I want."

I'm not sure what to do. Or if I'm going to get out of this apartment alive.

But as I approach Dallas' body, I formulate a plan.

EIGHTY-EIGHT

I move out of the band of light and into the darkness of the apartment.

Dallas' body lies ahead of me, a shadowy shape on the floor.

I hadn't planned on coming back. Facing his body again.

But since I'm here, I need to make it worthwhile.

For Dallas. For Stanley. Heck, even for Tyler.

Why not?

"It's over here to the left, I think. But I can't see."

"Hold it."

I stop.

Aaron moves behind me. Something clicks, and a flashlight beam travels past me and illuminates Dallas' body, the pool of blood around his head an ugly red halo.

"To the left," I say. "I'm not going to stumble around in the dark."

He moves the beam that way, illuminating the baseball I wanted to give Dallas. Ron Santo's scribbled signature gleams in the half-light.

"Maybe it's to the right," I say. "Can you check over there?"

The beam travels down the length of Dallas' body, sweeping across the threadbare carpet until it finally lands on the package Hazel gave me. The sloppy wrapping, the off-center bow.

"That's it," I say. "That gift."

"That's it?"

"It is. Do you want to get it? Or do you want me to?"

Aaron laughs. "You get it. And try your damnedest not to do anything stupid."

My mind cycles through everything that's happened in the past twelve hours. The past six months. Hasn't it been a long series of me doing stupid things?

Taking a break from my marriage . . .

Coming to Florida . . .

Leaving Dallas' apartment so he was alone when a killer—Aaron?—came to the door . . .

Driving across the causeway . . .

Driving back . . .

Sending Jordan and Mackenzie out on the Intracoastal . . .

What difference does it make if I do one more stupid thing, which might end everything once and for all?

"Okay," I say. "I'll try my damnedest."

I start forward—

—but instead of going to the right, I dive into the darkness on the left, hitting the floor very close to Dallas' body.

Aaron shouts. "Hey—"

I manage to get my hand around the ball. In one motion, I roll onto my back and throw it as hard as I can, aiming right for Aaron's head.

He sees it coming and tries to duck. But he's not fast enough.

The ball nails him in the temple, sending him reeling backward toward the door of the apartment.

As soon as he hits the floor, letting go of the Glock, I jump to my feet.

He's scrambling for the Glock and, in the process, drops his heavy flashlight. I grab it at the exact same time Aaron wraps his fingers around the butt. Before he can point the gun in my direction, I pull back and swing the giant flashlight directly at his hand. The Glock goes flying across the room. I've swung so hard I fall on top of Aaron.

From the floor Aaron kicks at me, connects with my lower body, and sends me flying back to the floor. Somehow I manage to keep my grip on the flashlight.

We both start to rise at the same time.

He gets to his knees and reaches for his own gun.

He fumbles ever so slightly. Something on the gun catches on the fabric of his jeans, giving me the tiniest opening. . . .

I don't even think.

I act.

I push myself up, flashlight in hand. I swing again, aiming squarely for Aaron's head.

The flashlight connects with a sickening thump, catching him on the side of the head. For a moment, he remains upright, hand clutching the butt of the gun but not moving.

I rear back, prepare to swing again—

But I don't need to.

Aaron's grip loosens, and his arm falls limp to his side. A split second later his entire body tips over, a falling building crashing to the floor.

When he hits the floor, he lies still.

Absolutely still.

EIGHTY-NINE

A new fear—*terror*—grips me.

I've killed a man.

I drop the flashlight, and it thuds dully against the carpet, rolling away.

I take a knee next to Aaron, feeling for a pulse in his neck. Before yesterday, I'd never taken someone's pulse even once, and now I've done it three times—twice in this apartment.

Panic races through me as I fail to locate a pulse. My fingers move one way and then another, the tips against Aaron's clammy, sweaty skin.

"Come on. Come on . . ."

I keep pressing, willing a pulse to appear. As if it's magic.

"Please . . ."

Then—finally—I feel it. A small beating sensation below the skin.

"Yes . . ."

I lean closer. Aaron's chest moves. Air whistles in and out of his nose. His breathing is shallow but steady.

"Thank God."

I almost collapse to the floor in relief. I feel empty, drained.

Outside the open door a flock of pelicans soars past in a graceful

V. It's quiet enough to hear the steady, eternal, rhythmic beating of the waves against the shore.

It's almost peaceful.

But then I sense something on the edge of my hearing. Over the sound of the waves, I hear the sound of something tearing. It's like fabric being ripped . . . two things being torn apart. A second later, a giant popping sound echoes down the walkway, followed by a loud crash in the yard below.

I'm up, stepping over Aaron and onto the walkway, where the sun is bright enough now to make me squint. My fellow tenants are still gathered downstairs. Alaina points frantically to my right.

She says something I can't hear.

I don't need to hear it. I follow her gaze and see another chunk of the building has fallen away. I don't have much time left.

I rush back into the apartment, find the gift on the floor, grab the baseball too.

Once again, I step over Aaron's prone form. He looks weak, pitiful. He's completely at the mercy of whatever fate may befall him.

The sight of him ignites a burning rage in my chest. We wouldn't be in any of this mess if not for him. He descended on us—worse even than the hurricane—and brought disaster upon us. Three people are dead.

Maybe more . . .

Our lives have been forever changed. . . .

We'll never forget what's happened here.

I want to spit in his face. Instead, I step over him and out onto the walkway.

Alaina puts her hands on either side of her mouth and shouts, "Hurry, Jake!"

"Yeah, yeah. I get it. . . ."

The building's about to go. I need to get out of here.

But something deep down inside stops me in my tracks. I look back to where Aaron's low breathing continues. His face is placid, but a trickle of blood runs out of his right ear.

He needs help. *Serious help.* Mackenzie's words overcome me. *You and Mom always tell me to do the right thing, Dad. . . . Maybe we should put that into practice when we have the chance.*

"For fuck's sake."

I launch Hazel's gift over the wall. It spins like a Frisbee in the air, landing at Alaina's feet. Whatever it is—even if Hazel's completely lost her mind—it's out of the building now. It's safe. Alaina looks up, and I toss the baseball—much easier to throw than the gift—to her. To my surprise, she catches it like a pro.

I turn around, go back for Aaron.

I bend down, give his cheek a few gentle slaps. "Hey, man, time to wake up." He doesn't move. "Aaron?"

He emits a low whimper, but his eyes remain closed. Not even a flutter.

The building groans again.

"Shit."

It's not going to be easy. Not easy at all.

Not after no sleep and nothing to eat and all the stress of the last day.

Maybe we should put that into practice when we have the chance.

I have to try. He's a human being. A shitty one, but still . . .

I put his arm on my shoulder. "Aaron, can you help me out, man?"

Nothing.

"Aaron?"

His arm goes from my shoulder around my back of its own accord, tightening his grip. A small miracle.

"I'm going to lift you. And we're going to get out of here."

I work my left arm under his legs, take in the deepest, longest breath I can, and then try to stand.

My back and legs scream. Every muscle, tendon, and bone is stretched to its absolute limit.

I get halfway up—and don't think I can make it farther.

I'm going to drop him. We're both going to crash to the floor.

I wobble, Aaron growing heavier and heavier in my arms.

My left knee buckles. I'm about to go down.

"You . . . got . . . it . . ."

I begin to sink.

". . . got . . . it . . ."

Somehow—someway—I stop sinking. My back and legs get injected with a shot of iron.

I take another deep breath, adjust Aaron's weight in my arms. I grunt like a weight lifter.

My knee rises. My back straightens.

I reach my full height again, his weight still absurdly heavy in my arms.

I turn, making sure not to bang his skull against the doorframe, and head out the door of Dallas' apartment.

NINETY

Alaina's voice reaches me on the walkway. "Jake, you need to get out of there."

She can't possibly hear my response, but I deliver it anyway: "No shit."

I'm almost to the stairs when a piece of the ceiling above Aaron and me breaks loose, scattering plaster around my feet.

I stop. "Shit." I can't go back to the other staircase. It's too far, too dangerous. . . .

If I go forward, more of the ceiling might fall on top of us. The whole building might go. . . .

I have no choice. I have to keep going.

I kick debris out of my way as I make my way to the stairs. When we all carried Catalina down, there was a group of us.

But it's just me now.

I go slowly. Very, very slowly. One step at a time.

On the second landing, I stop, try to gather my strength. I want to put Aaron down and catch my breath. But there's no time.

I keep going. What other choice is there?

Halfway down the last half of a flight, I miss a step, almost stumble.

After what feels like twenty years, my feet hit pavement. I've made it to the garage. Momentum is the only thing carrying me forward at this point. As soon as I step onto the lawn, Nina and Kiara rush toward me, help me lower Aaron to the ground.

My arms feel limp and useless. I walk a few steps away from Aaron and fall to the ground.

I don't care that it's wet. I don't care about the sun in my eyes. I just want to rest. I'm flat on the ground, staring at the sky. I don't know if I can ever get up again.

My chest rises and falls.

Nina's face appears over me, hovering like a heavenly body. "What are you doing, Jake?"

"Dying."

"What on earth made you carry that asshole out of the building?"

"I couldn't let him die. Even if he is a bad guy." I huff and puff a few more times. "He's pretty out of it. I smacked him. Hard. He'll need a doctor."

"I wanted to come up and help you, but with the building about to fall and everything, Kiara said . . ."

"It's okay. . . ."

A tremendous noise begins. Louder than anything we heard all night.

The ground shakes so hard it feels like we're having an earthquake.

Or another storm is bearing down on us, ready to swamp the island once and for all.

"What the—"

I lift my head, push my body up so I can see.

Like we're staring through waves of heat, or we're seeing a shimmering mirage, the entire building wobbles. Windows pop, sending glass shards and hurricane shutters flying into the air. The windows glisten in the light like diamonds.

The gray stucco cracks. Countless seams run across the facade of the building like capillaries.

"Oh, my God," Nina says.

I watch—both fascinated and detached. It's like watching a movie, or footage of a disaster thousands of miles away.

Except it's right here. Right in front of us.

I was just inside there, and barely made it out.

The building continues to shimmy from one side to the other. The movement speeds up, and pieces of the building start to go, falling down to the ground and exploding into dust.

In a matter of moments, everything starts to fall in on itself. Like a ship being sucked into a whirlpool.

In one sudden, terrible moment, the entire thing collapses with a tremendous roar, sending a gigantic plume of dust and dirt into the air, as though a bomb has exploded.

I turn away, duck my head. Feel bits and pieces of debris fall down on me like hailstones. My face is pressed against the wet ground. I inhale the loamy scent of mud and rain.

Eventually, the debris stops falling.

I dare to lift my head. Our former home has been reduced to a pile of rubble. I try not to think of all that went down with it. Most importantly, Dallas' body.

If there'd been more time . . . if it'd been safer . . .

The police will find him. Someday. Return his body to his sister in Chicago.

What matters is that everyone who is still alive made it out.

Everyone gathers together. We all stare in shock at the massive mess before us. Mouths hang open. Hands are lifted to chests. No one says a word.

I look around, take a quick mental inventory. I see everyone, even Catalina, on the roofing sheet off to the side. Ethan under the tree.

Hazel leans against the shed, her body supported by the cinder block structure. She holds the gift. Alaina must have given it to her.

"Are you happy now?" I call.

Hazel waves the wrapped box in the air. "Open it, Jacob. See how crazy I really am."

NINETY-ONE

Everyone gathers around me.

It's like an impromptu birthday party.

I want to object, but Hazel's eyes—watery and bloodshot—gaze at me.

Hard.

I can't say no. She's too determined. And I went through hell to get the thing. I might as well finish the job and open it. Even if I can't comprehend what could be inside that would be worth killing for.

"Okay, fine." I rip the paper, taking a quick glance at everyone around me. "After everything we've been through, I guess we're all in this together. We might as well do this together too."

"Maybe there's buried treasure on the island," Sawyer says.

Hazel shushes him with a wave of her hand.

The wrapping paper gets caught in a breeze and flutters away. The leather box underneath looks like it came from a department store in 1968. I work my dirty fingernails under the lid and lift.

Inside is a thick stack of old papers. The paper is yellowed with age, and the type is fading but still readable. I put my hand on top to keep them from blowing away. No doubt a strong wind could turn them to dust.

I'm baffled. I look into everyone's faces and see they all look slightly confused. "What is all this, Hazel?"

"It's proof."

"Proof of what?"

Hazel straightens, her spine stiffening. She looks six inches taller and ten years younger.

"It's proof," she says, "that *this* island and all the land on it rightfully belongs to the Native people who first lived here. By Florida statute, their claim to this property supersedes any claim made by the developers, builders, agents, and bankers who have sliced and diced this place over the years. If—*when*—this documentation gets into the right hands, the land will be returned to the rightful owners. To do with whatever they want."

"Holy shit," Kiara says. "Wow."

"That's incredible, Hazel," Nina says. "This is such important work you've done."

Hazel goes on. "The people who first called this island home will finally have back what is rightfully theirs."

Several of us turn to Alaina. Her skin has flushed pink, but she doesn't say a word. My own response surprises me. My heart feels lighter. Like it's been pumped full of air.

Home.

I may never have a home again.

Or a family.

And all nine of us will have to move, start over completely.

But as a result of Hazel's hard work, an entire group of people—besides Alaina, people we don't even know—will get their ancestral home back.

Maybe that's the real reason we went through hell last night. Maybe that's what all this trouble was for. To save these papers. To give people back their home . . .

Alaina finally speaks. "Maybe . . . maybe I'll get to live here again someday." She sniffs, and I see now that tiny tears are forming in the corners of her eyes. "Maybe I'll have a place to call home someday." She wipes her eyes. "For my daughter." Alaina turns to Hazel. "Thank you so much."

Hazel basks in the praise. "Once again, historians save the day." She lifts her arm in the air like she's leading us into battle. "We're really like Superman."

"Alaina," I say, "you should be the one to hold on to these papers. You and Hazel can make sure they get into the right hands." But when I turn to Alaina with the box of papers . . . she's looking away from me.

She's looking toward the water. . . .

She glances back at me and then takes off *running*.

"Alaina?"

She throws words over her shoulder, and they come to us on the wind. "I . . . see . . . something . . . a boat. . . ."

A boat?

A rescue boat?

That would mean . . .

I hand the box to Nina and take off across the lawn, following Alaina to the water.

NINETY-TWO

9:51 A.M.

I catch up to Alaina at the water's edge.

She turns around when she hears me coming. "Jake, look."

A police boat approaches the island, its aluminum hull slicing through the gray waves.

"They're heading for the dock," Alaina says. "We're saved, Jake. We're going to get out of here."

The boat turns parallel to the shore, cruises slowly to the small dock that sits behind what used to be our apartment building. Several people stand at the enclosed helm, but we can't see them clearly.

Alaina and I move up the shoreline as the boat gently bumps against the old tires anchored to the dock.

A familiar uniformed figure emerges from the helm, ties a line from the boat to one of the pilings. Sgt. Fernandez. As Alaina and I step onto the dock, she turns our way and waves in an unusually friendly manner.

"Mr. Powell." She takes both of us in, her hands resting on her gun belt. "I need an assessment of the situation here as soon as you can give it. More help is on the way—there's a fire department craft coming. But I don't want to bury the lede." She turns back to the boat. "I know what you're really curious about. . . ."

There's more movement at the enclosed helm. Two figures.

I allow myself to hope. . . .

Hope is all I have. . . .

First Jordan and then Mackenzie step out onto the bow. Sgt. Fernandez helps each of them down to the dock.

I'm running—pounding—down the dock.

Fernandez barely gets out of my way.

"Dad!"

The three of us come together, forming a tight, unbreakable family unit again.

Our words are jumbled. They don't matter.

Our heads touch. I don't know how long we hold one another without speaking.

Finally, words come again.

"Are you okay?" Jordan asks with tears in her eyes.

"I'm fine. I'm fine. We're all okay. But what about you? I saw the dinghy. It was upside down in the water. What happened?"

We loosen our grip on one another. I take a step back and look them over for real.

Their clothes are different. Jordan wears a Ketchum Island PD sweatshirt, Mackenzie a long-sleeved Florida State T-shirt that looks like it could hold two people her size. It's obvious they've been in the water. Their hair looks damp and not as perfect as normal.

"You should have seen it, Dad. Mom was so badass."

"What?" I turn to Jordan. "What happened?" But it's Mackenzie who answers.

"We got swamped by a wave. Thank God we were close to the mainland. The boat went over. Dad, we had to *swim* to shore. In a hurricane."

"I suspect a lot of details are being left out."

"Oh, yeah, totally. She grabbed me, Dad. Mom did. She held me above water, and then we started paddling for the shore. About ten gallons of water went up my nose. But we made it."

"I never should have let you out of my sight."

Jordan grips my arm. "You did the right thing, Jake. We made it. That's all that matters." She nods at Fernandez. "And help is here."

Just then a chugging sound reaches across the Intracoastal. We all turn to look. Sure enough, the promised fireboat approaches. Paramedics, more cops.

I let out a long breath. "It's over. It's finally over."

"And something else is just beginning," Jordan says. I look into her eyes, and see she means it. We're going to start over. We're getting a new beginning.

I pull Jordan into my arms and behind her back reach for Mackenzie, dragging her into our embrace.

We all clutch one another. Again.

We did it.

We made it.

And now I'm never letting go.

ACKNOWLEDGMENTS

Thanks once again to everyone at Berkley for their hard work on my behalf. Special thanks for the publicity and marketing wizardry of Loren Jaggers, Jin Yu, Hilary Tacuri, and Tina Joell.

Thanks to Jen Carl for working on my newsletter and to Kara Thurmond for keeping my website going.

Big thanks to my excellent editor, Tracy Bernstein, for her hard work and dedication to making the book better.

Big thanks also to my wonderful agent, David Hale Smith, for his wisdom and guidance. Thanks to Naomi Eisenbeiss and everyone at Inkwell Management.

Thanks as always to my family and friends.

And thanks to Molly McCaffrey for everything else.

STORM
WARNING

DAVID BELL

READERS GUIDE

QUESTIONS FOR DISCUSSION

1. At the beginning of the novel, the characters have to choose between leaving and staying as the hurricane bears down on them. What factors would you weigh if faced with the prospect of evacuating in response to a potential natural disaster?

2. Jake is torn between his desire to return to his family in Ohio and his desire to stay and help his fellow tenants. Have you ever had to choose between your loved ones and other people you knew who might have been in greater need?

3. Jake feels loyal to his neighbors because they've become like a surrogate family. Where and when have you had the experience of finding community beyond your family?

4. Jake and the others underestimate and dismiss Hazel because of her age. Have you seen older people treated this way? If you've been on the receiving end, at what age did it start?

5. Each of the tenants in the building has a secret or a story that explains why they ended up living on the island. Whose backstory did you find the most surprising? The most sympathetic?

6. The buildings on the island and the people who live there have been neglected because a developer is interested in the land. Have you witnessed this tension playing out where you live? If so, in what ways?

7. At one point Jake uses an autographed baseball against the killer. What everyday object do you own that you could utilize in self-defense?

8. Jake and Jordan have encountered difficult times in their marriage and their careers. Do you think they can put their family back together?

9. Jake is an everyman, but he fights to protect his neighbors. What real-life stories have you heard about a "regular guy" summoning bravery in the face of challenging circumstances?

Photo © Glen Rose Photography

David Bell is a *New York Times* bestselling, award-winning author whose work has been translated into multiple foreign languages. He's currently a professor of English at Western Kentucky University in Bowling Green, Kentucky. He received an MA in creative writing from Miami University in Oxford, Ohio, and a PhD in American literature and creative writing from the University of Cincinnati. His previous novels include *The Finalists*, *Kill All Your Darlings*, *The Request*, *Layover*, *Somebody's Daughter*, and *Cemetery Girl*.

VISIT DAVID BELL ONLINE

DavidBellNovels.com

 DavidBellNovels

 DavidBellNovels

Ready to find
your next great read?

Let us help.

Visit prh.com/nextread

Penguin
Random
House